K. T. Talbot

Unleashed Desires

K. T. Talbot

Unleashed Desires

Lesbian Romance

édition el!es
www.elles-books.com

Cover Photo:
© Kesu – Fotolia.com
ISBN 978-3-95609-153-7

Acknowledgements

To Alison, thank you so much for your advice and tireless effort, your assistance was invaluable. We spent many long hours working on this, but the most special part was becoming much closer friends. For all of this I thank you.

To two of my dearest friends, Cheryl (Sugar) and Mary for your honest opinions and advise. Thanks for letting me talk endlessly about my book while I was writing it and not allowing you to read it until it was complete. Thank you for being there.

To Allan, your expertise was greatly appreciated and a blessing. Thank you for your support on this project.

Thanks to all my family and friends who offered their wonderful support and encouraging words.

Also, thanks to Gloria, because without her vision, I do not think I would have had the courage to pursue my dream of being a published author.

SPECIAL THANKS

To my wife Heather, who from the very beginning was always supportive. You encouraged me and gave me confidence to follow my dream during this entire journey. I love you for that. Your support and input was a welcomed asset to my writing and I am forever grateful to have you by my side. I love you Heather, now and always.

CHAPTER ONE

After having worked all week and filling in two extra shifts for a sick colleague, Karen was looking forward to the weekend off. Being a nurse at Brockville General Hospital in a very busy emergency room had given Karen great satisfaction and pleasure over the past nine years. She had seen many disturbing severe injuries, but being able to help others was Karen's passion.

Since it was a rainy day Karen took a long hot bath, grabbed a good book and curled up in her large chaise longue. An opportunity for a relaxing day did not arise often. There were always chores to be done when you owned a house. Either the yard needed mowing or the garden needed tending, and in the winter she needed to shovel snow off the walkways.

Karen's home in the country was only fifteen minutes outside the city of Brockville. The drive back and forth was beautiful and allowed Karen enough time to get herself energized on the way to work or to unwind on her way home. Her two bedroom bungalow was set back from the road and nestled amongst several pine trees.

Karen loved people and enjoyed getting together with her friends and family, but once she was home she was so comfortable and relaxed that she found it difficult to make herself go out again.

Karen took a sip from her freshly steeped tea and looked outside. The trees had lost their leaves and had covered the ground with a protective blanket for winter. Even the pine trees had left a sandy golden blanket of needles on the ground. It was a rainy November day. The skies were an unsettled mix of grey and blue.

A number of bird feeders hung from the big pine trees full of enticing pieces of corn, nuts, and a variety of seeds. There were also a few suet balls inviting the downy woodpeckers to join in the bountiful buffet.

Numerous types of birds arrived each day to take advantage of this banquet of food. The blue jays were making their voices heard with their distinctive call. Many other birds fluttered about with excitement. It was truly a delight to watch all of them get along for the most part enjoying one common necessity, eating. But throw in a squirrel or two and watch the scurrying that goes on. Seldom did Karen find time to take pleasure in simply sitting and watching the wildlife that had found a safe haven in her yard. Nature was so beautiful, and Karen had her own piece of God's beauty just outside her window.

While she watched a pair of 'love doves' that cuddled in close to each other on a branch and softly released their comforting coo, Karen felt a bit melancholic. They always seem so content nestled in so cosily together. Someday I would love to share moments like that with someone special, she thought.

Just then the phone rang and interrupted her thoughts.

"Hello."

"Hi, Karen," said the voice on the other end.

"Oh, hello, Julie. What a great day to be lazy, isn't it? Especially after this busy week."

"Yeah, it is. I thought I would put on a pot roast and let it cook all day. Would you like to join us for dinner and play cards afterwards?"

"I would love to come for dinner. What can I bring?"

"Nothing. All is taken care of. Come around five o'clock."

"What about dessert?"

"Just bring yourself."

"Okay, I will see you tonight."

Julie had been a great friend for about seven years. Karen had met her the day Julie was hired as a nurse. They had instantly become friends.

Karen made herself a fresh hot cup of tea and nestled back into her lounge chair. She read for hours. Before she knew it, it was time to get ready to go to Julie and Rhonda's for dinner.

Rhonda was Julie's partner. They had been together just over three years and were very happy and very much in love. Karen had many acquaintances and friends. Some, many in fact, were lesbian. She often found herself curious and intrigued by lesbian relationships, but she could never see herself with a same sex partner. However, she envied Julie and Rhonda's relationship and admired the respectful way they treated each other.

Karen had dated a few guys over the years, but had never developed any serious relationship or found herself willing to take that special barrier down and let herself be free to make love. To be thirty-four and still a virgin was rare and almost embarrassing. When she finally gave herself completely to the one she loved she wanted it to be special. She had never been attracted to anyone enough to pursue a relationship to that level.

Karen rang the doorbell to Julie's house, a bottle of red wine in one hand and a bottle of white wine in the other. Holding them out she said, "I didn't know if white or red is supposed to go with a pot roast, so I thought I would play it safe."

"You weren't supposed to bring anything," Julie reminded.

"I couldn't come empty handed. You know me," Karen defended herself. "Where is Rhonda?"

"Upstairs. Putting on a different shirt."

Just then Rhonda came in and took both bottles from Karen. "I bet we can decide which one goes better with the pot roast. By the time dinner is over we will have our verdict," Rhonda predicted.

They all had a good laugh, and the bottles were opened before Julie had Karen's coat hung up.

"Dinner smells wonderful! I haven't eaten much all day anticipating your scrumptious pot roast," Karen announced.

"Well, there is plenty, so nobody needs to go hungry." Julie invited them to sit down at the table.

Dinner was delicious as usual. They all had a glass of both the red and white wine, so they could make an educated decision as to which went best with the roast.

Rhonda pretended to be a wine connoisseur, swishing it around inside her mouth, first the red and then the white.

Julie and Karen laughed at Rhonda's facial expressions.

"Okay, how about this ..." Rhonda stood up, took a sip of the white, held it in her mouth, leaned over to Julie and passed it between their mouths only wasting a small dribble. "Did that taste the same as your white?" Rhonda asked.

"No, actually it tastes like more," Julie countered with a huge grin.

Karen observed her friends' playfulness. What a wonderful couple, she thought. I wish I would find someone and have the happiness that Rhonda and Julie share. Watching them banter back and forth, flirting and teasing, making goofy faces, acting like teenagers in love seemed so natural. Karen began to long for someone to treat her special and look at her with eyes that sparkled the way Julie's and Rhonda's did, when they looked at each other.

Rhonda turned to Karen and changed the topic. "Karen, you have been a faithful fan of our hockey team again this season."

"I enjoy it. And knowing almost everybody on the team makes it a lot more fun to watch."

"Yeah, most of the same group is back. We have a new player by the way. This gal teaches Physical Education at Thousand Island Secondary School."

"Julie told me. But every time I have been there she hasn't been."

"Jessie has had some commitments with the school lately. From now on she should be there most of the time."

The evening passed quickly. They had been playing cards for hours when Karen looked at her watch and discovered it was after ten. "I had better get my butt in gear and head home."

"Is it that time already?" Julie asked.

"I was pretty lazy today. I have a whole list of things to get done tomorrow morning. Thanks again for a wonderful evening." Karen gave them both a hug and a kiss good-bye. "Julie, I will see you at work and Rhonda, I will see you Thursday evening at hockey."

The week went by quickly. Before too long Thursday had arrived. Julie and Karen met in the bleachers.

"The new girl is supposed to be here tonight," Julie informed Karen.

"I am excited to see how she plays. Is Rhonda going to listen to our opinion and bench her if we say she is no good?" Karen teased.

"I have only seen her play a few times. She had to miss a number of games in the beginning of the season because of her new teaching job. However, when she played, she was quite impressive," Julie stated.

"Those must have been the games I missed because of work. I will judge her tonight, and we will make our decision then," Karen joked.

Just then the ladies came out to warm up. Rhonda took her position as goalie in the net. Rhonda was the captain of the Rideau Rocket's ladies' hockey team. She was a strong player and loved the game. They took turns shooting the puck at her. Karen was watching for the new player so she could critique her. Jessie was wearing number nine. Her skating skills are certainly impressive, Karen thought. The Rideau Rockets are lucky that Jessie had chosen them.

Just then the new player looked up, straight into Karen's eyes. For a few short seconds they held a fiery gaze.

Something unfamiliar stirred inside Karen. It was as if the new player was casting a spell on her.

Jessie, who had only been with the team since the middle of September, delivered her best performance so far on this night. She was out to impress. Not only was the team pleasantly surprised with her exceptional game, but one spectator in particular was more than a little intrigued with this new player on her all so familiar local team.

Karen was unable to take her eyes off of Jessie. When the game was over she bent over to Julie. "You can let Rhonda know that I give my approval of the new player on the team. She looks like a keeper."

"After tonight's game Rhonda probably knows that Jessie is an asset." Julie smiled.

They got up, and after their good-byes Karen left as she usually did. Julie always waited and walked out with Rhonda.

Later that night Karen had trouble falling asleep. In her mind she kept replaying the moment when her eyes had locked with the eyes of the new player. Neither of them had been able to look away. Karen felt intrigued by this mystery woman on the hockey team. Who was she? She decided to make a point of going to watch more games this season.

Karen attended two more hockey games with Julie in the next couple of weeks, each time keeping her eyes glued on player number nine. Thursdays had become the focus of her week.

This Thursday the Rideau Rockets were playing a strong team from Kingston which held the top position in their league. Karen found herself watching the clock while eating her dinner. Time did not seem to be passing fast enough. What was only ten minutes felt like thirty. She couldn't wait to see if Jessie was playing today. She was not sure why, but this fascination with the new player was very strong. Ever since this brief moment they had shared during that first game three weeks ago there had been an excitement in Karen that she could not explain and did not understand.

Finally it was time to leave. After checking her hair one last time, she headed out the door. On her drive she listened to the local sports news.

"The T.I.S.S. Pirates Girl's High School team won their basketball tournament yesterday in Windsor," the announcer said. "The new coach, Miss Carmichael, has brought the team to new heights. Miss Carmichael has come to us from a small community northwest of here called Mattawa. She has proven to be quite the coach for our young ladies, who seem to look up to her and respect her. Well done, Miss Carmichael."

Karen's thoughts drifted off. She didn't hear any more of the radio broadcast. Instead she started to picture Jessie on the court – taking charge with her bold assertiveness and leading her team into the championship. I am pretty sure Sophie plays for this basketball team, she thought and decided to call her niece tomorrow to find out.

Karen arrived at the arena and parked her car without even remembering her drive into town. She had gotten completely lost in her thoughts and was surprised to find herself in the parking lot already.

Inside the arena she found Julie in their usual spot in the bleachers.

"Hi, Julie." They exchanged a hug and kiss on the cheek as usual.

Karen wasn't there more than ten minutes before the ladies were out on the ice warming up. Intently Karen searched for Jessie. Where is she? Where is she? Ah, there she is. Good, she did make it! She had been concerned that after the travelling involved with the basketball tournament Jessie would not be up for a hockey game . . . if in fact this Jessie and Miss Carmichael were one and the same person.

Once Karen spotted Number 9 she took a deep breath and relaxed.

Watching Karen watch Jessie was fun for Julie. It was like watching someone enjoy window shopping for that one item you want but you know you shouldn't have. And yet, you are looking over every inch of it when you think no one is watching . . .

Jessie looked up into the stands to see if Karen had made it this evening. So far she had not yet been comfortable enough with the other members of the team to go around asking questions about this woman. She did not want to draw any additional interest to herself and her personal life. After all she was a school teacher and didn't need any negative publicity brought to her over her sexual preference.

She spotted Karen in her usual seat next to Julie. Jessie watched her as often as she was able to, hoping she would be looking back. Finally they spotted each other at the same time. Just as in the past, the intensity and warmth they drew from each other's eyes was unbelievable.

For a moment Jessie forgot where she was. She got hit in the side of the foot with a puck. That brought her back to the ice and the warm-up.

Karen could not help but give Jessie a big smile without even realizing it.

"Julie, didn't you say that Jessie is new in town?"

"Yeah, she moved here at the end of the summer. Right before the school year started."

"That's right. You said she taught at T.I.S.S. What does she teach?"

"Remember, Karen? I said she teaches PE. I swear, either you don't listen to what I say, or you just like talking about Number 9 all the time."

Karen realized that Julie had a valid point. All she wanted to do was talk about Jessie. She remembered everything she had ever been told about her; still she wanted to hear it over and over. Her information on Jessie was limited, therefore she was always hoping Julie would have something new to tell her about Number 9. After all, Rhonda did play on the same team.

"Ha ha, very funny! I do listen to you. You just never mentioned Jessie's last name."

"I think Rhonda said her name was Carmichael, Jessie Carmichael."

"That would be right then," Karen said with certainty.

"What would be right?"

"On my way here tonight the sports news mentioned her and the T.I.S.S. Girls' High School basketball team winning the tournament in Windsor yesterday."

Julie nodded. "It sounds like that is one and the same, Miss Jessie Carmichael."

Karen beamed. Jessie Carmichael, Karen thought. I like the sound of her name.

The final score was three to two for the Rideau Rockets. With her speed and energy Jessie had made it an exciting game to watch. Jessie herself scored one goal and had one assist.

Usually Karen would leave as soon as the game was over, while Julie would wait around for Rhonda and chat with the others who were waiting for their partners or friends. Tonight however Karen was a bit slower in heading out. "The game was exciting tonight. A great deal of action and very tense."

"Yes, it was most enjoyable watching all aspects of the game," Julie teased.

Karen got a puzzled look on her face. "What do you mean, 'all aspects of the game'?"

"You know … the game, the players, the spectators, the interactions …"

"What are you talking about? What interactions?" Karen's face turned red. She was pretty certain that Julie had seen her watching Jessie very closely during the whole game. She knew exactly to what Julie was referring. "I think that the fans' involvement and cheers help the players during the game."

"Well, you certainly did your share of cheering tonight, especially when Number 9 scored her goal."

"With her being the newbie on the team I wanted her to feel that her efforts were noticed and appreciated."

Julie decided to leave it at that. She had a notion about Karen's true motivation, but did not want to scare her away from her feelings.

Karen waited with Julie a bit longer and was just about to leave when she saw Jessie coming out of the dressing room. The way her short red hair curled up around the bottom of her black ball cap seemed to add brightness to her soft brown freckles hidden beneath the rosy flush she had from playing hockey. Karen was stunned. She literally froze and could only smile, as Jessie walked closer and said hello.

Julie slowed Jessie up. "So, was it you we heard all about on the sports news tonight?"

"Oh, did we make the local sports broadcast?"

"Yes, apparently you and the T.I.S.S. Girls' basketball team did well in a tournament … where did you say that was Karen?"

Karen could not believe Julie was doing this to her. Her mind went blank. "I believe I heard it was in Windsor."

Jessie stepped closer. "That's right. The girls made me very proud."

Julie smiled to herself. Finally the two had at least spoken to one another. It wasn't much, but you had to start somewhere. "Congratulations again. You played a great game tonight."

"Thanks, I had fun. It's very nice to finally meet you." Jessie shoved her hockey bag farther back on her shoulder, winked at Karen and headed off.

Karen watched Jessie walk away so self-confident. What a raspy, deep, sultry voice she has, she thought. That voice along with Jessie's smoldering brown eyes made her knees weak. She had never had anyone affect her this way. Karen was perplexed and uncertain of the unsettling feelings that simmered within her.

Jessie could not believe how beautiful Karen was up close. Her complexion was so smooth, her skin so soft. Her eyes, which she had looked into from a distance on a few occasions, were even more breathtaking up close. They were the soft blue of the sky on a clear summer day. She really had to get to know this woman! Finally she had a name, Karen, to go along with the face she kept seeing in her dreams, the face that often kept her awake at night.

CHAPTER TWO

Julie and Rhonda had been tossing around the idea of hosting a party for the hockey team in celebration of the approaching holiday season. Although Karen was not on the team, she attended most of the games and was friends with most of the girls on the team.

"Let's include her," Julie suggested. "Judging by the questions she has been asking about Jessie lately, I bet there is an underlying interest that needs to be explored. I want to give it a little push in the right direction."

Rhonda was concerned. "Julie, you wouldn't be trying to play matchmaker here, would you?"

"Hell, yeah! I think Karen is on her way to discover a whole new world."

"Do you really think Karen may have a sexual interest in Jessie?" Rhonda asked.

"I believe she is much more interested in her than she realizes." Julie paused a moment. "Karen is treading unfamiliar territory here. I think she wants to meet Jessie and at the very least get to know more about her. All she does is talk about Number 9 and what a great player she is and how the team is lucky to have her. So all it takes for me is to get the ball rolling . . ."

The next morning at work Julie and Karen spent their break at the hospital cafeteria as they often did to get off their feet. It had been a busy morning. Karen decided on a fresh fruit cup and hot tea, Julie had her usual bowl of cereal and an order of toast.

Sitting down at a table, Julie started the conversation. "Great game last night. Exciting to watch."

Karen nodded in agreement without hesitation, her mouth full of fruit.

"Rhonda and I are hosting a party in a few weeks to celebrate the holidays."

"I don't remember the last time you and Rhonda threw a party. It has been quite some time."

"You're right. I think it was back in early February. We have decided on December 18th, two weeks from Saturday. You can come, can't you?"

"I will have to check the schedule to see if I have to work."

"I already checked for you when I was checking my own. We are both off that weekend. We can even sleep in the next morning in case we get a little wild and foolish," Julie said with a mischievous grin on her face.

Karen hesitated. "It is such a busy time of year with shopping and decorating."

Julie pushed a little harder. "Yeah, Rhonda and I discussed that. But it is still a couple of weeks away. People will have time to schedule other seasonal duties around it."

"I would love to come. I will simply have to make an extra effort to get my shopping done early. Actually that way I won't have to fight the crowds later." Karen smiled, pleased to avoid the Christmas rush. "Who else are you inviting?"

"Rhonda's entire hockey team and their partners, spouses, and a few other friends."

Karen picked up her tea casually and nodded in approval. "It should be a good time. Those women like to party. Besides it will be a good opportunity for everyone to get to know each other, especially Jessie. She only knows the girls on the team and not really anybody's significant other."

Break time was over. They headed back to work. Julie was immediately called to care for a patient who had just arrived in the emergency room, while Karen had to finish up some paperwork.

Karen was all smiles and cheerful the remainder of the day. As soon as she arrived home she marked the date on her calendar – December 18th, party – meet Jessie. Each time she thought of the date, an unfamiliar jittery sensation twitched in the pit of her stomach. Karen didn't understand what this woman was doing to her. She could not put her finger on it. All she knew was that she was attracted to Jessie in some strange way. It was an attraction she had never experienced before.

The days passed quickly. It was Thursday night, ladies' hockey night. Karen decided not to go home from work for dinner before the game. Instead she wanted to grab a bite at a burger joint and get some serious shopping done. Having planned ahead, she brought herself a change of clothes which she put on before leaving work. It was shortly after 5:00 p.m. when Karen walked to her car. She took in deep breaths of the cool evening air. What a beautiful night, she thought and looked up into the clear dark sky.

The Thousand Islands Shopping Mall was her first stop after taking time for a burger and fries. Karen was on a mission. She had a list of places to go to and pick out the ideal Christmas gifts for her parents. She also needed to get something for Julie's party on the 18th. There was enough time left before Christmas to shop for the rest of her family and friends.

Karen was tired and needed a few minutes to recoup from shopping before going to the game. She bought a cold drink and headed over to the hockey arena.

Rhonda and Julie had come to the rink a little earlier, because Rhonda wanted to extend party invitations to her teammates. Rhonda was putting her gear on, when the girls started to come in. Jessie was not there, yet.

"Can I have everyone's attention," Rhonda shouted loudly, after she had her entire gear on. "Hey, girls, listen up. Julie and I are having a party at our place for you gals and your partners, spouses, and significant others."

Rumblings and laughter erupted in the locker room.

At that moment Jessie entered. "Hey, everybody, what's going on?"

Carla spoke up. "Rhonda was just telling us that she and Julie are having a party for the team."

"Let me clarify," Rhonda interrupted. "I said the team and your partners, spouses, and significant others. We want everyone to come."

"Sounds great. I would love to get to know what makes some of you clowns, oops, I mean gals, tick." Jessie had all the players in the dressing room laughing and tossing things at her.

"I like your sense of humor," Rhonda commented. "You fit right in with the rest of these comedians."

"When did you say this big bash is taking place?" Jessie asked.

"December 18th, two weeks from Saturday."

"Oh, damn! I have a basketball tournament that day; one we are hosting here in town."

Rhonda took a deep breath. "Will you be able to make it to the party?"

"You don't want to miss a party hosted by Rhonda and Julie," Carla added. "They are always great fun."

"Tournaments do run late sometimes. But it's scheduled to be over by five. Even if it runs a bit late I should be able to make it by around eight o'clock or so."

"Perfect." Rhonda exhaled with relief. It looked like things were going to work out nicely. "Okay everybody, let's get out there and play like you are ready to party. Let's go!" Rhonda had just stirred the team up enough to get them pumped to play a fantastic game.

When Rhonda came out on the ice for her warm-up, she looked up at Julie and signaled her that Jessie was able to attend the party.

Julie began to laugh. Her matchmaking idea was in motion! She reached over and punched Karen in the arm with excitement.

Baffled Karen looked at her. "Ouch, what was that about?"

Julie giggled. "Nothing, I just love Rhonda so much!"

"You and Rhonda are very lucky to have each other. I am envious of your relationship." Karen sighed. Someday I hope to experience the same happiness with someone, she thought.

Karen had planned on wrapping some of her presents on Saturday and putting up her Christmas tree. When the phone rang at five-thirty in the morning it startled her. It was the hospital. Someone had called in sick. They needed her to come in for an extra shift. After dragging herself out of bed and turning on the kettle for her morning tea, she hopped in the shower. Soon she was refreshed and ready to head off to work.

Actually it wasn't a bad day at work, and the time went by fairly quickly. When Karen got home she was tired. However, she still wanted to get her tree up and decorated, so she called her sister Joan for help.

Joan was only three years older than Karen. Growing up they had not been close, but that had changed since they had both moved away from home and got their own lives.

"Hi, Joan. I was planning on putting my Christmas tree up tonight, and wondered if you would give me a hand with the decorations."

"Sorry, Karen, but Sophie is home tonight. We were looking forward to spending time together." Sophie was Joan's daughter. Being a teenager, she was not often up for a night in with her parents.

"Bring Sophie along. It would be great fun having the two of you here decorating and singing carols." Karen was hopeful. "What do you say? Ask Sophie if she would like to join us." Karen could hear Joan yell up the stairs to Sophie.

"Actually, Karen, Sophie thinks it would be a blast. What time do you want us?"

"Well, it is almost six o'clock now. How about seven?"

"Seven works for us. See you then."

Karen hung up the phone, prepared soup for a quick dinner and got some treats ready to serve her guests.

It wasn't long before the doorbell rang. "I am so glad you both were able to make it on such short notice. I don't enjoy decorating my Christmas tree alone."

Sophie jumped in right away. "Aunt Karen, you really need to find someone. You deserve to be happy and not alone all the time."

"Is that so?" Karen tugged on Sophie's shirt collar. She pulled her close to give her a kiss on the cheek. "What makes you think I am lonely and unhappy?"

"Aunt Karen, I didn't mean you were unhappy! You are one of the happiest people I know. What I meant is that you should have a companion, someone to share special occasions with."

"Well, if I had a companion, then I wouldn't have this special time with my favorite niece and sister, right?" Karen teased Sophie a bit longer, although she knew Sophie had a point. She did want a companion to share special times with. She always figured it would happen when the time was right.

Over the course of the evening the singing got a little crazy and loud. "It's a good thing I live out in the country so my neighbors can't hear us." Karen put the final ornament on the tree and brought in eggnog and snacks.

"Hey, Aunt Karen, would you be interested in coming to our basketball tournament in a couple of weeks?"

Karen immediately felt a tug in her stomach. "A basketball tournament?"

"Yeah, on December 18th," Sophie confirmed.

"Roger and I are looking forward to it," Joan intersected. "We have been unable to attend any games so far. But we have heard a lot about Miss Carmichael."

"Miss Carmichael is an awesome coach," Sophie added with enthusiasm. "And she has a great sense of humor."

Karen knew the party was on that same night. "I would love to come and watch. Joan, call me and let me know when the games are, and I will watch with you and Roger."

"Great. I'll take any chance I can get to spend time with my baby sister." Joan stood up. "Come on, Sophie. We better get going, or your father will think we got lost." They all chuckled and headed toward the door.

"I can't thank you two enough for your terrific company and your help. I really enjoyed it. The singing was pretty special for sure!" Karen could not resist one last jab at the vocals. They all hugged and kissed good-bye.

"We had fun, too, Aunt Karen. Thanks for including me." Sophie gave Karen one more squeeze and told her that she loved her.

As they were leaving they were surprised to see that it had started to snow.

"What a perfect ending to a tree decorating evening with family." Karen wrapped her arms around herself, rubbing them to keep the chill off as she watched her company head out the driveway. After they were on the road, Karen gave Roger a quick call to let him know Joan and Sophie had just left her place so he wouldn't worry.

Karen came back inside and made herself another cup of tea. She slipped into her pajamas and wrapped herself in a housecoat. Putting her feet up, she relaxed on the couch, admiring her Christmas tree. How nice it looked! Her thoughts turned to Miss Jessie Carmichael. Karen took a sip of tea and sighed. Why do I like her so much when I don't even know her?

She set her tea aside and fell into a peaceful sleep.

Snow fell steadily for two days and made everything shimmer and appear clean and pure. It certainly helped put the feel of Christmas in the air. Everywhere decorations and pretty lights were hung up, and holiday tunes were playing. Karen loved this time of year. She enjoyed all facets of the season except for the crowded shopping. But thanks to Julie's and Rhonda's party she had her Christmas shopping done and almost all gifts wrapped.

Due to another extra shift at work Karen had missed the hockey game the previous week. No wonder she was looking forward to this weekend. She hadn't been this excited about an outing in a long time. Saturday couldn't come soon enough.

Jessie's schedule had been crazy. She had basketball practices after school every day and road trips for games a couple of times a week. Basketball and volleyball practices kept her busy, but they also kept her fit and feeling vibrant. Jessie loved her job, although it consumed a lot of her time.

Jessie lived in an apartment in town. It worked convenient with her extracurricular activities. She intended to go home for the holidays to see her family in Mattawa for Christmas break. But before she needed a couple of extra days to finish her Christmas shopping. Due to her obligations she was far behind. When she got home to her apartment after teaching all day, she simply wanted to go over the game plans and mark papers.

Jessie was very excited to be going home to see her family. Along with her parents, her brother Tom still lived in Mattawa with his wife Sharon. Jessie talked to them regularly.

Her brother Tom was her best friend and her biggest fan. His support of her lifestyle was amazing to Jessie. He had been by her side through all of it. When she had told her parents, Tom had held her hand, giving her strength. And when her former partner Lynne had left her for another woman two and a half years ago, Tom had come to be with her. He had held her while she had cried. He had always been there for her, and Jessie would be there for him if he ever needed her. Tom and Sharon had been married for four years. They wanted children, but had not been able to conceive, yet. As Tom always said, "It sure was fun trying."

Feeling exhausted and a bit lonely, Jessie dialed Tom's number. "Hey Tom, how are you keeping up?"

"Pretty good, Jess. Good to hear from you."

"Are you ready for Christmas? Which really means: Do you have my presents bought, yet?" Jessie teased.

"Always the comedian." Tom snickered. "So, tell me, any new love interests I should know about?" Tom always probed into Jessie's love life, hoping she would find someone that he felt was good enough for her sometime soon.

"I have my eye on a woman that comes to watch our hockey games. She has a beautiful smile and is very attractive. I can't stop thinking about her." Jessie admitted. Her name is Karen."

"Have you asked her out?"

"No. I am not even sure she is gay."

"Since when has that ever held you back? Have you lost your touch? What is taking you so long?"

"There are lots of things I don't know about her. I don't even know her last name. Maybe she is married or has a partner already? What does she do for a living?" Jessie blurted out.

"Okay, slow down," Tom stopped her. "Sounds to me like you are thinking too much. Why not act first, think later? That is what you always did." He laughed.

"Yeah, and look where that got me. I have a lot of questions. I will ask Julie and Rhonda at their party on Saturday night."

"Will this woman be there? Or can you invite her?"

"No, it is for the hockey team only. But I plan on finding out a lot more about Karen, and I will make this party no matter how tired I may be after the tournament. I have to make the time to socialize and meet new friends," Jessie explained with new determination.

"Well, Sharon is calling me. I'd better get going. Keep me informed. Ask her to the party anyway. I love you, Jess."

"Love you too. Bye, Tom."

Jessie needed this Saturday night for her own sanity. It would be good to be with other lesbians and to see her teammates with their partners. She wanted to meet everybody. Jessie considered Tom's suggestion of asking Karen to the party.

On Tuesday Jessie was going over some drills with the girls in her class. About twenty-five minutes into the period Jessie was watching Hope getting ready for the pass. She was in a good position, just outside the key. Sophie passed the ball to Hope.

"Nicely done, girls. Excellent set-up," Jessie praised.

Hope caught the ball. With a firm hold she went for a lay-up. When Hope came down, her foot landed on the side. Hope went down to the floor so fast Jessie knew she had been hurt.

Jessie rushed over. "Hope, don't move. Stay put for a moment."

"It hurts like hell! Ohhhhh, shit! It hurts!" Hope was yelling and holding her leg.

"I know it does," Jessie sympathized. "Just take a few deep breaths for me."

"Ah, hell. It hurts!"

"Hope, look at me. Take a deep breath," Jessie repeated. "Okay, now let me have a look." Jessie looked up. "Sophie, can you please get the cold packs from the first aid kit in my office? Hurry!"

Within seconds Sophie was back.

Hope's ankle was swollen. Once she pulled down the sock, the entire ankle was already turning black and blue. "Hope, I have to take you to the ER."

"I can't walk, Miss Carmichael." Tears streamed down Hope's face.

"Just try to be calm and keep the cold pack on it." Jessie stood up, blew the whistle and motioned for the class to gather around. "I need someone to gather up the equipment and put it away."

Instantly hands went up. Everyone volunteered to help. Jessie picked two of the girls for the job. "Obviously class is over, but I expect you girls to be responsible enough to spend the rest of this period in the library or put your next half hour to good use." Jessie's tone told the girls that she was serious. "No goofing off. I don't want to hear about anybody misbehaving or getting into trouble." Jessie dismissed them. "Sophie, can you please help me get Hope over to the bench?"

"No problem." Sophie was immediately ready to help out.

"Hope, tell Sophie which coat is yours, and she will get it for you. I need to advise the secretary to call your parents. I will be right back." Jessie turned to Sophie. "I am going to need help getting her to the car. Do you mind?"

Sophie replied without hesitation. "No, I don't mind at all."

Jessie pulled up just outside the hospital's emergency entrance.

"Stay here, Hope. I will get you a wheelchair." All Jessie could think about was taking care of her student. She headed in through the automatic doors. Just inside there were three wheelchairs. Jessie grabbed one and headed back out to get Hope. Once they had manoeuvred Hope into the wheelchair, Jessie took her inside and then ran back to park the car.

Jessie returned so quickly, Hope was surprised. "Wow, that was fast!"

"I didn't want you waiting here in pain, so I ran. Besides, the extra exercise won't hurt," she joked, trying to take Hope's mind off her pain.

Hope smiled. "You are in great shape, Miss Carmichael. I pray that I'm in as good a shape as you are when I'm your age."

"My age?" Jessie grinned. "I will take that as a compliment. But that won't get you any higher grade than you deserve!" she joked.

Hope was feeling much more relaxed and laughed out loud, however, the pain in her foot and ankle made her wince.

"Come on, let's get you treated." Jessie wheeled Hope over to the admissions window.

Much to her surprise the lady behind the window was Julie. Pleased to see her familiar face, Jessie relaxed a bit.

"Hi, Jessie. What brings you in today? Nothing too serious, I hope," Julie queried.

"Actually I have brought in one of my students. She may have sprained her ankle. I need to get her checked."

"Okay, let me get some information from you." Once they had filled out as much of the paperwork as they could, Julie gestured to the chairs. "Have a seat. Someone will be with you shortly."

Jessie and Hope sat in the waiting room for no more than ten minutes. The double doors opened and a nurse came out. With a friendly voice the nurse announced Hope Harper's name. Both Hope and Jessie looked up. You could have knocked Jessie over with a feather if she hadn't already been sitting down. There stood Karen.

Karen couldn't believe who she saw sitting in her emergency room. No wonder Julie had insisted she handle this one. Karen forced herself to remain focused on the patient.

Jessie jumped up. "This is Hope Harper. She is one of my students. I am Jessie."

"Yes, I know, Jessie Carmichael, hockey player and physical education teacher." Karen held out her hand. "I am very pleased to officially meet you. I'm Karen, Karen Andrews." Forcing herself to take her eyes off Jessie, she looked towards Hope. "Hope, let's go and take a look at your ankle." Karen steered the wheelchair over to the double doors. Smiling she turned to Jessie. "I will be back to get you shortly."

"Okay, I will be here." Jessie was going nowhere.

After they had disappeared behind the doors, Jessie was the only one in the waiting room. She couldn't keep herself from doing a little happy dance, not knowing that Julie was watching her the whole time.

Jessie sat there going over the vision of Karen in her mind. She had always been turned on by a woman in uniform, and Karen definitely did her nurse uniform justice. What lovely legs she had, so firm, so smooth and silky in her white stockings and moderately short skirt. Jessie envisioned running her fingers over those legs, caressing them, inching higher and higher up Karen's thigh . . .

"Miss Carmichael?"

Jessie did not hear her name. She was deep in her daydream.

"Miss Carmichael?" A lady was standing there looking at her.

"Yes." Jessie blushed. She was thankful her thoughts could not be heard.

"Hi. I'm Hope's mother, Beth Harper. Is Hope doing okay? Where is she?" Beth inquired.

"She should be back any minute. They took her to get X-rays of her ankle," Jessie informed Beth. "Hope took a nasty fall today on the court. I think she may have sprained it. I really don't know. It may even be broken. I felt it was best to bring her here and get it checked out."

"I am very grateful. Thank you." Beth appreciated Jessie's actions.

The double doors opened again. Karen appeared. Jessie was still standing with Beth. "Karen, this is Beth, Hope's mother."

"Nice to meet you. Come right this way." Karen gestured for them to follow her. They reached Hope's bedside. "Hope has a badly sprained ankle. Sometimes this is more painful than a fracture," Karen explained. "I will see if Doctor Stratton is available now to come and talk to you."

She left.

The doctor came in and explained what Karen had already told them. "I will be sending Hope home with crutches. She needs to stay off her foot for a few days and take it slowly for a couple of weeks. Hope will be fine, but she will definitely not be playing in the tournament this weekend."

Neither Hope, nor Jessie were pleased with this information. This would be a big setback for the team.

Hope and her mother left together.

Jessie felt no urgency to get back to the school at this point. She waited for a convenient time to approach Julie. "I didn't know you worked at the hospital. I guess it never came up in our conversations."

Julie's opportunity had arrived. "I suppose you didn't know Karen was a nurse either?"

"No. Actually, I had no idea. It is nice to see that you two can work together and still be such good friends."

"Karen is a wonderful person. She makes it easy."

"I am sure Karen would say the same about you."

Just then Karen came in behind Julie. She was returning a clipboard with a patient's updated file. "Hey, I heard my name. You are mentioning only good things, I hope," Karen joked playfully.

"I was just telling Jessie what a pain in the butt you are," Julie retorted.

They all laughed.

Karen looked at Jessie. What beautiful eyes . . .! Breathtaking . . .!

"Well, I really should be going," Jessie announced. "Thanks again for your help Karen."

"No problem. I'm glad I was here," Karen replied, "and don't always believe what Julie tells you. She is known for her mischievous ways." Karen winked and left the room.

Jessie was caught off guard and had to catch her breath.

"Are you both coming to the hockey game on Thursday?" Jessie asked Julie.

"I am for sure. As for Karen, she has had to work some extra shifts lately. Otherwise she'll definitely be there."

"Great, see you Thursday."

Julie and Karen headed out from work that night both in high spirits.

"You thought you were pretty clever earlier today, didn't you?" Karen accused her colleague.

Julie grinned. "I have no clue what you are referring to."

"Yeah, you do! You knew exactly that Jessie was in the waiting room today, when you called for me."

"I have no control over who comes into the ER. Isn't it our job to help those in need? I think you took care of them both very well." Julie laughed. She was pretty proud of herself.

"Very funny. I must admit it was nice to see Jessie outside the hockey rink. She seems very nice."

"Well, Jessie wanted to know if you were coming to the game on Thursday."

"Did she? Or are you just making that up? Besides, why would she care?"

"Not sure. I have my suspicions," Julie teased. "Nevertheless, I am telling the truth."

"What are you talking about? What suspicions? Maybe she would just like to have a few more connections. She is still fairly new around here."

"That could very well be." Julie had a sense it was more than friendship Jessie wanted, but left it at that, especially since she had witnessed Jessie's happy dance earlier.

"Anyway, see you tomorrow. Say hello to Rhonda for me."

The next two days were trying for the basketball team. Hope showed up for support, but could not do anything more. The girls were discouraged knowing that Hope would not be playing. Jessie explained the new strategies she had worked out. Although the girls didn't play as well without Hope, they gave their best. The team still had a good shot at the tournament. Never give up! was what Jessie taught her girls, and that was what she lived by.

Hockey night couldn't come soon enough. Jessie needed the game to release her tension. She was feeling anxious about Saturday's tournament and the fact that it was being hosted by her school. Most of the girls' parents were expected to come. Many of them she had already met, but there were still a lot she had yet to meet. She wanted her girls to do well and have fun.

Jessie arrived at the rink. Rhonda was already there. She always came early to get her goalie gear on.

"Do you still plan on coming Saturday night?" Rhonda asked.

"I am looking forward to it," Jessie replied. "Would it be okay if I brought someone to the party?"

Rhonda was surprised. "Sure. Sounds like it will be a good turnout. Initially we were a little concerned because of the holiday season, but that doesn't seem to be an issue."

"Did Julie mention my visit to the ER earlier this week?"

Rhonda smiled. "Yeah, how is your student doing?"

"Hobbling on crutches and loving the attention."

They both laughed. The other teammates started coming in. It was getting loud. Everyone seemed to be in good spirits.

While she was going out onto the ice Jessie immediately checked the bleachers and gave a wide grin and a wave to Karen and Julie. Both ladies waved back.

The girls were on the ice doing their warm up exercises and drills, all taking shots at Rhonda in the net. The game began. The first two periods went well. The Rideau Rockets were ahead 2-0. When the second period ended, Karen stood up and put her coat on.

"Are you going for a coffee?" Julie asked.

"No, I have to go pick up Sophie at the mall tonight. Joan and Roger are busy and asked if I could bring her home," Karen explained. "Please say hi to Rhonda for me."

"And to Jessie, if I see her?" Julie teased.

Karen smiled. "If you see her, of course."

"You are still coming Saturday night?" Julie reminded Karen.

"Definitely," Karen confirmed. "Do you need me to bring anything or come over early and help you get ready?" Karen offered.

"Would you have time to prepare a veggie and dip platter?" Julie asked. "It is the one thing I forgot. Rhonda reminded me on our way over here tonight."

"No problem." Karen was pleased to be able to help.

"You are the best. I knew I could count on you." Julie got up and gave her friend a big hug. "Come prepared for a good time."

"Okay, see you then." Karen intentionally did not tell Julie she was going to watch the basketball tournament on Saturday.

Julie sat by herself, hoping her efforts would pay off with Jessie and Karen.

When the ladies came back out for the third period, Jessie was disappointed that Karen was not there. She had planned to ask Karen out for a coffee after the game and had also intended to invite her to the party on Saturday. Now she wouldn't see Karen until after the Christmas break. She was going home to Mattawa on Tuesday and would not be back until after the New Year. Jessie's heart sank.

CHAPTER THREE

Saturday had finally arrived. The sun was shining; the temperature was reasonably mild. There was no snow in the forecast.

Sophie had called Karen the previous evening and confirmed that her first basketball game was scheduled for 9:30 a.m. and that Joan and Roger would meet her at the school by 9:00.

Karen was ambiguous as to why she was a bundle of nerves. Why am I so antsy? It makes no sense to feel this agitated about Jessie's tournament. It's not like I am playing! she thought and quickly corrected herself. I mean Sophie's tournament. Jessie just happens to be her coach. Lucky for me I get the pleasure of watching them both.

Karen got up early and made the party dip Julie wanted. She laid out her clothes for the evening, so they were ready for her when she got home. She would pick up fresh veggies later allowing for enough time to cut and clean them.

Karen left early to pick up coffees for Joan and Roger and a French Vanilla Cappuccino for herself. The parking lot was already full, as there was one game scheduled to be played before Sophie's. Karen found a spot, parked, and headed towards the school. At the school's entrance she noticed Joan right away.

"You didn't have to get us coffee," Joan greeted, smiling.

"But I am sure glad you did!" Roger added with his smug grin.

They exchanged hugs and headed inside. Karen and Joan followed Roger as he led them to the gymnasium. There were still plenty of good seats available. They got themselves settled where they had a good view of the whole court and were quickly brought up to speed on the game that was just about finished. Cornwall was beating Kingston seventy-six to sixty-six. There were still ten minutes left to play.

Karen began to relax. How silly to be so nervous about coming to watch, she thought. The first game was over, Cornwall won. The T.I.S.S. girls were coming out to warm up as was the Cardinal team they would be playing against. The sound of bouncing balls echoed throughout the gym. Karen scanned the court looking for Sophie. There she was, sporting the number four on her team jersey. Seeing Sophie made Karen proud. She got a lump in her throat and became choked up with emotions.

Joan looked over at Karen and slapped her on the leg. "You stop that right now! Otherwise you are going to have me crying," Joan scolded.

"I'm sorry, it is just that I am proud of her, and I don't get to see her like this very often." Karen took a Kleenex to dab her eyes. "Okay, now I am fine."

They both giggled and went back to watching the activity on the court. Karen searched the court for Jessie.

Jessie had just entered the gym from the changing rooms. Now she blew her whistle. Immediately the girls gathered around her to go over the game plan. You could tell by the way the girls responded to Jessie, that she had their respect. The moment she entered the gym she was in control.

Jessie finished her pep talk with her team. The girls huddled closer and proudly delivered their team cheer. The Cardinal team followed suit. Both teams seemed very enthusiastic and ready to play.

Soon the game was underway. Watching those young girls with all that energy had Karen's adrenaline pumping. She looked at Jessie, who remained calm and cool. Jessie yelled her commands out sharp and clear. There was no question as to what she was expecting from the girls. Her direction was very precise.

Jessie wore a very attractive black polyester Nike track suit. There were three narrow white stripes down each leg that widened at the bottom, with a zipper on the outside of each leg that was half undone. She dresses very stylish. Her pants fit snugly and nicely form to the shape of her buttocks. A nice handful, Karen thought, blushing.

The jacket, also black, had one wide and one narrow white stripe down each arm. Jessie wore a white V-neck shirt that could be seen below the bottom of the black polyester jacket about an inch. The only other part of the white V-neck that could be seen was directly at Jessie's cleavage. What an attractive woman she is, Karen couldn't help but think. Jessie certainly knows how to dress.

Jessie seemed to be oblivious to all the spectators. She was totally focused on the game. Sophie's team was down eight points going into half-time. The whistle blew, and the teams cleared the floor.

Once the game had stopped, the sound of voices increased in volume. Karen found herself listening to the conversations around her. Joan and Roger were involved in their own assessment of the game and discussed Sophie's performance. They were very proud parents and justifiably so. Sophie was a great young lady. The people in the stands were parents and friends of the players. Karen could hear casual conversations around her. Some talked about how well the team had been doing this season compared to the past few years. How they were grateful Mr. Boswell had retired this year. That it was time for the school to have a change. What a welcome addition Miss Carmichael was. That the students really liked her and showed significant improvement in their skill. At the same time they were having genuine fun.

Another conversation within earshot was less flattering for Jessie. A certain man had heard Miss Carmichael seemed to spend her spare time with women. This fellow did not elaborate, he only lifted his eyebrows in a sceptical gesture, implying an additional accusation. "As long as she keeps her personal life away from our girls ..." In other words, out of sight, out of mind.

Overall, the consensus was that everyone liked Jessie and appreciated her talent and her support of the kids.

Is Jessie a lesbian? Karen thought to herself. I wonder if Julie and Rhonda know. Maybe she has a partner? Karen became uneasy with this possibility, unsure as to why.

As Karen had watched the game, she had noticed Hope was there in her team uniform, but still relying on her crutches to get around.

She was showing great team support and was encouraging her team-mates from the sidelines.

Sophie, all smiles and energetic, happened to look up and spot Karen with Joan and Roger. Her hand went up sending a big wave off to Karen. Karen automatically returned the wave, and so did Joan.

Sophie's enthusiasm caught Jessie's attention. Jessie looked up to see what had distracted her student. She spotted Karen waving and smiling at Sophie. Jessie could not believe Karen was in the stands. Karen was wearing a white knit, tight fitting, low cut sweater that emphasized her very appealing, well-endowed bosom.

Karen did not notice Jessie starring at her. She was too occupied by Sophie for the moment.

Jessie noticed Karen was sitting beside a woman. She wondered who this woman was and if perhaps Karen was involved with someone after all.

The second half was about to start. Jessie had to get herself and her girls focused again. "Sophie, back in the game, please. Okay girls, let's give our cheer and get back out there. Let's show them how it is done." Jessie clapped her hands and blew her whistle. "Let's go!"

The girls gave their loud energetic cheer. With great passion they got back into the game. The lead kept going back and forth. Jessie on occasion would look up to see Karen watching the game intently. Karen and the woman beside her were both cheering for the girls. Having fans really got the players pumped. As a matter of fact, one fan in particular got the coach pumped, as well.

When the game got close, Jessie paced the sidelines, back and forth, back and forth, arms folded, and then she shouted out a command and clapped her hands. "Let's go!"

Is Jessie gay? Karen wondered again, not that it mattered to her one way or the other.

The game had only two minutes remaining; the score was eighty-two to eighty for Cardinal. Jessie called a time-out. The girls gathered around her, hanging onto her every word.

Jessie instructed the girls how she wanted her strategy played out. "Come on girls, there are a lot of people here to see what we can do," she finished. "I have faith in all of you."

Not only were the girls able to pull off Jessie's strategy once, but twice in a row. They won the game by two points.

Karen watched Jessie as she picked up her clipboard and headed out. Joan and Roger got up, stretched and went to wait for Sophie.

Before she left the gym, Jessie looked up one last time. She felt like Karen was checking her out. She wondered at the possibility that Karen could be interested in her. However the woman with her was a concern.

In the changing room Jessie informed the girls that their next game was at 12:30. If they won that one, they would play the finals at 3:45.

"Great job out there girls," Jessie praised. "You made me very proud. I need everyone to be back here by 12:00 to warm up. See you then. Please don't eat a heavy lunch." She dismissed them.

"Sophie, you have a couple of fans here today I noticed," Jessie commented.

Sophie giggled. "Yes, my mom and dad are here with Aunt Karen."

"Karen is your aunt? She was the ER-nurse when I took Hope over earlier this week."

"I'm not surprised. She seems to always be there. Aunt Karen is great. She's lots of fun and very kind-hearted."

"She sure helped us out that day," Jessie praised.

"I guess that's why she makes such a great nurse," Sophie said with a huge smile. "I had better get out there. They are waiting for me." Sophie left quickly.

Jessie was left to her own thoughts. So the other woman was Sophie's mother. She now remembered having met her parents a few months back at Parent/Teacher-Night. There had been so many parents that evening that it was difficult to remember them all.

Jessie went over the team strategy one more time and got herself a quick bite to eat. Since T.I.S.S. was the host team of the tournament, she had to make herself available in the gym in case she was needed.

Karen and the others went out to Kelsey's Restaurant for a light lunch. Karen was glad to be a part of the day out with her family.

Other than her parents, this was all the family she had. Karen respected both Joan and Roger and admired the way they had raised Sophie.

"You guys had us worried, Sophie. We thought you were going to lose it. What an exciting finish!"

"We were all really nervous. Mrs. Carmichael took the time out, laid out the plan and we were able to follow through," Sophie praised.

Over lunch they talked mostly about the tournament and wondered how the rest of the day would unfold. Hope's inability to play was unfortunate for the team. However, winning the first game had given the players much needed confidence.

Karen kept wondering what Jessie was doing with her time off between games. She was anxious to get back. She enjoyed watching Sophie play, but observing Jessie on the sidelines was heart-warming in some bizarre way.

"Miss Carmichael noticed Aunt Karen in the stands this morning," Sophie said suddenly.

"Oh, what do you mean?" Joan asked.

"Well, when she took Hope to the ER this week, Aunt Karen was on duty," Sophie informed.

Karen spoke up. "Yes, I did meet her earlier this week at the hospital. She seems like a nice person. She definitely has compassion for her students."

"That is good to hear," voiced Joan. "It gives parents much relief to know that their children are left in the hands of people who care and who do their job well."

"I heard a few comments about your coach today that concern me," Roger spoke up. "Some people think she is queer. If she ever touches you inappropriately, Sweetheart, let me know."

"Dad, please don't start. I like her, she's not like that," Sophie defended Jessie.

Karen didn't know what to say. Finally she took Sophie's side. "I like her, as well. She seems very nice."

"I don't know if it's true. All I'm saying is to watch yourself. If I ever find out she so much as looks at you the wrong way …" Roger pointed directly at Sophie.

"We better get going. I am supposed to be back soon." Infuriated Sophie got up and stomped off.

The ride back to the school was quiet. Karen was surprised by Roger's behavior. She had no idea he harbored such feelings.

Time had gone by quickly. Before too long the girls started to file back into the gym. The tournament was running about ten minutes behind. When Sophie and her family arrived, Karen took her jacket off and hung it over her arm. She scanned the gym looking for Jessie. When she spotted her, Jessie was on her way towards her.

Jessie knew this might be her only chance to talk to Karen before the holidays. "Hello, Karen."

"Hi, Jessie. You have your hands full today, haven't you?" Karen gestured towards the court.

"You bet. I love it though," Jessie confessed.

"Jessie, I believe you have met my sister Joan and her husband Roger." Karen introduced them casually, trying to include them in the conversation.

"Yes, at Parents' Night. So good to see you again," Jessie said, pleased Joan was Karen's sister.

"You have done a great job with the girls. Your coaching ability certainly shows," Joan praised.

"They make it easy for me." Jessie laughed and rolled her big brown eyes.

"Well, we should get to our seats," Roger said. "Coming, Joan?"

Joan turned to Jessie. "Good luck to you and the team."

Off they went. Sophie had already gone to join her friends.

Jessie loved the sweater Karen was wearing. It showed her figure nicely. Jessie knew Karen would be wearing this the next time she showed up in her dreams. Probably tonight!

Karen felt a bit uncomfortable and waited for Jessie to say something.

"So, did you notice Hope is here showing her team support?" Jessie asked.

"I noticed that earlier, yes. She was right in there, cheering them on. True team spirit," Karen stated.

The whistle blew from behind them. The referee waved to Jessie to come and get the team warmed up.

"I have to go now, but maybe I can see you after the tournament?" Jessie asked.

"Actually, I will be leaving right after this game. Unfortunately, I won't be able to stay and watch the last game," Karen informed with disappointment on her face. "I still have things I need to do today. I wish you all the best with the tournament though," Karen said supportively.

"Thanks, I appreciate that. I guess I had better get going. See you around then," Jessie said, turning to walk towards the court.

Karen located Joan and Roger and settled in for another good game. She was thrilled about her conversation with Jessie and hopeful they would become friends. What an attractive woman she is. Her complexion is flawless, and that track suit beautifully forms her figure. These thoughts passed through Karen's mind again. I still hope to see her at the party, but Jessie didn't mention anything about going to Julie and Rhonda's. I bet she'll be too tired after a day like this to go out and party.

Joan cut into Karen's thoughts. "You must have made some impression on Miss Carmichael," Joan remarked.

"Jessie just wanted to thank me again for helping Hope and her at the hospital the other day."

Jessie gave Karen a game to remember. The girls seemed to be having fun and were enjoying playing as a team. One thing even Roger commented on was how the players used each other and counted on their teammates to do their jobs. No player was trying to take over and do it all on her own.

Karen could not believe how fast this game had passed. There were only a couple of minutes left, and Sophie and her team were ahead by twelve points. Karen was disappointed she was going to miss the championship game, but could not let Julie down either.

After the game Jessie was busy tending to tasks at hand and people asking her questions. Karen did not get a chance to say anything more to her before she left. She waved at Sophie and wished her all the best in the finals. "Give me a call tomorrow, and let me know how you did. Good luck!" Off she went.

CHAPTER FOUR

Karen headed to the grocery store to pick up the fresh vegetables for the party. Driving home she felt self-conscious and confused that she was so consumed by thoughts of Jessie. Once the groceries were in the house, Karen went back out to fill the bird feeders. Karen began humming, joining in the birds' chorus of chirps and whistles. She loved feeling a part of something as beautiful as the nature that surrounded her.

Back inside, she turned on some rock'n'roll tunes, cranking them loud enough to make her hips feel the beat. The vegetables took some time to clean and cut up. After arranging them on a platter, Karen focused on getting herself ready. She changed her mind on the outfit. The one she had chosen earlier no longer seemed to match her mood. Karen decided on something a little more casual and dressed it up with a couple of accessories.

It was almost seven o'clock when Karen headed out. On her drive she wondered if Sophie's team had won the basketball tournament. She hoped they had. Everyone had put so much effort into it.

By the time Karen arrived at Julie and Rhonda's, there were already about eight or ten people there. That was good. Karen never liked to be the first to arrive. Julie met her at the door and helped her with the platter. Karen put down her cooler, took her coat off and handed Julie the Christmas ornament she had picked up as a hostess gift.

"What a beautiful decoration! That is so sweet of you! You are always so thoughtful! And, thanks so much for doing the veggies and the dip for me, Karen." Julie was truly grateful of Karen's efforts.

"No problem. I wouldn't have offered if I didn't want to help." Once her coat was hung up Karen and Julie exchanged hugs and kisses as usual.

Just then Rhonda arrived. "Hey, I want my share of the warm fuzzies going on in here." They laughed as Rhonda gave Karen a big hug. "I don't have to tell you this, but make yourself at home," Rhonda instructed.

They headed towards the kitchen where people seemed to have gathered. Karen quickly greeted everyone and mixed herself a drink.

Jane and Sharon were there. They were a cute couple that had started dating about six months ago. Then there were Janet and Martha. They seemed like a nice couple. Karen didn't really know them that well. She had only met them a few times. Mary managed to get John to come with her. Not many of the guys usually came. Probably because some were a little uncomfortable when their wives got more stares from the girls than they did.

John however always fit in and seemed very secure in his own relationship. He usually had a good time. There were also Heather and Connie from the hockey team who each came alone.

Karen felt comfortable. She knew everyone who was there. The doorbell kept ringing, and people kept arriving. It was starting to get louder. Groups of people now spread around the living room and the kitchen. It was just after eight. Still Jessie had not arrived. Obviously her day must have been too tiring. Karen was extremely disappointed at this realization, but she could not let it show. Julie and Rhonda would question her, if they saw her moping. Karen decided to make the best of it and party like she came to do.

Just then Julie entered the room. "Is anybody interested in playing charades?"

Along with Karen there were seven others willing to embarrass themselves, which made two teams of four. Julie and Rhonda each picked their teams. Karen was on Rhonda's team, as well as Barb and John. Julie had Martha, Jane and Connie on her team. Julie went over the rules, and the game began.

Karen was on her second drink and felt pretty relaxed. Even those that were not really playing were yelling out their guesses.

Once again it was Karen's turn. She had to act out "pain in the neck".

Everybody was laughing and talking loudly. Nobody heard the doorbell ring. Jessie let herself in and followed the sound of the laughter. She opened a beer for herself and searched for the cause of the noise. Just then she spotted Karen acting out a charade in the center of the room. Jessie moved closer to get a better view and was happy that she had made the effort to come tonight.

It took a bit of exaggerated effort on Karen's part to get the team to guess the word "pain". The "in the" came pretty easily. Karen could not help herself and immediately turned her back to everyone, stuck out her behind and pointed to it. Everybody yelled "ass" and laughed. They were clapping for themselves, proud that they had it. Then Karen turned and signalled they were wrong. She was laughing out loud. Redoing the last word again, "neck" was just as easy as "ass" for them to figure out, but not nearly as funny.

Karen was not aware that Jessie had entered the room. Once she finished, she grabbed her glass and decided to have one more drink before switching to tea.

Jessie had watched the whole charade and was laughing with everyone else at Karen's actions. Karen had a great personality. She was funny, smart, polite, well liked and good looking. Jessie was smitten. Karen was wearing a navy pair of slacks with fine pinstripes, along with a white blouse that had a blue jay embroidered over the left breast. The blouse was unbuttoned just enough to show a lace camisole, drawing attention to her breasts.

Karen was mixing her drink when Jessie came up beside her.

"Hey there, I didn't know they were having live entertainment here tonight," Jessie said playfully.

"The pay is bad, but the fringe benefits are pretty good," Karen remarked laughing. Looking up she discovered it was Jessie standing there. Her stomach instantly had butterflies.

"Now what fringe benefits would Julie and Rhonda have that would interest you?" Jessie played along, hopeful and curious about the answer.

"If I told you, I would have to kill you," Karen quipped.

They both laughed.

"You sure are quite the performer," Jessie praised, not getting the information she was looking for.

"I couldn't help myself. Opportunity knocked, and I was unable to resist." Karen was leaning against the wall. Jessie stood beside her. She was wearing flattering black slacks with a black T-shirt under a light blue fleece jacket. She looked comfortable and relaxed. Everything looked good on her. "So, tell me, did you win the tournament?" Karen asked.

"Unfortunately no, we didn't. We lost the last game by six points."

"That's too bad. Your girls played so well today," Karen sympathized.

"Yes, I am very proud of them. They gave it a good go."

Just then Julie walked into the room. "Hey, you finally made it," she said to Jessie.

"Just in time to catch the star of the show with her charade." Jessie gestured towards Karen.

"You caught the main act, did you?" Julie laughed.

"It was the only act I saw, but I am glad I didn't miss it."

"Okay, okay enough." Karen blushed.

"Let me go and grab Rhonda another beer." Julie left the room thrilled with the fact the two of them were talking.

Twenty minutes later Rhonda discovered Karen and Jessie in the kitchen. Jessie was sitting on the counter; Karen was making herself a cup of tea. She was familiar with her friend's kitchen. She had put the kettle on to boil and was getting a mug from the cupboard along with the teabags.

Jessie was watching Karen's every move. Karen on the other hand seemed to be oblivious of the effect she had on Jessie.

"Are you gals doing okay in here?" Rhonda asked. Karen was always a little naive. How long would it take her to figure out it was a woman that was going to make her truly happy?

"Yes, just great!" Jessie answered quickly, and Karen agreed.

"These seem to be going down pretty good tonight." Rhonda grabbed another beer from the fridge.

At that moment Connie came in. "Jessie, some of us are about to play a new game. Martha is going to teach it to us, but I need a partner. Come on and play, be my partner," she pleaded.

"I'll have to pass. I'm really tired from the tournament today. Besides, I'm enjoying my visit with Karen."

Connie left the room, but not without sending Karen an unpleasant look that clearly conveyed her jealousy.

Karen felt a little awkward, but it wasn't like Jessie couldn't have gone if she had wanted to.

Rhonda and Jessie smiled at each other and continued their conversation.

"Your Christmas decorations are absolutely beautiful. Who is the one with the creative touch?" Jessie complimented.

"That would be Julie. She has the patience for that. I help her, but she knows what looks good."

"She certainly has the knack for it," Jessie praised again.

Karen was almost done making her tea and listened to the conversation.

"How long have you and Julie been partners?" Jessie inquired.

"Believe it or not, it has only been three and a half years. The best three and a half years of my life," Rhonda said smiling. "I wish I would have met her ten years ago."

Jessie also smiled. "It isn't meant to happen until its time. Fate put you together when the timing was right for both of you." Jessie's expression changed.

"Hey, why so serious all of a sudden? What's wrong?" Karen jumped in, concerned for Jessie.

"Nothing." Jessie forced a smile.

Just then Julie hollered for Rhonda. "Well, I'd better go and see what she needs." Rhonda turned and left.

Karen came over to Jessie and gently rubbed her arm in a compassionate manner. "Are you sure you're okay?"

"Yes, I am absolutely fine. Simply a flashback of a bad memory. My ex-partner always had to do the decorating when we were together,."

Karen didn't know what to say. "This seems to be a sore spot," Karen said reluctantly, still rubbing Jessie's arm in an attempt to comfort her.

"A little." Jessie admitted. "I always wanted us to do things together, and she wanted full control of the reins most of the time."

"That doesn't sound like a fifty-fifty relationship to me," Karen sympathized.

Jessie could hardly refrain from pulling Karen into her arms. She longed for the comfort of Karen's body next to hers. She could smell the soft fragrance of her perfume. And with Karen touching her arm, it was driving Jessie crazy.

Jessie jumped off the counter to get Karen to stop touching her before she could no longer control her desire. "Our relationship was never fifty-fifty. Lynne is in my past, and I want to keep it that way," Jessie said firmly.

Karen decided to lighten the mood. "Okay then, so what plans do you have for the holidays?"

Jessie smiled again. "I am going home to Mattawa. I am leaving on Tuesday. I still need a few days here to do all my shopping and wrapping."

"I am way ahead of you. I got most of mine done before tonight. I only have a bit of wrapping to finish up," Karen bragged.

"You do remember that I am a teacher. I work two more days, and then I am on holidays until after New Year's. There are some perks to my profession," Jessie rubbed it in teasingly.

"You are very lucky. And yes, I am jealous," Karen confessed. "I have to work the entire week. Additionally I took a four-hour-shift on Christmas morning for a co-worker who has children." Karen wrinkled her nose and threw up her arms. "Why do I do such things?"

"Probably because you are such a nice person. It is your nature to help others in need."

"And you know all this about me already?" Karen had a second cup of tea. Jessie joined her this time. "I must tell you though, after Christmas morning I do have holidays booked. I also will be off the following week," Karen said with satisfaction. "That's good, because I need to find someone who can trim a few branches off the trees along my driveway. They are interfering with the globe lights."

Jessie saw an opportunity and jumped on it. "Why don't you let me come and do it for you?"

"I couldn't ask you to do that."

"No, really, I don't mind! I can come home a few days early, and we can tackle it together. I know how to use a chainsaw. If you don't have one, I can borrow my brother Tom's. You could save yourself some money. My fee could be dinner and wine."

"I would love for you to help me, but I don't want you to cut your visit home short."

"Honestly, I love my parents dearly, but a few days at home with them, and I will thank you for letting me come to help."

They both laughed.

Karen accepted the offer. Both satisfied with the arrangement, they raised their mugs and tapped them together, then began sipping their tea.

People were starting to leave the party. Julie and Rhonda were great hosts and saw their guests off at the door. As usual, Karen volunteered to help clean up and grabbed a garbage bag. Jessie offered to assist. Together they went around the house, Karen holding open the garbage bag and Jessie picking up the scattered paper plates and plastic cups and tossing them.

"Many hands make light work, that's what my mother always says," Karen commented.

"Smart woman, your mother."

Karen found herself staring at Jessie, once again mesmerized by her strikingly dark eyes and her easy nature.

They found an empty case and began gathering the beer bottles.

"Aren't you two just a handy pair to have around," Rhonda commented, glad to see the mess was disappearing before her eyes.

"Don't get too excited. There is still a lot to clean up in the kitchen," Jessie remarked.

"Not a problem. Why do you think I keep Julie around," Rhonda joked, knowing Julie could hear her.

The laughter got even louder when Julie came running across the room and jumped into Rhonda's arms. Both landed on the couch. "You will pay for that comment," Julie threatened.

"I sure hope so."

"Will you two get a room, or at least wait until your guests have left?" Karen joked.

"No, I think this is great fun. I finally get to see a side of Julie I haven't seen before," Jessie admired.

"Don't encourage her. Run now, before she shows you more," Karen teased again.

They all went into the kitchen, tidying up quickly, chatting and laughing.

"Ladies, it has been a long day, so I am going to head out." Jessie turned to Karen. "It has been good talking with you. Can I get your phone number? When I get back from Mattawa I will give you a call, so we can arrange to cut those branches."

Karen wrote it down and gave it to her. "Great, but I don't have a chainsaw. Are you sure your brother won't mind?"

"Trust me, he will be fine with it." Jessie turned to the hosts, who had walked the two of them to the door. "Thank you for the invitation. It has been a great time. Enjoy your holidays."

"Thanks for coming, Jessie." Julie reached out and gave her a hug.

Rhonda did the same.

A little awkward Jessie looked at Karen.

Karen's arms were already reaching out to give her a hug, as well. "Enjoy the holidays with your family. See you after Christmas."

"I will call when I get back." Jessie turned to leave.

Karen quickly put on her boots and coat. "I have to get going, too."

"Are you sure you don't want to stay and fill us in on what you two talked about all night?" Julie pried.

"I am sure you have more important things to do than to worry about our conversation."

"Not really." Julie winked at Rhonda.

"Nothing that can't wait," Rhonda agreed.

Karen laughed at the two of them. "You two crazy girls truly deserve each other. I must get going. I had a great evening. Thanks again for everything."

They exchanged hugs and kisses. Karen headed out the door.

Julie and Rhonda left the rest of the dishes for the morning. Instead they decided to call it a night and enjoy their playful mood.

CHAPTER FIVE

The snow fell steadily for the next couple of days, although it was not amounting to much. Julie and Karen were kept very busy and did not get an opportunity to spend their breaks together. The ER was continually busy. People visiting for the holidays from out of town were coming in with colds and flus or injuries from falling on the ice and snow. Patients came and went in a steady stream.

When Tuesday arrived Karen found herself thinking of Jessie making the long drive to Mattawa on her own. The roads were cleared, but the heavy holiday traffic was another thing. She prayed for Jessie to have a safe trip. She knew Jessie missed her family and hoped she would have a great vacation. What surprised Karen most was the fact that she was so looking forward to Jessie's return.

Jessie was on the road by ten o'clock. The traffic was already busy. It seemed everyone had somewhere they needed to be. She was in no hurry and took her time. Her thoughts soon turned to Karen. Jessie kept envisioning Karen in her nurse's uniform and in the tight knit sweater from the basketball tournament, not sure which one put the biggest smile on her face. She was looking forward to spending the holidays with her family, but she couldn't wait to get back a few days early to spend time with Karen.

When Jessie arrived at her parent's home, it was already nightfall. Christmas lights sparkled beautifully in the darkness. Her parents were standing at the door waiting to greet her with open arms. They were so proud of their daughter. Happy she had arrived safely, her mom took her coat, and her dad brought in her suitcase and then went a second and a third time to retrieve all the parcels from the car. This was Jessie's first trip home since mid-August. They all had a glass of wine and sat around the Christmas tree. Jessie told them about the small town of Brockville and her school, the students and the hockey team. She talked to her parents every week, but they wanted to hear it all again.

"What is for dinner anyway? It smells delicious!" Jessie inquired.

Her mom laughed. "Homemade biscuits and stew."

"One of my favorite meals."

"Like we didn't know that already," her dad teased, as they headed off to the kitchen.

Dinner was excellent. There was homemade chocolate cake for dessert. After helping with the dishes and the clean-up, Jessie excused herself. She took a cup of tea to the living room to enjoy the quietness. She took pleasure from the glow of the fireplace and the lights on the tree. Her parents joined her after a while. The family was enjoying the time together. After an hour Jessie headed off to bed after kissing her parents good night.

Karen and Julie had both been able to get off work an hour early. Karen followed Julie home just like they had planned it earlier in the week. Rhonda was already there and had just finished putting together some snacks.

On Christmas Eve they always exchanged gifts. To Karen Julie and Rhonda were like sisters. Exchanging Christmas cards and presents had become a special part of her holiday tradition. The tree lights sparkled like diamonds, when Karen and Julie entered the living room. The two women stood there taking it all in, enjoying the stylish decorations and the ambiance.

Rhonda joined Karen and Julie in the living room with drinks almost as soon as they sat down. "A toast to great friends and to happy and safe holidays."

Karen lifted her glass. "The two of you have been wonderful friends to me." Karen's eyes began to glisten as tears formed. She felt overwhelmed.

"What's wrong, Sweetheart? Where is this coming from?" Julie wrapped her arms around her dearest friend.

Karen sniffled and wiped the tears from her eyes. "It's the season. I'm feeling a bit lonely. I had hoped I would have found someone to share my life with by now."

"You will, Karen. When the time is right, it will happen for you," Julie assured. "God is picking a real special partner for you."

Karen smiled at her friends and cleared her throat. "I know. Anyway, enough of that. Let's exchange presents.

"Now you're talking," Rhonda quipped, trying to lighten the mood.

They shared many appreciative words and some laughs over the gifts.

"So, when is Jessie coming back to town?" Rhonda asked all of a sudden.

"I'm not sure. She said she would call me," Karen replied.

"This project she is helping you with, is there anything we can do for you?" Rhonda probed.

"No, I think we will be able to handle it. There are just some branches that need trimming. Besides I want you two to enjoy your time off together."

"Keep us in mind if you have to fight her off with one of those branches that she is helping you trim," Rhonda teased.

Julie was no help. The two of them high-fived each other and laughed like kids.

Karen threw one of the couch pillows at them. "Jessie doesn't know that many people. I think she is looking for a friend. I like her," Karen tried to convince them.

"Karen, seriously, don't you see the way she looks at you?" Julie asked.

Karen revealed her innocence. "What are you implying?"

Rhonda got up to get another beer and came back almost instantly. "Well, my dear, be sure to let her down gently. She will be crushed when she finds out you just want friendship."

Karen's mouth dropped open. "I am not interested in Jessie that way. Julie, you should know that." Karen sounded like she was trying to convince herself. "I think you two have your minds working overtime on this for no reason. You are just saying this because I told you I was feeling lonely. Jessie has done nothing but be kind to me. I am taking the friendship she has offered me," Karen explained. "Look, I have to get going, or I will be late for Joan, Roger and Sophie. I will give you a call in a couple of days." Karen got up.

"We love having you over. Thanks again for the gifts. Enjoy your holidays. Be sure to call," Julie said at the door.

Rhonda came out on the front step and took in the fresh night air. "Merry Christmas, Karen." She gave her a hug and watched her drive away.

"Now that is truly sad," Rhonda said to Julie. "That girl really has no idea."

"Not everybody can be as happy as we are." They went inside and cuddled on the couch.

The doorbell rang. Sharon and Tom had finally arrived.

Jessie opened the door and welcomed them with open arms. "Come on in. Let me take your coats."

"What is this, my kid sister has turned into Suzy Homemaker?" Tom teased.

"No, she is just trying to be helpful for a change. After all, it is the holidays," Jessie defended her reputation. "Don't expect this all the time."

The whole family was finally together. This was the reason Jessie had come home.

Everyone had drinks. Different conversations were going on around the room. As soon as Tom had Jessie alone, he inquired about Karen. "So, Jess, have you worked up your nerve to ask the nurse out?"

This brought a huge smile and a slight blush to Jessie's face. "No." She hit him in the arm. "But I wish."

"You really have lost your touch. There was a time when you were out with a different girl every other month."

"Those days are behind me. I am a respected teacher now. I have to be a good role model."

"Being a good role model and being lonely are two totally different things," Tom reminded.

"I know. I am really attracted to Karen, but I still don't know how she feels," Jessie confessed.

"Tell me about her," Tom insisted.

"She is very funny, smart, and attractive. Her smile just melts me. I saw her at the basketball tournament. As it turns out, her niece is one of my students. And on top of that, she was also at the hockey party I attended." Jessie was beaming.

Tom knew his kid sister was falling in love. "Didn't you get to ask her out when you were at the party together?"

"Not exactly. But I need a favor from you." Jessie hesitated. "I need to borrow your chainsaw, and I need a quick refresher course on how to use it."

"Slow down here," Tom got serious. "The chainsaw?"

"Yes, the chainsaw. Karen has some branches she needs cleared. I offered my services and your chainsaw. I guess you could say it's a package deal."

"And what do you get out of this deal other than hard work?" Tom inquired.

"Dinner and wine, not to mention time spent with Karen."

"Nice going. Now that is what I expect from you," Tom praised. "But you haven't used a chainsaw for a few years now."

"That is why I need you to run over a few things with me. Refresh my memory on the ratio of oil and gas, when to turn the choke off, that kind of stuff."

"I don't have a problem with you borrowing the chainsaw. I just want you to be careful," Tom indicated with genuine concern. "I will clean it up and go over everything with you in a couple of days."

"Great. I haven't told Mom and Dad yet, but I am returning to Brockville earlier than I had planned. Originally I was staying until New Year's Day, but now I plan on leaving on the 28th."

Christmas Day went by quickly. Everyone had gotten to spend quality time with their families and friends. Jessie had told her parents she was leaving early, and they were not pleased to have their little girl leave them again for another long period of time. At this point Jessie was not sure if she would be able to make it home over the March break, or if she would have to wait until Easter. But Jessie's parents understood and were thankful that she still called every week and that she still wanted to come home to spend time with them.

Jessie headed over to Tom and Sharon's to get the chainsaw. Tom was in the garage cleaning it.

"Hey, Jess. This thing needed a bit more TLC than I thought," Tom said with a smile. "I haven't had it out since late October. I still need to top it up with the fluids."

"Tell me how, and I will do it. What better way to refresh my memory than with a good ole fashioned, hands on experience," Jessie insisted.

Step by step Tom gave Jess instructions. Before long the chainsaw was purring like a kitten. He had her cut a few pieces of wood that were lying in the yard and gave her some pointers. Tom knew Jess was responsible and didn't worry about her. He was proud of his sister for so many reasons, but mostly just because she was who she was.

"Just be careful. Don't show off or do something stupid," Tom advised with a grin.

"Me, showing off? Never!" Jessie laughed out loud. They went inside to have a cold drink. Soon after, Jessie said her good-byes and was on her way.

Karen had spent Christmas morning working. Later she headed to her parent's place where the rest of the family was gathered. It was a wonderful time. She was happy to be a part of such a loving family. After presents were exchanged and stomachs were filled, Karen was about to head home when Joan invited her over for leftovers the day after Christmas. Karen accepted. She was officially on holidays until after New Year's.

The next day Karen was up early and decided to go for a walk on the snowmobile trail not far from her home. There were tracks in the snow where someone had been out on skis. The sunshine on the white snow was brilliant, causing her to squint. She was thankful she was wearing sunglasses.

Karen got lost in her thoughts. I wonder how Jessie's holidays are going. Mattawa is a fair distance. I hope she drives carefully. Remembering her conversation with Julie and Rhonda a few nights earlier, she shook her head telling herself that those girls were reading way too much into the reason why Jessie wanted to help her out.

They have forgotten why single people need friends to do things with, she thought. I am certain Jessie doesn't look at me the way they implied. But what if she does . . .? Karen blushed. She found Jessie very attractive and easy to talk to. She felt drawn to her in a way she couldn't understand. Could I kiss her passionately? she wondered. Better yet . . . do I want to . . .?

Suddenly Karen was distracted by a couple of squirrels chasing each other. Karen began to hum aloud to keep from having to answer the bizarre questions she had just asked herself. Uncertain of when Jessie was returning to Brockville, she had better spend time doing some house cleaning.

Karen's house was spotless by the time she left to go over to Joan's. When she arrived, Joan and Sophie were enjoying a cup of hot chocolate together.

"Your house doesn't look too bad considering Roger's family visited earlier. So, what would you like me to start with? Vacuuming?

Dusting? The dishes?" Karen asked, ready to get the work done and out of the way.

Sophie quickly spoke up. "My room, Aunt Karen. You can start there."

They laughed.

"I would probably be there the rest of the day," Karen retorted.

"You are right about that," Joan added.

"Hey, hey. It isn't that bad," Sophie defended. "I keep it a lot better now that I'm older."

Before too long the house was back to normal. After the work was done, they went for a short walk to get some fresh air.

"So, Karen, do you have any other plans for the rest of your holidays?" Joan asked.

"Not really. I am having a friend over at some point. We are going to tackle a small project outside."

"Why didn't you ask? Roger is always willing to help – once I volunteer him of course." Joan laughed.

"It isn't that big of a deal. Jessie said she would help."

"Jessie? I haven't heard you mention her before. Do I know her?"

"Yes. You all know her. Jessie Carmichael, Sophie's teacher."

"I didn't realize you two had become friends. That's great." Joan sounded pleased.

"We have talked on a few occasions, and she offered her help, so I accepted."

"I like Miss Carmichael. You both have a lot in common. You both have a great sense of humor, enjoy other people, are always willing to help out . . . stuff like that," Sophie said.

Karen smiled. A warm rush passed through her. She didn't understand why, but she was pleased that Joan and Sophie immediately were okay with Jessie being a part of her life.

It wasn't too long after they returned that dinner was ready. All agreed that leftovers were just as good if not better than the first time.

Around nine o'clock Karen headed home and was in bed shortly thereafter. She grabbed the pen and paper on the nightstand to create a grocery list of the items she should have on hand for Jessie's visit. Karen decided to have spaghetti with garlic bread and wine. Dessert would be a homemade blueberry cheesecake. Karen admitted to herself she was a bit nervous about cooking for Jessie, but her cooking usually passed as acceptable.

CHAPTER SIX

Jessie was eager to get back to Brockville. Her drive was enjoyable. Traffic was not nearly as bad as it had been going to Mattawa before the holidays. Jessie was in a great mood. She had her tunes cranked and was singing her heart out. She was happy knowing she would be able to see Karen soon.

Jessie arrived home around seven o'clock and chose take-out food for supper. She ran out, picked up a burger and onion rings and devoured them at home. She hadn't realized just how hungry she was. Her mom had done her laundry for her, so she put it away. Once that was done and the gifts were unpacked, she called Karen.

Karen had just finished chopping vegetables and throwing them into the spaghetti sauce. It needed to simmer for a couple of hours. Just then the phone rang.

"Hi there, Karen?" the voice on the other end queried softly. "This is Jessie."

Karen froze for a second. She hadn't expected it to be Jessie. "So good to hear from you. Are you back in town?" Karen tried to keep the delight and nervousness from coming through.

"Yes, I got back today."

"How were your holidays?"

"Fine, thanks. It was great to see everybody. How about yours?"

"My holidays were very enjoyable also. How long a drive is it to Mattawa?"

"It varies with the traffic. Roughly six or seven hours. I don't mind the drive." Jessie couldn't wait any longer to find out. "So, I was wondering if you had decided when you wanted help with the trees."

"Joan has offered Roger's assistance in case we need it," Karen tossed out even though Roger was the last person she wanted around Jessie.

"From what you described, I think we women can handle it without too much trouble," Jessie said with confidence.

"Okay then, if you are sure. Do you have plans for tomorrow?"

"Tomorrow is good. What can I bring to contribute to dinner?"

"I promised you dinner and wine for helping me. You are to bring nothing."

"Okay. I just thought I would offer," Jessie happily agreed. "What time should I be there?" She enjoyed listening to Karen's voice.

"If we start after lunch that will give us lots of time."

"Sounds good to me."

Karen gave Jessie her address with directions.

When they hung up the phone, both women were pleased and looking forward to the following day.

Karen was in the middle of putting blueberries on the cheesecake when the phone rang again. Still happy from her conversation with Jessie, she answered. "Hello."

"Karen, hi, I haven't spoken to you since Christmas Day when you called. So, what's going on?" Julie greeted.

"Right now I am in the middle of topping off a blueberry cheesecake, and I have spaghetti sauce simmering."

"Sounds good. When should we come over?" Julie joked.

"Too bad. It is for tomorrow night's dinner. Jessie is coming to help me with the trees. Would you like to join us?" Karen asked hesitantly.

"We've already made dinner arrangements for tomorrow, but thanks for asking. I know it is last minute, but we were wondering if you have plans for New Year's Eve."

"New Year's Eve? I thought you guys were going to Mary and John's party."

"We were supposed to, but Mary's mom is not doing well, so they cancelled," Julie explained.

"Oh, I'm sorry to hear that. I had a quiet evening planned at home with a couple of movies, popcorn, and, of course, my Crown Royal whisky," Karen confessed laughing.

"We were going to invite you over here, but why don't we join you there? We could pick up some Chinese food for dinner. What do you say?"

Karen was uncertain if she wanted to give up her quiet movie night, but she could watch a movie any time. After all, this was New Year's Eve. "Okay, that sounds good to me. I will call you beforehand and confirm everything." Hanging up the phone, Karen finished her cheesecake and called it a night.

Jessie was not familiar with the countryside outside of Brockville. She had the directions in hand along with Karen's phone number in case she took a wrong turn. But first she travelled to a small park and got the chainsaw out of the trunk of her car. Not wanting to be embarrassed in front of Karen, she needed to make sure she could start it. She turned the switch on, set the choke and gave it two quick pulls. It started right up. Jessie breathed a sigh of relief and giggled like a little girl.

The drive to Karen's was quite picturesque. It reminded Jessie of Mattawa. The road that Karen lived on was paved, although in need of repairs. When she pulled into the lane, she was in awe of all the pine trees.

"What a lovely place," she whispered to herself. "Oh, how I miss living in the country." Jessie parked the car. When she got out, she took a moment to listen to all the birds singing so happily. She noticed a flag hanging from a pole on a tree that read "Welcome". And that was exactly how she felt. The peacefulness was breathtaking.

Karen had not heard Jessie arrive. When she walked by the window, she spotted Jessie standing in the driveway. Karen watched as Jessie took a moment to enjoy the surroundings. Karen was elated at the sight.

She went to the door and greeted Jessie. "Please come in."

"What a wonderful spot you have!"

"Thank you. I like it here," Karen said, pleased that Jessie appreciated the beauty.

"I can certainly see why you would." Jessie was wearing a hooded grey sweatshirt under a navy quilted vest with a pair of navy wind pants that zipped at the bottom over a pair of work boots.

My God, even in work clothes she looks adorable, Karen thought. Her red hair was curled around the bottom of her ball cap. Her bangs reached down just enough to touch the top of her eyebrows. Then there they were, those big brown eyes, bright with excitement. Karen was once again drawn to them.

"Have you already had lunch? I could make you something quickly." Karen didn't want to put her volunteer helper to work without offering her something.

"I ate about an hour ago. Thanks for asking."

"Well then, do you want to have a drink first or just get out there and get the work done?" Karen asked with a nervous giggle.

"If you are ready, we should probably get to it," Jessie suggested.

"Great, I am ready." Karen grabbed the heavy plaid jacket she always wore working in the yard. She was already wearing her black wind pants. Before long she had her boots on and work gloves in her hand.

They headed outside. Jessie retrieved the chainsaw.

Karen explained which branches she needed to have cleared away. Both went to work. Jessie held her breath in hopes that the chainsaw would start. On the second pull it started right up. They were both excited, gave each other a high-five, and the work began. Karen gave the initial instructions. Jessie buzzed through the limbs pretty easily. As Jessie cut the limbs away, Karen dragged them over just inside the bushes where she had a pile of brush already started. Karen made a number of trips. Each time she returned she could see the progress they were making.

Finally Jessie's arms were getting a little tired from the chainsaw, so she shut it off.

"Is everything all right?" Karen asked.

"Uh-huh," Jessie acknowledged a little out of breath. "I just need to check the gas and oil levels." She did not want to let Karen know her arms were tired.

Karen picked up another load of brush and headed off across the yard.

Jessie also loaded up with brush and followed. "You really have a beautiful spot here."

"I'm glad you like it. Living in the country is not for everyone."

"That's true. But I grew up on the outskirts of a small town. I love the country."

"What about now? Do you live in town?" Karen asked.

"I do. In an apartment for now. I thought it would be easier, at least until I get my first year behind me and see how things go," Jessie explained.

"Do you like teaching at T.I.S.S.?"

They made their way back across the yard to the driveway.

"I really do. The students are great for the most part, and the staff has been very helpful and friendly."

Jessie filled the chainsaw up with gas. Remembering Tom's instructions, she also topped up the oil for the chain. By now Karen had gathered up another load of brush and was headed back across the yard. Jessie gave a quick pull and was back to cutting. It was hard to talk with the chainsaw roaring, but they managed a little conversation and a few laughs while they worked. They had been out for a couple of hours, so they were both glad to see the job coming to an end. Jessie had only a few more limbs to cut off, and her job would be done.

While Karen was across the yard with her arms full of branches, Jessie took a closer look at the remaining task. The last bunch of branches was intertwined together. It was difficult to see where exactly to cut first. Jessie made an educated guess and started. After a couple of cuts something came loose. One of the limbs from behind was released and sprang fast and furious from the branch that was holding it. The limb caught Jessie on the side of her neck, just behind the bottom of her right ear. The switch startled her. It caused her skin to sting. She let out a squeal.

Karen came running. Jessie immediately shut off the chainsaw and almost lost her balance. Karen grabbed Jessie just in time to help steady her.

"Oh shit, that hurt!" Jessie confessed as she was putting the chainsaw down.

"Are you alright? Let me take a look at that." Concerned, Karen reached over.

Jessie stepped back. She was embarrassed. "Don't worry. I'll be fine." If her face had not already been red from working outside, Karen would have been able to see her blush. "Pardon my language by the way," Jessie realized her outburst.

Karen laughed. "No need to apologize. You have the right to curse a bit."

Jessie smiled innocently.

It took Karen by surprise. Suddenly she felt a little weak in the knees. She had to catch her breath. "Please, let me take a look at your neck. I just want to be sure it isn't cut."

Jessie reached up to touch the hurting spot and winced. When she took her hand away, she had blood on her fingers.

"Let me take a look, please."

"Okay, but I will be fine," Jessie repeated stubbornly.

Karen saw that it was an open wound. "I don't think you need stitches, but I won't know for sure until I get it cleaned up. Come on. Let's go inside."

"I only have two more limbs to cut, and we are done." Jessie reached for the chainsaw.

"No, no, no. You are done now. I need to clean that cut."

"I am not leaving the job this close to being done. It will only take me a couple of minutes," Jessie negotiated.

Karen wasn't pleased with the fact that Jessie wanted to finish, but she could see her determination. Jessie took down the remaining branches. Karen quickly picked them up and tossed them in a neat pile just beside the driveway. She would haul them over to the other pile later. Together they put everything away and headed inside.

"May I have a glass of water?" Jessie asked once they were back inside the house.

"Absolutely." Karen quickly got the water. "Have a seat on the couch and relax. I will be right back." Karen pointed to the living room.

Jessie could feel her neck throbbing. She was glad to sit down.

Karen returned and gently pulled Jessie's hair back. "I am going to clean this up." With a warm cloth she tenderly dabbed the blood from the wound. Once the blood was gone, Karen could see the injury was not as bad as she had originally thought. "No stitches required. It is a nasty little cut, but you will survive."

"I am glad to hear that." Jessie laughed and turned to look at Karen. Karen was right there, so close that she could see the sparkle in her eyes. They were so blue. Jessie felt the strong urge to pull Karen closer. She wanted to taste the sweetness of her lips. Quickly she turned her head away to resist the temptation.

Karen continued cleaning the cut with an alcohol swab. Jessie could feel the warmth of Karen's breath softly dancing across her neck.

"Are you almost finished?" Jessie asked, unable to control herself much longer.

"Yes, I will just put some ointment on it and cover it with a bandage."

While Karen finished, wild sensations tingled over Jessie's body. The warm soft caressing of Karen's breath was driving her crazy.

"Done." Karen got up from the couch.

"Thank you. Now, can we break into that wine you promised me?" Jessie teased, gesturing in a begging manner with both hands locked together.

They laughed and headed for the kitchen. After they both washed up, Karen got the glasses out while Jessie opened the wine.

"Are you hungry?" Karen asked Jessie as she stirred the spaghetti sauce that had been simmering in the slow cooker all day.

"I am always hungry," Jessie joked. "But if you don't mind, I would like to relax with a glass of wine first." She didn't want to have the evening pass by too quickly.

It had started to get dark. Karen turned the globe lights on outside. They both looked out the window and admired the work they had done.

"Wow, that looks so much better," Karen complimented.

Jessie turned to Karen. "To a job well done!"

Karen poured each of them a second glass of wine, then put on the pot of water for the spaghetti. She pulled out a pan and began cutting the garlic bread. Before too long, dinner was served. The wine was once again topped up. They chatted easily and comfortably over dinner. Both enjoyed each other's company. They shared many laughs and learned about families, friends, work, and life interests.

Jessie felt relaxed and took pleasure in simply listening to Karen.

Her next question caught Jessie off guard. "If you don't mind me asking, do you have plans for New Year's Eve?" Karen asked.

"I was originally spending it in Mattawa, but since I came home early, I don't have any plans. I don't know anybody well enough, yet, that I would go and crash their party."

Karen laughed. "Julie and Rhonda are coming over with Chinese food. We are planning to play some board games. Why don't you join us?"

"That's an unexpected invitation. If you really don't mind . . ."

"We would love to have you."

They both cleared the table, and Karen put the dishes in to soak. "I can do them tomorrow."

"No. I am not leaving the dishes for you. I will help," Jessie insisted.

"They can wait until tomorrow," Karen protested.

They started to laugh. "We squabble like we have known each other for years," Jessie said. "I won't leave without helping, so let me dry."

"All right then." Karen threw her arms up. "Are you always this persuasive?"

"I have my ways." Jessie grinned devilishly while raising her eyebrows in a flirtatious manner.

Laughing, Karen began to wash the dishes. Once they were done, they had a cup of tea. "Are you going to be okay to drive home?"

"Yes, I'm fine." Jessie said with certainty.

"I can't thank you enough for all your help today. It was a lot of fun. I do feel bad that you got injured."

"It only hurt for a while. After my nurse fixed me up, I felt all better." Jessie laughed. Her compliment caused Karen to blush. "Besides, I really enjoyed it. Any more projects I can help with?"

"Not right now. Do you know your way back to town? I don't want you to get lost."

"Yeah, I should be good."

Jessie was ready to leave. Karen reached out to give her a kiss on the cheek along with a hug good-bye like she did with all her friends. Jessie felt the warmth of Karen's breath on her cheek and held Karen a bit longer than necessary.

Karen followed her outside onto the step and waited until she drove off.

On the drive home Jessie replayed the day's events in her mind. Even her little injury had been worth it. It was intensely exciting to have Karen get that close to her, literally breathing down her neck. Remembering how much it had aroused her brought the thrill back into her body. She quivered at the thought of where it could lead . . .

Karen felt some aches and pains from hauling the brush all afternoon. She decided to soak in a bath for a while. She then slipped into her flannel pajamas and nestled into bed. Karen was grateful she had gotten to know Jessie more today. She liked Jessie's bubbly personality along with her generous nature, and she was impressed that Jessie seemed to enjoy the outdoor work as much as she did.

Karen recalled the look on Jessie's face earlier that afternoon when she had taken care of the wound. At that moment she had felt a sense of longing and desire from Jessie.

Oddly enough she didn't mind. No one has ever looked at me with such loving eyes, Karen thought. Am I leading her on if I am enjoying the attention, although I know I cannot return her affection?

She was drawn to Jessie. Something had stirred inside her, something uncertain, confusing. What did this mean?

CHAPTER SEVEN

The morning of December 31st Karen slept in until nine-thirty. This was late for her, but it felt good not having to get up and rush off. She turned on the coffee machine and picked up the phone to call the girls.

"Good morning," Rhonda answered.

"Good morning right back!" Karen replied very peppy.

"Well, aren't you in a good mood! What happened?"

"I am always in a good mood, you know that."

"I can't argue with that my friend," Rhonda said in agreement.

"Listen, I hope you don't mind, but I have invited Jessie to join us for New Year's Eve. She came home early from Mattawa to help me trim the trees, and she didn't have plans for New Year's Eve."

"Hey, that's great. We will give her a call and see if she wants to hitch a ride with us."

"Excellent. Do you have any idea about what time I can expect you?"

"My best guess would be between six and six thirty."

"Sounds perfect. Do you have Jessie's number, because I don't?"

Rhonda checked her list for the hockey team on the fridge. "Yeah, I have it. Do you want it?"

"Sure, just in case something comes up and I need to call her." Karen jotted the number down.

After she got off the phone with Rhonda, Karen enjoyed a relaxing cup of coffee. She then headed outside to drag the last of the brush to the pile. Once that was completed, she stood at the top of the driveway and admired the work she and Jessie had done together. A sense of accomplishment and pride came over her. Jessie had really helped a great deal, and Karen was extremely grateful.

After getting cleaned up, she headed into town to pick up peanuts, chips, and veggies with dip for the night and added a few party favors along with streamers and balloons. The day flew by.

Karen had gotten home a little later than planned. She had intended to take a short nap, instead she found herself exploring her feelings for Jessie. Thinking about Jessie instantly brought a smile to her face. She had feelings for Jessie. She couldn't deny that. But I'm not a lesbian, she thought. It must be a different kind of attraction. Maybe infatuation?

Just after six o'clock Karen mixed her first drink of the evening. While she lit the candles and turned on the fireplace, Karen hummed to the music she had playing.

The ladies arrived close to seven o'clock. Rhonda announced their presence by blowing the horn like a mad woman. Jessie was in the car, as well.

Karen went outside and helped with their coolers and the Chinese food. Once inside Karen gave hugs and kisses with her hellos.

"Come in, come in." Karen motioned for them to head for the kitchen. "I have cleared a spot on the counter for us to set up the bar." She pointed to her open bottle of Crown Royal.

Julie spoke up immediately. "Okay Jessie, Karen is probably too polite to say this, so I will fill you in on our arrangement."

"Here we go!" Rhonda winked at Karen. They both laughed.

"You're the 'newbie' here. I only want to help you feel comfortable," Julie began.

Jessie was already having fun watching how these three friends carried on with each other. "Okay. Fill me in, I want to know."

"Nobody waits on anybody. We all get our own drinks, help ourselves to the food, ice, whatever. Don't be shy."

"Just make yourself at home, relax, have fun." Karen smiled.

"I think I can handle it. Thanks again for including me. I am glad you extended the invitation." Jessie looked directly into Karen's eyes.

"I'm glad I asked," Karen said with a flirtatious grin.

Rhonda opened her cooler and got out a beer, offering one to Julie, who accepted.

"Hey, doesn't she have to get it herself?" Jessie pointed out.

"I like your sense of humor. You suit our little group," Julie approved.

All chuckled.

Karen showed Jessie where to find a few things around the kitchen as Jessie made herself a Caesar. "That looks good."

"Here, try it," Jessie offered.

Karen took a sip and loved the cocktail.

"If you like, I will make you one."

"I may take you up on that a little later."

Jessie wore a pair of snug fitting black jeans, along with a black long sleeved V-neck shirt with three small buttons that went down from the V. Karen caught herself looking Jessie over. She certainly was an attractive woman.

"Does everyone want to eat or shall we wait for a bit?" Karen asked.

Since the food smelled inviting, they made up their own plates and took them to the table. Dinner was great. The conversation was even better. Julie asked Jessie about herself, and the more she told them, the more they wanted to know.

Karen took pleasure in listening to Jessie's soft, sultry voice. Then Jessie turned the table on all of them, and they each took turns sharing parts of their lives, all the while indulging in second helpings of Chinese food and drinks.

"I will do the dishes." Jessie volunteered and started to pick up the paper plates.

"Aren't you the funny one," Karen teased.

Julie had brought a couple of board games. Rhonda and Jessie rearranged the living room furniture so they could play in the middle of the floor. Julie put on a pot of coffee. Unfortunately she had to get up for work the next morning, and so she volunteered to be the designated driver.

Karen arranged a mix of disco and rock'n'roll CDs and cranked the volume. "Let's party!" she hollered, moving and grooving to the beat.

Rhonda and Jessie joined in the dancing, and before long Julie was taking part.

Jessie watched Karen's every dance move. The white short sleeved V-neck shirt Karen wore bounced up and down freely with her firm breasts as she danced around the living room. Jessie noticed that her feelings for Karen were stronger than she wanted them to be. However, she could not seem to help herself. She was falling in love with this woman and wanted to be with her.

After a couple of songs Julie poured a cup of coffee for herself and a beer for Rhonda and headed to the living room to set up a game. Karen agreed to let Jessie make her a drink, joking that she might regret it in the morning. Two teams were agreed upon, Julie and Rhonda against Karen and Jessie.

Ten-thirty rolled around. Karen remembered the snacks. "Time for a break. I have to get the snacks out. I didn't buy them for nothing."

"I will help if you need a hand," Jessie offered.

Rhonda and Julie took advantage of their time alone to cuddle in front of the fireplace.

"What can I do?" Jessie asked.

Karen pulled out the peanuts and chips. She pointed to where the bowls were. Jessie dug them out and filled them up. Karen retrieved prepared veggies from the fridge. Jessie stuck her head into the living room to see if she could get the other gals anything. Seeing the two of them cuddling and kissing made her want Karen even more. How she missed being held and touched.

She went back into the kitchen and watched as Karen put the veggies on the platter with such care and precision. Jessie's heart melted. The overwhelming feelings she had for this woman prompted her to reach out and gently run her fingers through Karen's hair. Her hair was so soft and silky. The sensation that passed through Jessie's fingertips shot through the rest of her. Jessie hadn't even realized what she had done until she noticed the surprised expression on Karen's face.

Quickly Jessie pulled her hand away. "I apologize. I couldn't help myself. You are just so beautiful."

Uncertain how to respond Karen turned and looked at Jessie. She smiled. "Flattery will get you almost anything, except that. I'm not gay. I don't want to hurt your feelings, but I want to be perfectly clear."

"Of course." Jessie's heart sank. She appreciated Karen's honesty, although she felt like she had just taken a hard blow to the stomach.

The blush in Jessie's cheek revealed her embarrassment.

Karen made an attempt to smooth things over and get past the awkwardness. "I love our newfound friendship, Jessie," she started. "I am sorry if I have misled you in any way."

"No, no, you haven't. I don't know what I was thinking. You just . . . I just . . ." Jessie was lost for words.

Karen took her hands. "Listen, I really like you, Jessie. I want us to be friends."

"I want us to be friends, too. I'm sorry if I crossed the line. I just wasn't sure how you felt, and I was so very hopeful."

"Well, I'm flattered! Really, I am. But I have never been with a woman, nor do I see myself ever being with a woman sexually." Karen wanted to sound convincing, but who was she really trying to convince?

"Where do we go from here?" Jessie asked hesitantly, not sure she wanted to hear the answer.

"We are both adults. I hope we can continue enjoying our new friendship," Karen said cheerfully, trying to lighten the mood.

"Sounds reasonable." Jessie was relieved that she had not ruined one of the best relationships she had ever had.

"So, let's go back in there and whip those girls' asses at the next game!" Karen suggested and picked up the platter of veggies.

Jessie followed with the chips and nuts. "Okay ladies, my partner says we are going to whip your asses this round!" Jessie announced as they entered the living room.

Karen froze for a moment when Jessie referred to her as her partner, even though Jessie's reference was strictly pertaining to the game.

The games continued. Apparently what happened in the kitchen had no lasting effect on their friendship. Relieved Jessie saw that things were going to be fine between them. She wanted this more than anything. She did not want to lose Karen as a friend.

"Well, have we beaten you enough?" Karen asked after winning the last two games.

"I still think the two of you cheated," Julie accused jokingly.

"We should stop while we are ahead," Jessie added. "Besides it is close to midnight."

"Yes, right, time to quit and leave you two to lick your wounds."

Now eleven forty-five, they packed up the game. Everyone had a drink to toast to the New Year. Rhonda turned the television on so they could watch the countdown. Jessie was sitting by the fireplace and watched as the soft glow of light caressed Karen's cheek.

Jessie was deep in thought, replaying those few moments from the kitchen over and over in her mind. She was no quitter and was not about to give up so easily on Karen. She wanted her friendship, yes, but deep in her heart she knew that they were meant to be together as more than just friends.

Rhonda and Julie were standing in the middle of the living room and motioned for Jessie and Karen to join them. They all counted down the last ten seconds of the year.

"Happy New Year!" they all cheered.

Julie made a toast. "To a new year with new beginnings." She looked directly at Karen, who was all smiles, and gave her a wink. She pulled Karen closer, gave Karen a kiss on the lips and wished her happiness in the New Year.

Rhonda had given Jessie a kiss, and then she kissed Karen. Now Rhonda turned to Julie. "Okay, Sweetheart, it's our turn." They put their drinks down, embraced and took pleasure in a long, deep, sensual kiss.

Jessie turned to Karen who was staring at her. Before the situation got uncomfortable, Karen set her drink down and came over to Jessie. Jessie had waited for this moment all evening. Now she was not certain how to handle it.

Without saying a word, Karen took Jessie's hands and held them in her own. They looked into each other's eyes, the tug more powerful than ever before.

"I want you." Jessie leaned forward and pressed her warm soft lips onto Karen's.

Karen was thrown off guard by the look of desire in Jessie's eyes. Just as Jessie was about to pull away, Karen found herself leaning into her. She pressed her lips harder against Jessie's. Jessie was as surprised as Karen was. When their lips parted, their eyes met. No words were spoken.

Karen blushed from head to toe. She waved her hand up and down. "I must be too close to the fireplace." She turned away, leaving Jessie standing there.

Jessie's knees were about to give out. She grabbed the closest chair and sat down. For a woman who doesn't like women she sure fooled me, she pondered. If she would give me a chance, I know I could please her. I'm not giving up that easily!

Oblivious to anything else, Rhonda and Julie were still enjoying their New Year celebration.

"Okay, you two get a room!" Karen had always admired the love they shared, but watching them necking made Karen strangely embarrassed in the company of Jessie.

"Is all this lip-smacking driving you crazy with envy?" Julie asked.

"Between the smacking and the moans, yes," Jessie admitted, laughing.

Karen contemplated what had just happened to her. Jessie's delicate, tantalizing fragrance lingered in the air. She still felt her soft and moist lips tenderly caressing hers. Why do I have such feelings? she wondered. I know I'm not gay!

"I guess we can wait till we get home," Rhonda winked at Julie, interrupting Karen's thoughts.

"That would be appreciated," Karen agreed and left the room.

Julie had to work the next morning, so they quickly tidied up and put the living room back in order. Julie went out to warm up the car. Karen, not wanting to look directly at Jessie, quickly gave Julie and Rhonda their hugs. Then, without eye contact, she awkwardly did the same with Jessie.

"I will see you at work in a couple of days," Karen said to Julie.

"Don't forget, hockey starts back up again this week," Rhonda reminded Karen and Jessie.

They all left together. Karen watched from the window as they drove off.

Then she took a deep breath and sat down. Her hands started to tremble. What was happening to her? She knew the feelings that stirred inside of her were like nothing she had ever felt or experienced before. I'm scared, she thought.

CHAPTER EIGHT

The first day of the New Year was a blur for Karen. After a restless night she was unable to focus on anything. Even the simplest task seemed complicated. Karen kept remembering the kiss, and each time she did, the feelings resurfaced. Watching Jessie laugh and joke ... Looking into Jessie's eyes ... Kissing her soft, sweet lips ... She wanted to hide, but was unsure why. If I could just identify my feelings, she wondered. Am I ashamed or embarrassed that I enjoyed the kiss? Am I gay? No, I'm confused. It has been a long time since I kissed anyone. Maybe I am just enjoying the attention? Yes, that must be it! It's reassuring that I am appealing to someone. Perhaps there is hope for me after all ...

She spent the day at home and didn't answer her phone on the four occasions it rang.

Sunday, January second, was the last day of the holidays before most people returned to work. Karen had to get out of the house. Being alone with her thoughts was driving her crazy. She needed to see Joan and Sophie.

Roger was watching football on television, so they sat down in the kitchen where they could talk without disturbing his game.

"Tea?" Joan filled a kettle and put it on the stove.

Sophie got herself a soda. "Did you and Miss Carmichael get all the work done?"

Karen had forgotten they knew about Jessie's visit. Her face flushed. "Yes, we did. Jessie was a great help," Karen praised. Unable to prevent it, she smiled. "It looks fantastic. I am so glad to have it done."

"So how is Jessie?" Sophie asked with a laugh.

"Sophie, that would be 'Miss Carmichael' to you." Joan gave her a gentle slap on the shoulder on her way past to tend to the tea.

"Jessie is doing just fine. She had a great vacation with her family."

"Where does her family live?" Joan asked. "Did you mention it before? I must have forgotten."

"In a small town called Mattawa. Just before you get to North Bay."

"Well, for people like Jessie ..." Joan coughed.

Immediately Karen froze, assuming the reference was to Jessie being a lesbian.

"What do you mean, 'people like Jessie'?" Karen was ready to defend her friends.

"Oh, excuse me," Joan said when she finished coughing. "I was going to say for people like Jessie who had to travel over the holidays, the weather sure held off and made for better driving conditions," Joan finished.

Why am I so fearful? Karen thought. She felt like her emotions were on display and everybody could detect her feelings for Jessie. Would my family support me if I was a lesbian? Karen contemplated.

"You are right about that." She tried to change the subject. "So Sophie, did you go partying with your friends on New Year's Eve?"

"Yeah, Mom and Dad went out with friends, and I went over to Hope's party."

"How is Hope doing? Her ankle probably healed enough for her to get back into gym class tomorrow."

"Actually, she is coming along pretty well. She is looking forward to the upcoming volleyball season. So am I."

"You have always been good in sports, Sophie. I know you don't get it from our side of the family," Karen joked.

"I agree, Aunt Karen. It definitely came from Dad's side."

Joan cut in. "You never said what you did for New Year's Eve? Did you go out?"

"I had friends over. We played board games," Karen disclosed the information.

"Sounds like fun. Let me guess, Rhonda and Julie?"

"Yes, as a matter of fact it was, and Jessie."

"Jessie also?" Joan smirked.

"Yes, why?" Karen repeated.

"No reason. You just seem to spend most of your time with them these days," Joan pointed out.

"We have fun together. Rhonda and Julie are my closest and dearest friends. I have been off from work, and that is what you do: You spend time with friends." Karen got defensive. On the other hand this was an opportunity to explore Joan's feelings. "Do you have a problem with them . . ." Karen began to fidget. "Or the fact that they are lesbians . . .?" she managed to get out.

"No, not at all. I think the world of Julie and Rhonda." Joan set Karen's mind at ease at once.

"Everybody talks about Miss Carmichael being gay, too," Sophie mentioned quietly, not to let her dad hear her.

"And how do they know this?" Karen asked, curious.

"A couple of girls in our gym class are lesbians. They say they have pretty good 'gaydar', and that she is definitely gay."

Joan laughed out loud. "What the hell is 'gaydar'?"

Karen had often heard Julie use the term, and nine times out of ten Julie was right.

"You laugh, but it's true. They seem to be able to 'tune in' to other homosexuals. Anyway, I don't care one way or the other. I really like her," Sophie added.

"Well, it has been most enjoyable spending time with Jessie. I really like her," Karen confessed, surprised at herself for saying it and pleased that Jessie being a lesbian didn't seem to matter to Joan or Sophie one way or the other.

"Anyone I have talked to seems to really like Miss Carmichael. All Sophie's friends' parents have nothing but good things to say about her," Joan added.

"What are Roger's feelings on the subject? Has he toned down any since his outburst the day of the tournament?"

Joan hesitated. "He has issues. He is quite vocal on the subject. He goes on about how unnatural homosexuality is and how queers should go for counselling. You really don't want to get him started on the subject. He refers to them as perverts. He doesn't understand it. I think it scares him."

Karen felt uneasy and a bit nauseated. She loved Roger like a brother. Times had changed, but the phobia was still out there, just not as pronounced as it once had been.

She got up and placed her mug on the counter. "I am going to head home. I have to work tomorrow, and I haven't slept well for a couple of nights. I am going to try to lie down for an hour or so. Bye Roger," Karen yelled to the next room. She got her hugs and kisses and left.

Jessie was pressing her clothes for work the following day when the phone rang.

"Hey, Jess, how are you?" Tom asked. "I haven't heard from you, and I was curious how the chainsaw worked."

"I had no trouble at all. I did have a branch want to take me on though." Jessie laughed, as she recalled the incident.

"You didn't get hurt, did you?" Tom asked concerned.

"Don't worry. I had a good nurse taking care of me."

"I forgot Karen is a nurse. You probably made it out to be worse than it really was just to get her attention."

Both laughed.

"I lapped it all up, and she left me wanting more," Jessie admitted freely.

"I bet she did. So, are you dating, yet?" Tom wanted his sister to find happiness.

"No. Unfortunately that may never happen. But I am not giving up." Jessie sounded a little disheartened.

"What does that mean?"

"Well, I brought the New Year in at Karen's along with a couple of lesbian friends. Over the course of a great evening, I made a stupid move and may live to regret it."

"Now you have my curiosity peaked."

"Promise you won't laugh?"

"I promise. Now tell me."

"I reached over, ran my fingers through her hair and told her she was beautiful."

"And?" Tom waited eagerly.

"And that is when she politely told me that flattery would get me almost anything, except that. And then she added, 'I'm not gay'."

"Ouch! That hurts," Tom sympathized. "That takes the wind out of your sails in a hell of a hurry."

"By the time I left for home, I think I put some wind back in the sail or at least a small gust of air!" Jessie continued.

"What happened? What did you do?"

Jessie knew that she could tell Tom anything. "Let's just say I left her with something to think about when we saw the old year out and the New Year in."

"You kissed her?"

"You bet I did. I was not about to let an opportunity like that pass me by."

"That's my girl! She didn't slap you, did she?"

"Actually she seemed to respond in a favorable manner. I am hopeful."

"You sly devil. I taught you everything you know," Tom bragged. "Keep me posted. I like her already, and I don't even know her."

"Thanks Tom." Jessie suddenly felt tears well up in her eyes. "Listen Tom, I have to go, but I will call you again soon." Jessie needed to get off the phone and let her emotions settle.

"Okay, take care of yourself, and remember that I love you."

Getting back to work was good for Karen. She was happy to be back helping others with their troubles and getting her mind off her own. The first few days it was hard getting back into a routine after the holidays. Karen and Julie only managed to have one break together because they were so busy.

Karen was having difficulty facing the reality of how Jessie's kiss had made her feel. Her mind was whirling with recurring thoughts. She desperately wanted Jessie as a friend. Still she was afraid to see her or to talk to her. Friends played a huge part in Karen's life. When a special one came along, she didn't want to just turn her back when the road became bumpy.

If she called Jessie, she didn't want to lead her on and give her false hope. On the other hand, if she didn't call, then Jessie would feel she had gone too far and pushed her away. What was she to do? She needed time and decided that she was going to take it.

So for the next couple of weeks Karen kept pretty much to herself. She did not go to the hockey games and did not answer her phone when she recognized the number on the other end as Jessie's. She felt like she was hiding. In fact that was exactly what she was doing. Out of sight out of mind? That wasn't true at all; Jessie was always on her mind.

Jessie was not handling the silent treatment very well. The first week after the holidays she managed to keep herself occupied with planning the volleyball season. It was another busy schedule. Volleyball was one of her favorite sports. On her first day back she posted sign-up sheets for tryouts. Then she worked late a few evenings getting her classroom courses prepared for an in-depth look at the human anatomy coming up in a few weeks.

When Karen did not show up for the second week in a row to cheer on the hockey team, Jessie needed to talk. As soon as the game was over, she approached Rhonda. "Would you mind if I come over for a beer?"

"Not at all." Rhonda put her arm around Jessie's shoulders in a comforting gesture.

When they arrived at the house, Rhonda got beers for everyone, and they sat around the kitchen table.

"I hope you don't mind, but I need to talk with someone," Jessie began.

"We are here for you." Julie covered Jessie's hand with her own and gave it a light squeeze. "Is this about Karen?" The answer was obvious.

Julie's question took some of the stress off Jessie. "Yes. You have seen her at work. How is she?"

"Honestly, she is not quite herself these days. I have tried to talk to her a couple of times, but she isn't opening up."

"She must hate me. She doesn't answer the phone, and now she is not showing up for the hockey games."

"Karen couldn't hate anybody. She is not that kind of person," Rhonda reassured.

Julie patted Jessie's hand for comfort. "We have known for years that Karen is a lesbian, she just hasn't realized it, yet. We have often teased her about it, but now we feel she has met that special someone and is having trouble dealing with it."

"She told me she wasn't gay, but I feel it," Jessie declared.

"That is her defensive shield. This is all new to her. She needs time to sort it out for herself in her own way." Rhonda said knowingly.

"Do you suggest I should just wait?" Jessie asked desperately. "I can't wait much longer without talking to her. I am ready to explode. At the very least I want her friendship."

"Then you need to tell her that. Just take this slowly. Give her time," Julie advised. "I would talk to her for you, but I don't want to get in the middle. Besides, that way Karen has someone to turn to when she is ready to talk."

CHAPTER NINE

Saturday morning was sunny and beautiful. Karen was relieved it was the weekend. Evading Julie was getting more and more difficult. As for Jessie . . . she knew she should call her to talk this out. Yet she could not make herself pick up the phone and dial the number. Wanting some fresh air, Karen decided to go for a walk. She had just gotten her coat on when the phone rang. Checking the number, she knew it was Jessie. Her heart melted; she wanted to hear Jessie's voice. She picked up the receiver.

"Hello Karen?" Jessie waited for a reply. "Karen, are you there?"

Hearing Jessie's raspy voice instantly flooded Karen with a desire she could not ignore. She hung up the phone. I need some fresh air; I'm definitely in need of a walk, Karen thought, putting on her boots and heading outside.

The sun felt wonderful on her face. She thought of Jessie and began to smile. Hearing Jessie's voice made her realize how much she had missed her. This rush of excitement and turmoil at the sound of her voice . . . I know I want more than friendship from Jessie. How much more? Where do I go from here? I can't keep hiding. I miss her, Karen thought to herself. She needed to call her. They had to work this out.

Jessie's heart ached when she heard the dial tone instead of Karen's voice. But she was not the type to give up. Karen was at home, and it was a great day for a drive.

Jessie stopped by a coffee shop and picked up two French Vanilla Cappuccinos. She knew those were Karen's favorite. Not knowing what she was going to say exactly, the drive to the country allowed her time to get nervous.

When she turned onto Karen's street, the bright sunlight caused her to reach for her sunglasses. Not too far ahead a pedestrian was walking along the side of the road. As she approached, Jessie recognized Karen. Her heart started racing. Her hands began to sweat. Oh, how she had missed her!

No other cars were coming in either direction, so Jessie slowed down and pulled up alongside Karen. Jessie lowered the window and held up a cup of cappuccino. "Can I interest you in a peace offering?" she said with a wide smile.

Karen looked up and noticed Jessie behind the wheel. Smiling back at her, she accepted the cup. "Absolutely." Steam escaped her lips, as her warm breath met the cool air.

"Hop in," Jessie invited.

Karen opened the door and got inside.

Jessie broke the silence. "What a perfect day for a walk."

"It is colder than expected. The sun is deceiving. I'm glad to get a ride back."

In no time they were back at Karen's place. Karen invited Jessie in and offered her a seat by the fireplace.

Jessie loved the appearance of Karen's rosy cheeks and her tousled short blonde hair. Karen's eyes were so blue she found it hard not to stare at her. "I called you several times," Jessie began.

Karen didn't know how to answer. Instead she watched Jessie crossing the room. Jessie wore a crewneck shirt with wide stripes of navy blue and bright yellow, along with plain navy track pants with a plain navy zipped jacket and a white ball cap.

"It has been pretty busy at work lately, and I have been tired." Karen hated not being completely truthful, but she couldn't tell Jessie she was avoiding her intentionally.

"I thought I would see you at the rink. You haven't been to the games either," Jessie pointed out. "Are you dodging me?" Jessie asked her directly.

Karen could not lie. "I won't lie to you Jessie. I am having a hard time trying to decipher my feelings for you. I cherish our friendship, and I worry that you might want more than what I am willing to give."

"I respect and understand that you are confused. Whatever happens, Karen, I don't want to lose your friendship. Having you in my life is the best thing that has happened to me in a very long time," Jessie confessed.

"I feel that way too. I just don't think I can give you anything more than friendship."

"That is all I am asking. I will take what you are willing to give me. If friendship is where we draw the line, then I am okay with that," Jessie was relieved. At least they were speaking again.

"Are you really okay with that?"

"Do I want more? Absolutely! If there ever is a time when you change your mind, I want to be the first to know." Jessie spelled it out, not wanting to leave any room for misunderstanding.

They gave each other a long hug. Both took a deep breath. They were relieved they had salvaged their friendship. For now it was Karen who led the direction in this relationship. Although deep in her heart Jessie knew that one day she would have her completely.

Karen prepared a light lunch. Meanwhile Jessie brought her up to date on what had gone on in school the last couple of weeks.

"... and by the way our hockey team has lost the last two weeks."

"Ouch, that isn't good," Karen sympathized.

"We lost because our good luck charm wasn't there to cheer for us," Jessie teased.

"I was going to say that." Karen laughed. "What is that expression? 'Great minds think alike, but fools seldom differ'."

Jessie had missed Karen's sense of humor. She was glad that Karen felt comfortable enough to let her stay for a couple of hours. It was already dark when she headed for the door.

"I had better get going; I don't want to wear out my welcome."

"I am glad you came to see me. I kept putting our talk off, but I didn't want to speak over the phone either. I apologize," Karen explained once more.

"Let's move forward and see where it leads us." Jessie looked directly into Karen's eyes.

"I agree." Karen gave her a soft kiss on the cheek and saw Jessie out.

Karen needed to talk with Julie. She was sure Julie would be angry since she had been avoiding her, as well. At work on Monday they spent their break together. Karen was relieved with Julie's warm reception. What Karen did not know was that Jessie had called Rhonda and Julie on Sunday and explained what had taken place. Julie was happy that things were working out between them. Julie figured Karen would come around; it was just a matter of time.

"How is Rhonda?" Karen started up the conversation.

"Rhonda is great. How are you doing?" Julie asked her.

"I'm good." By the expression on Julie's face Karen knew that wasn't enough for her closest friend. "Okay, honestly I have had a rough couple of weeks. I am sorry for not being myself," Karen blurted out. She felt guilty for avoiding Julie.

"I am here if you need to talk." Julie grabbed Karen's hand and squeezed it.

Julie's sincerity and the look of understanding made Karen realize Julie was aware of her inner struggle.

"Karen, hi it's Jessie. The Leafs are playing the Sens tomorrow night. Would you like to come over and watch the game?"

"Sounds like fun." Karen jotted down Jessie's address and realized she drove by Jessie's apartment every day on her way to and from work.

She arrived with her Senators jersey on, two bottles of beer in one hand and a bag of Doritos in the other.

Jessie opened the door and immediately started laughing. "We could be in trouble here."

"Already? I just got here."

"I had no idea that you were an Ottawa Senators fan."

"Don't tell me you cheer for the Toronto Maple Leafs," Karen huffed playfully. "In that case this could prove to be a very interesting evening." Karen looked at the collection of Leaf memorabilia that Jessie had on display.

Jessie opened one of Karen's beers for her and took the second one to the fridge. She grabbed one for herself and upon her return watched as Karen was consuming the display of Jessie's awards and trophies.

"It appears you excel in many sports. I am impressed with this exhibit of achievements."

"Don't be too impressed. I wasn't going to bring them with me when I moved, but I'm not ready to pack them away in a box just yet."

"You should be proud. I've wished from childhood that I could be a good athlete, unfortunately the best position for me to play is in the cheering section."

"From anything I have seen, you excel as a fan."

"I think so too. So why have I never received a trophy for it?" Karen sulked with a playful grin.

"Well, maybe you will someday. Come on, the game is about to start. You can show me what a good fan you are when your team loses," Jessie jabbed.

They moved over to the couch. Jessie put her beer down on the end table and went to the kitchen to retrieve a bowl for the munchies Karen had brought.

Karen sat at the other end of the couch, and they put the bowl between them. Jessie was on her best behavior all evening. Every once in a while she got a subtle whiff of Karen's perfume, but she managed to subdue her emotions and keep them well disguised from Karen.

Throughout the game the teams had taken turns being in the lead. On each occasion the gals teased each other over whose team was better. They both had a lot of fun. The Ottawa Senators won the game four-three, which gave Karen bragging rights.

When Karen got up to stretch, she noticed it had begun to snow. Shortly afterwards she headed home because of the weather.

Her drive home gave her the opportunity to evaluate how things had gone between them. Jessie had been true to her word and did not pressure her in any way. The problem was, Karen herself had trouble. Watching Jessie laugh and joke made Karen's heart ache with the desire to once again feel the touch of Jessie's lips against her own. She had had to make a conscious effort to grab for the Doritos when Jessie wasn't reaching for them, for fear that one touch would cause her to give in to her unspoken desires.

Whenever Karen let her guard down and even remotely considered the possibility of letting herself explore the pleasures Jessie offered, she remembered Roger and the harsh words Joan had conveyed, describing his feelings on the subject, queers need counselling, it's unnatural, they are perverts. Roger had no use for homosexuals. Karen thought the world of Roger and could never see herself jeopardizing the wonderful relationship she had with him or Joan.

Once Karen got home she needed to unwind. Her thoughts were racing in every direction. She grabbed the shovel and cleared the newly fallen snow off the front step and the walkway. Still a little tense, Karen decided to take a quick shower, crawl into bed and watch TV. She was trying to keep her mind busy so she would not constantly think about Jessie, but it wasn't working. As soon as she closed her eyes, there was Jessie's smiling face looking at her with those long gorgeous lashes over those big beautiful brown eyes. Seeing Jessie's face caused a stir inside Karen which she tried hard to ignore.

CHAPTER TEN

The following day Julie and Karen were unable to take any breaks together during work. They met up later at the hockey rink. Julie was sitting in their usual spot watching the cleaning of the ice.

"Hey, Karen." Julie rose to give her hug. "What a crazy day at work today! I sure hope tomorrow is a little quieter!"

"Did you and Rhonda plan anything for the weekend?"

"We may tackle cleaning out a couple of closets, a chore we have been putting off. We will see how we feel. Right now I am too tired to be overly ambitious about anything. Actually I am surprised to see you here."

"I promised Jessie last night that I would be here to cheer them to victory. She told me they have lost the last couple of weeks."

"So she called you last night? Bring me up to date."

"No, I went over to her apartment. We watched the hockey game together," Karen explained.

"That's nice. I'm glad to see the two of you are hitting it off so well," Julie said sincerely happy for them.

"Yeah, me too." Karen blushed. "Jessie is a lot of fun to be around. She is such a nice person. I really like her. One big problem though . . . she's a Leafs' fan." Both laughed aloud.

Just then the girls came out onto the ice to warm up. As usual Jessie looked up immediately to see if Karen had made it to the game. They acknowledged each other with smiles and waves.

Julie watched and wondered how much longer Karen would be able to fight the inevitable.

The Rideau Rockets won. Afterwards Karen waited with Julie for the players to come out. Most of the girls were wearing smiles. Jessie and Rhonda were no exception.

"See, I told you that you were our good luck charm." Jessie dropped her hockey bag, grabbed Karen around the waist and gave her a hug.

A bit self-conscious of who was watching, but thrilled to experience the joy Jessie was feeling, Karen enjoyed the moment of tenderness. "With the way you all played tonight you didn't need good luck. You gals were awesome," Karen complimented them both.

"Yeah, the whole team played well tonight," Rhonda added winking at Julie.

"Would anybody be interested in going out for a beer to unwind?" Jessie asked.

Rhonda and Julie both answered at the same time. Rhonda said yes, Julie declined, because she was too tired.

"I have to agree with Julie tonight," Karen replied. "It was a tough day today. I need to get home and call it a night."

Jessie was disappointed, but she totally understood. "Rhonda, if you want, you can come with me, and I will take you home afterwards."

"Sounds good. Is that okay with you, Honey?" Rhonda asked Julie.

"Of course, I just can't tonight, I'm sorry."

They walked out to the parking lot together discussing the game. Julie said good-bye and got into the car. Rhonda tossed her hockey bag into the trunk, and then went around to the window to give Julie a quick kiss on the lips.

Suddenly from across the parking lot they heard some guys yelling obscenities at them. "Hey, you dykes, get the hell out of here or better yet come on over, and I will show you how to be with a real man."

They could see the guys were standing around having a few beers in the parking lot.

Another one yelled "Damn queers", and yet another started up, "I like watching two women have sex. Come on lesbos, give us a show."

Karen became very nervous and not at all comfortable with the situation.

Julie just rolled her eyes. "See you at home later. You better get going before there is trouble. Love you," she said to Rhonda and pulled away. At the road she stopped for a moment to make sure there was no trouble for the other girls.

Jessie had loaded her hockey bag already and started the car.

Rhonda called them assholes, told them to get a life, and then got into Jessie's car.

Jessie and Karen acknowledged that they had better get going, said good night quickly, and they both drove away.

Karen had never experienced this sort of behavior before. How could people be so nasty?

Julie caught up with Karen the next day. "Rhonda and I have decided on a movie night tomorrow. We would like you and Jessie to join us. Are you available?"

"I have to check my schedule." Karen lifted her eyebrow teasingly.

"Can you find room in that busy schedule for a couple of close friends and a movie? Please!" Julie begged.

"Sounds like fun. What time?"

"Around seven o'clock."

"Great. Have you asked Jessie, yet?" Karen asked curious.

"Rhonda and Jessie talked about it last night when they went out for a beer."

Karen wanted to talk to Julie about the episode in the parking lot, but she didn't want to bring it up and spoil Julie's day.

The afternoon was hectic but not unbearable like the previous day and passed quickly.

A movie night required casual attire. It appeared everyone had the same idea because they all wore either flannel comfy pants or track pants with T-shirts. Jessie was already there when Karen arrived.

Julie made a huge bowl of popcorn with lots of butter, while they all stood around the kitchen chatting.

Jessie observed Karen. She watched her talking and laughing with Rhonda while she was nibbling at the popcorn before Julie had even added the butter. My heart aches for her, Jessie thought to herself. How much longer will I be able to refrain from touching her? I want the opportunity to show her how I could please her in many different ways. Oh, how I could …

"Hello? Earth to Jessie!" Rhonda said with volume. She had already called Jessie's name twice without a response.

"Huh, what?"

"Wherever you were, it must have been good. I called you three times before you heard me."

A subtle pink color crept into Jessie's cheeks. "Yes, in fact it was good. It was very, very good." Jessie tossed a couple of pieces of popcorn at Rhonda causing them all to laugh.

"Care to share your thoughts with us?" Julie pressed.

"No, I will keep them as my own thoughts, thank you." Jessie grinned wryly. She looked over at Karen who was also blushing. It was as though she could read her mind. Time to change the subject. "So, which movie did you pick for tonight?"

"'Desert Hearts'," Julie replied with a straight face.

Jessie's face turned stone sober. She knew that Karen would not be at all comfortable watching that movie with the three of them. She couldn't let them do that to her. "Are you sure you want to watch that one?"

"I can't wait. We haven't seen it in a while."

"It's a great movie. I would enjoy it, just not tonight."

"'Desert Hearts'? Never heard of it," Karen said. "What is it about?"

"It's a really good love story," Julie said.

"But if the three of you have already seen it, why pick that one?"

Rhonda and Jessie stayed quiet, letting Julie handle it, since she was the one who had gotten them into this situation.

Julie grabbed Karen's hand. "You're right. We can save it for another time, or you can take it home to watch it if you want to."

Jessie breathed a sigh of relief. To make Karen sit and watch a lesbian love story with three lesbians would not only make Karen uncomfortable but Jessie, too.

"What are our other choices?" Karen asked.

"We have 'Mama Mia' which is a chick flick, and we know all the music. Then there is an action movie called 'Transporter' or a comedy called 'Marley and Me'."

Jessie spoke up. "I have already seen 'Marley and Me'. It's fun, but I vote for either of the other two."

"Let's start with 'Mama Mia'. If we still feel like it we can watch 'Transporter' after that. If not, we call it a night," Julie suggested.

"Sounds like a plan." Rhonda grabbed the popcorn and headed to the living room.

Rhonda and Julie sat on the couch, while Karen and Jessie grabbed a large throw pillow and sat on the floor, leaning their backs against the couch.

'Mama Mia' was a fun movie right from the very beginning. They all sang along. For the faster tunes they were on their feet, cranking the volume and acting like school girls dancing and cutting loose.

"This is a riot!" Jessie exclaimed.

They all needed it after a rough week. The movie ended too soon. They refilled their drinks once again and decided to watch 'Transporter' next. Jessie squeezed onto the couch between Karen and Rhonda. There was enough room for all of them; it was just a bit cozier. Jessie's back was starting to ache from sitting on the floor.

The movie 'Transporter' toned the mood down immediately. It was an action drama. About an hour into it Karen found her eyes getting heavy. Every once in a while she caught herself when her head started bobbing. Finally, she gave into it and drifted off to sleep. Her head was leaning in Jessie's direction.

Jessie could hear Karen's breathing get heavier and knew she had fallen asleep. She wanted so badly to put her arm around Karen and let her lean on her.

It was as if Rhonda could read her mind. "Jessie, Karen doesn't look very comfortable. Why don't you pull your arm out from between the two of you and put it around her shoulders?"

"I don't want to wake her up. She looks so peaceful."

"She is a pretty sound sleeper. You won't wake her up."

"If she wakes up and is angry because I have my arm around her, you are taking the blame."

"I take full responsibility," Rhonda agreed, willing to take that chance.

Jessie moved her arm and put it around Karen's shoulders like Rhonda suggested. Karen leaned into Jessie with her head resting in the curve of Jessie's underarm and atop her breast. Karen's breathing got a bit louder, but it was not quite a snore. They were all giggling.

"Once Karen realizes she fell asleep, she will be so embarrassed," Julie remarked laughing.

Holding Karen felt so natural. Jessie felt like this was where Karen belonged, so she could protect her. Jessie wanted to kiss her on the forehead, but she did not want to push her luck. This was what she wanted; only she would have much preferred Karen to be awake and a willing participant. But for now she was happy just being able to touch Karen.

After a while Jessie herself was so content and comfortable that she started to nod off as well. Before too long the two of them were sound asleep. Jessie's head rested on Karen's.

Rhonda and Julie finished watching the rest of the movie. Afterwards they picked up the beer bottles and glasses. Neither Karen, nor Jessie stirred.

"Shall I wake them or you?" Rhonda asked.

"What if we leave them there for the night?" Julie proposed with a mischievous look. "Tomorrow is Sunday. They don't have to get up for work or anything."

"That's true. It is already really late anyway. I will get them a blanket."

Rhonda returned with a blanket and a couple of pillows. She propped Jessie up a bit, so she wouldn't tip over or kink her neck uncomfortably. She covered them both with the blanket. Julie and Rhonda stood starring at their two friends.

"They make a cute couple, don't they?" Rhonda asked.

"Yes, they do. I believe they have a great future together." Julie smiled.

Rhonda pulled Julie close to her and gave her a kiss. "You are such a romantic."

"I know, I can't help myself."

"Let's call it a night. Come on." Rhonda led Julie across the room.

They turned out all the lights, but left the fireplace on to keep their friends from getting chilled during the night.

The next morning Karen was the first to stir. She was warm and cozy nestled in the arms of Jessie, she just didn't realize it, yet. Karen's first instincts had her snuggling up closer; she was so peaceful and content. She opened her eyes. It took a moment for her to focus. Then she recognized where she was and what had happened. Here she was lying comfortably in Jessie's arms and very much enjoying the feeling. This felt so right, how could it be wrong?

Karen tipped her head back just enough to watch Jessie as she slept. Karen reached up and gently moved a lock out of Jessie's face. She ran the back of her fingers softly over Jessie's cheek. Jessie's complexion was flawless, with light brown freckles sprinkled over it. Her hair was messy, and her mouth was slightly open. She was perfect.

Karen didn't want to move. She would be quite pleased to stay in the comfort of Jessie's arms, but she did not want Jessie to wake and feel awkward about the situation. Slowly Karen wiggled her way out from Jessie's hold and made sure to cover her up, so she would stay warm. She leaned over and placed a gentle kiss on Jessie's forehead.

Karen fought with herself trying to decide whether to go home or to prepare coffee. Since she really didn't want to face the rest of the girls when they awakened, she decided to head home. She wrote Rhonda and Julie a note thanking them for everything.

Jessie heard the front door close and Karen's car start up. She sat up and pulled the blanket around her. She could smell Karen's perfume on it. Jessie had felt Karen brush her hair back and caress her cheek. What was it going to take to get Karen to see her both as a lover and as a friend?

Jessie got up and headed for the kitchen, keeping the blanket wrapped around her and drawing in the fragrance of Karen while she put the kettle on for hot water. She sat down at the kitchen table and read Karen's note. Karen thanked them all for a lovely time and said she would be in touch soon. "P.S. Julie, I have borrowed your movie 'Desert Hearts'. I like a good romance." Jessie smiled to herself wondering what kind of reaction Karen was going to have when she realized it was a love story about two women.

Jessie decided not to stay for coffee after all. She put "Ditto" after the first half of Karen's note, pulled the blanket up to her face to inhale Karen's aroma one more time and headed home.

Karen showered and had her morning tea. The whole time she was consumed with thoughts of Jessie's arms wrapped around her and that unspoken desire to explore more. I can see myself waking up next to Jessie more often, she thought. To herself she had to admit that she liked the feeling of Jessie's arms wrapped around her. She liked it very much. Too much, maybe …

She did not want to get ahead of herself and certainly did not want to lead Jessie on and get into something she was not prepared to carry through. Still, she was definitely considering the possibility of a deeper relationship with Jessie.

Later that morning Karen received a phone call from Joan. "Morning, Karen."

"Good morning, Joan,"

"I didn't say 'good morning Karen', just 'morning.' So far it is not really that good."

Karen could tell by the comment and Joan's tone that something was troubling her. "Okay, I get the point. Is something wrong with Mom or Dad?" Karen asked, now concerned.

"No, no, they are fine," Joan continued in a nervous voice.

"What is it then?"

"I don't exactly know how to tell you this without getting you upset." Joan loved Karen deeply and did not want to hurt her feelings, but thought she should know.

"Just tell me, Joan. Honesty has always been our policy."

"Well, you remember John and Martha Saunders, don't you?" Joan asked. "They are neighbors of Julie and Rhonda's a couple of houses down."

"Yes, I remember."

"John works with Roger at the plant and ..."

"And what? Joan, get to the point!" Karen was starting to feel a tug in the pit of her stomach, a feeling she did not like at all.

"Roger just received a call from John telling him that his sister-in-law is a lesbian."

"What?"

"John says he had always thought so, and now he is certain. He saw you leaving Julie and Rhonda's house early this morning. Apparently the school teacher left not long after you."

"I can expl..."

"Roger wants to go to the school and have Jessie fired. He considers her a bad role model for the students. Karen, Roger is livid. I have never heard him talk this way. I think he is ready to disown you, if this is true." Joan's voice quivered.

"He has no right to have her fired! Listen Joan, I can explain, it is not what you think!" Frightened for Jessie, Karen felt a flash of anger shoot through her. A multitude of thoughts darted through her mind: Is this what being a lesbian would be like? Dealing with people like John jumping to assumptions and pointing the finger with accusations? If I were a lesbian, I shouldn't have to defend myself. I have a right to be whoever I choose to be!

"Karen, he says you spent the night with Jessie," Joan continued.

"Joan, I did spend the night over at Julie and Rhonda's. Which I have done on several occasions in the past. We are friends. We were watching a couple of movies, and I fell asleep. They covered me up and left me on the couch for the night. What's the big deal?" Karen didn't feel the need to explain that she was curled up in the warmth and comfort of Jessie's arms all night and that she absolutely wished she could have stayed there all day, as well.

"Did Jessie spend the night with you?"

Karen had never lied to her sister and was not about to start. "Yes, she did. I didn't know that until I woke up this morning. Jessie was still sound asleep. Joan, I feel like a child having to explain my whereabouts to you. John Saunders should keep his nose out of other people's business."

"Roger is not happy with John either. He just wants to have the facts when he goes to work tomorrow and has to face him. Karen, I'm sorry for the mix-up."

"You are sorry for the mix-up? Joan, you don't know how much this hurts me. The fact is that you called and accused me of sleeping with another woman without even giving me the benefit of the doubt. And you have told me in the past that same sex relationships don't bother you." Karen was shaking. She often wondered if Joan would stop loving her if she were gay. She had been quite sure Joan would love her no matter what. Now she was uncertain.

Joan tried to calm her sister down. "Karen, I'm sorry. You are right. I should never have called. Roger was so worked up about it. I wanted to get him answers."

This was Karen's chance to find out for certain. "Joan, what if John was right. What if I did sleep with Jessie? What if I am a lesbian?" Karen put it out there, terrified of the answer, but she had to know for sure how Joan felt.

"Karen, you are my sister. I love you dearly and unconditionally." Joan truly meant what she said. Karen was her only sister. Never would she let anything come between the two of them, not even Roger.

"Do you really mean that?" Karen wanted to know if Joan would stand by her side.

"Without a doubt," Joan confirmed. "If Roger couldn't handle it, then that would be his problem, not mine. I love Roger with all my heart, but I love you also."

"I love you, too, Joan. Have Roger tell John Saunders to stop spreading rumors. He is jumping to conclusions and has no right sticking his nose into other people's business."

"I will pass on the message." Joan knew she had hurt Karen's feelings. She felt bad for having done so. "Would you like to come over for dinner on Wednesday?" Joan tried to smooth over the situation.

"No thanks, I can't on Wednesday. Perhaps some other time." Karen didn't want to see Roger. Roger's discomfort with lesbians was upsetting. Karen needed some time.

"Okay, some other time then. Give me a call soon, all right, Sis? I love you." Joan hung up the phone.

Karen was angry. Was it because she was being questioned like a child? Or was it because a nosy neighbor had gotten her family involved in her private life – a private life that Karen herself was uncertain of? Was she angry that Jessie was not there to help her through this? Karen was experiencing the hard reality of what life could be like if she were gay. Not everybody was as accepting as she herself had always been. Karen pondered the fact that she had tough choices to make. Should she let this opportunity with Jessie pass her by because people could be mean and hurtful? Did she want to spend the rest of her life being the brunt of people's sick jokes or rude comments about her sexual preference? Or should she hold onto Jessie and explore the possibility of finding true love and happiness?

Karen needed some fresh air. She went outside to fill the bird feeders. She stood there watching the birds take turns filling their bellies. When did life become so complicated? she thought to herself.

On Monday Karen was suspiciously quiet.

Julie switched breaks with another nurse, so she could talk with Karen.

She came up behind Karen and tapped her on the shoulder while she was standing in line in the cafeteria to get her toast. "Just wanted to let you know I was on break too."

"Okay, I will see you over at the tables." Karen got her order of toast and tea and found them a table.

Julie joined her almost immediately.

"Before you say anything, I want to tell you I had a great time on Saturday evening," Karen started.

"Rhonda and I both said it was the most fun we have had since we were at your place New Year's Eve. It seems like the four of us really click."

"Yes, we get along exceptionally well. I loved the movie 'Mama Mia'. Too bad ABBA is not a group of today and still pumps out more hits."

"I agree, they were great. So listen, why so quiet today? Are you mad at me for leaving you two asleep Saturday night?"

"No. I was a little surprised when I woke up in Jessie's arms, but I'm okay," Karen reassured Julie.

"You looked so comfortable there together. Rhonda and I decided to let you sleep instead of waking the two of you up."

"I apologize for falling asleep. Too many drinks, too much singing and dancing, I guess. Jessie fell asleep, too?"

"Yeah, not a half hour after you did. Guess you two didn't really enjoy the second movie." Julie laughed.

"No, it was great. I'm sorry that I left before you got up. I just didn't want to wake Jessie and make her feel uneasy about her morning bed head."

They both started to laugh. That was one of the things Julie loved about Karen: she could always see the humor in things.

"So, again, why so quiet?" Julie pushed, a little more seriously.

"No reason. I just have a lot on my mind." Karen wanted to talk about her situation, but was unsure how to go on about it. And certainly work was not an appropriate place.

"Can I help you with anything? You know you can talk to me."

"In fact, I really would like to have a talk with you, just the two of us over dinner," Karen suggested. "Are you busy on Wednesday?"

Julie made her face appear like she was really contemplating the question. That made them both giggle. "From what I can recall my appointment book shows that I happen to be available on Wednesday."

"Perfect. I will pick up pizza after work, and you can meet me at my place."

"We are going to your place for dinner?"

"Yeah, I don't want to fuss over dinner. On the other hand I prefer privacy. I definitely do not want a lot of people in a restaurant listening to our conversation."

"You got it, my friend. I will be there," Julie confirmed.

"I really need a good friend. It's good to know that I can count on you. Thanks." Karen gave her a hug as they got up and headed back to work.

Karen had a hundred and one things she wanted to talk to Julie about, all of which were racing around in her mind. She thought she should create a list so she wouldn't forget any of them on Wednesday.

CHAPTER ELEVEN

Jessie had a whole week planned on the subject of "The Human Anatomy". She was well prepared. But could one ever completely be prepared for all the comments and giggles from a classroom full of teenagers? One day down and she thought she had handled herself very professionally. Some of the comments were quite humorous to say the least.

Monday night Jessie decided to give Karen a call. The phone rang four times before Karen finally picked up. "Hey, Karen, I was just about to hang up. I didn't think you were home."

"No, I'm here. I was just down the hall folding a load of laundry."

"Sounds like fun. I have some here in case you are looking for something to do when you are finished with yours," Jessie teased.

"I would, but it's snowing. I just don't think I should drive in it, gee, sorry."

"Party pooper," Jessie came back.

"What can I say? All work and no play makes Karen a dull girl."

"Trust me; there is nothing dull about you." Jessie felt a rush of heat race through her, starting from the tips of her toes and then travelling with great speed all the way to the top of her head. Once she had said it she realized she probably shouldn't have. Quickly she tried to recover. "Karen, you have the quickest wit and brightest smile of anybody I know. Now, how can you call that dull?"

Karen was flattered, but a bit self-conscious. "Ahhhhhh, you are way too kind."

"I tell it as I see it," Jessie came back.

Karen giggled. "Then you had better get your eyes checked."

At first Jessie laughed. Then she turned a bit more serious. "You are always so hard on yourself Karen. You don't accept compliments very well, do you?"

"To be honest, no, I never really have. I get all self-conscious, awkward and uncomfortable for some reason. It is nice to hear them, I am just not a gracious receiver," Karen explained. It felt good to share that piece of herself, that honest moment, with Jessie.

"I could teach you. I am a teacher, remember."

"Good luck with that."

"I have lots of patience, and I don't give up easily," Jessie said to remind Karen she was sticking around for a while and not giving up on her. "Listen, I was wondering if you have plans for Friday evening."

"No, what do you have in mind?"

"I am doing lessons all week in class and will conclude the unit with a test. On Friday night I would like to grade the papers. That way I am done with it. I want to make it more enjoyable. I was hoping I could come out to your place."

Karen was excited by the idea of spending another evening alone with Jessie. "That sounds great to me. I am scheduled to get out at three o'clock on Friday instead of five. Why don't you come over for dinner?" Karen offered.

"No, no, I wasn't inviting myself for dinner. I just don't want to spend another Friday evening alone."

"Neither do I. It will be my pleasure to make dinner for us. If you want, you can bring the fixings for your famous Caesars." Karen thought this would make Jessie feel less like she was imposing.

Jessie was happy with the suggestion. "Excellent idea. What time?"

"Anytime you wish. If you want to come early and get started grading the papers, I will putter away at making dinner."

"I appreciate it."

"I am really glad you called to suggest it. I look forward to seeing you Friday. You are welcome to call anytime, Jessie. It is really nice spending time together."

"Am I going to see you on Thursday?" Jessie asked.

"I plan on being there."

"Great, we will have a better chance of winning with our good luck charm watching the game," Jessie teased.

She is so adorable, Karen thought. "What a smooth talker you are. You probably say that to all the girls."

"Hey now, easy!" Jessie retorted "I wouldn't say it if I didn't mean it."

"You are sweet, I will give you that." Karen imagined the smile on Jessie's face on the other end of the line.

"Sweet or not, I have to get going. I want to call Tom tonight and see how everyone is doing. I haven't checked in for a couple of weeks."

"Okay, I will probably see you Thursday, and if not, then Friday for sure."

"See you then." Jessie hung up and did a little jig in the middle of the living room. Oh, how I love spending time with that woman! she thought. Falling asleep holding Karen in her arms last weekend reinforced the fact that she wanted to spend the rest of her life with her. Everything feels right when I am with her. If only Karen felt the same, Jessie thought.

Karen hung up the phone and was all smiles. Simply talking with Jessie on the phone made her happy. Each day her feelings for Jessie were growing stronger. No matter how hard she fought to ignore those emotions or to pretend they were something less than they really were, Karen was painfully aware of what she really wanted. It certainly wasn't getting any easier to be just friends with Jessie. Her talk with Julie couldn't come soon enough.

Jessie decided to call her parents before calling Tom to tell them she was coming home for the Easter weekend. Maybe she would even be able to persuade Karen to meet her family. After speaking with her mom, she called Tom.

"Hi, Sharon. It's Jess. How is everything?"

"Everything is fine, thanks." Sharon chuckled. "You must have telepathy. Tom and I were just talking about you last evening. We were saying we hadn't heard from you, and Tom intended to give you a call."

"My ears were rather hot last night. I knew someone was talking about me. I'm just glad it was the two of you and not anybody else." Jessie thought the world of Sharon. She was a great sister-in-law.

"Sounds like you have developed some very broad shoulders, my dear. Have I told you lately how proud we are of you? We discussed that last night, too."

"Were you two bored last night with nothing better to do?"

Jessie had Sharon laughing. "You will never change, thank God. I love you and your sense of humor just the way it is," Sharon complimented. "Hold on Jessie, Tom is here wanting to say hi."

"Hey, Sis, how are things? We haven't heard from you in a while."

"Yeah, sorry I haven't called. Volleyball is keeping me busy. I have developed a social life, too, which is great."

"Oh, do tell. Does this social life include Karen by chance?" Tom inquired, hopeful for Jessie.

"Of course! We have been seeing each other a couple of times a week lately. I love it."

Tom's curiosity got the better of him. "Have the two of you …"

Jessie interrupted Tom before he could finish his question. "No, ah … yes, technically I have slept with her." Jessie started to laugh.

"I thought you would have a bit more excitement in your voice after sleeping with Karen," Tom said with disappointment. "Karen obviously isn't all you anticipated."

"I was just getting you going. What I mean is, we were at some friends together and both fell asleep on the couch while watching movies. She fell asleep on my shoulder, I drifted off, and our friends covered us up and left us there for the night. It was wonderful." Jessie sounded very excited telling the whole story. "The more time I spend with Karen, the more I want her. This is the real thing for me. Tom, I believe I have finally found the woman of my dreams. I love her," Jessie confessed. She felt relief and was elated to be able to share her deepest feelings with her brother and best friend.

"I can tell how happy you are. What about Karen's feelings for you?"

"Honestly I think she cares deeply for me. But this is all new to Karen. She is scared."

"Does she know how you feel?"

"Not totally. She knows I want her, but I don't think she realizes I have fallen in love with her."

"I knew at Christmas already that you were falling for Karen. I could tell by the way you spoke of her."

"I don't want to push too hard, because I care about her so much. But I don't know how much longer I can keep myself from letting Karen know how deep my feelings really are."

"I just don't want to see you get hurt. If you haven't been able to get to Karen by now, then I don't know if it is going to happen for you, Jess. You have always been pretty persuasive with women in the past. Never have you spent this length of time trying." Tom voiced his concern, even though his sister probably wouldn't want to hear it. "Maybe Karen is not going to come around to your way of thinking, and your dreams will come tumbling down around you."

"Karen is different. She is sweet and naive. She is worth the effort and definitely worth the wait. She's the one Tom, I know it."

"She must be pretty special to have you all in knots like this."

"Oh, Tom, I wish you could meet her. You will love her, too. I'm hoping to convince her to come home with me at Easter."

"We would really love to meet Karen. Besides, I need to give you my approval before anything serious happens," Tom teased. "Remember that after the last time your heart was broken I told you that I would have to give my blessing before you could give your heart to another. I'm your big brother, I have to protect you. It is my duty."

"Always looking out for me, aren't you? Well, there is no doubt in my mind that you will be pleased with Karen and happy to give me your blessing."

"Let me be the judge of that," Tom said with authority and humor. "Hey, March break is coming up soon. The perks of being a teacher must be nice."

"I am looking forward to it. I will miss the volleyball though. Our team is quite talented. We are second in the league," Jessie bragged. "The season ends with March break. We have a final tournament in Cornwall the last Friday before the break."

"Of course your team is doing well! Look who is coaching," Tom boasted. "Listen, Jess, Sharon is just about to go out the door, and I want to catch her before she leaves. I love you, kiddo. I will see you in a few more weeks."

Jessie hung up and held the phone to her chest. She loved Tom for wanting to protect her. She knew how lucky and blessed she was to have a brother who cared about her like Tom did.

Tuesday evening Jessie stayed late for volleyball practice. She enjoyed every minute of it. Jessie was in high spirits having talked to both Karen and Tom the night before. She felt her life was finally coming together the way she had always hoped it would.

Sophie was probably the most powerful player. Jessie was proud of her team and wanted to win the trophy. She had worked the girls hard. Now it was paying off for them.

Practice was finishing. Jessie had noticed that Sophie had been watching her closely. She was a bit curious as to why. "Sophie, come over here please." Jessie gestured with a wave of her arm.

"Yes, Miss Carmichael, what is it?" Sophie questioned.

"I was just wondering if everything is okay with you. You seem a bit preoccupied."

"No, I'm fine."

"Are you sure? I am a good listener. If there is anything you need to talk about, feel free to come and see me," Jessie offered.

"No, really I'm fine. But thanks, I appreciate it," Sophie replied.

"Okay, just know that my door is always open."

Karen got home from work and made herself a quick dinner. She intended to watch the movie 'Desert Hearts' that she had borrowed from Julie. Karen changed into her comfy clothes, turned on the movie and curled up on the couch with a Whisky and Pepsi which she felt she deserved after a hard day at work.

The movie began. It took Karen about fifteen minutes before she realized she was watching a lesbian love story. She was thankful she had not watched it with her friends, although she enjoyed watching it by herself now.

It almost felt as if she was getting away with something nobody else needed to know. The more she watched, the more she wanted to watch. Karen related to all the emotions and struggles that Professor Vivian Bell felt. She completely connected to Vivian's character, especially when it came to the love scene. Karen felt herself tense up, trying to fight her feelings, but knew she wanted to give in to the desire every bit as much as Vivian Bell did.

While watching the two women make love on the screen, she felt the warm wetness between her legs and became embarrassed. At the same time it excited her. She wanted to have this experience for herself and Jessie. Her desire for Jessie came strong and hard. She could no longer ignore her feelings after watching this powerful movie.

Suddenly Karen began to smile. Julie is such a prankster, she thought. I can't believe she wanted us to watch this movie together – especially with Jessie right beside me!

That night Karen fell asleep filled with thoughts of Jessie and the things she wanted to do with her. In the middle of the night she awoke to discover she was in a sweat and could not conceal the moistness between her legs. She lay there touching herself, stroking her soft mound gently. Slowly Karen slipped her fingers inside. A moan escaped her. Her back arched as she started a slow rhythm, moving her fingers in and out. Thoughts of Jessie swirled through her mind like a slide show. I want her, I so want her, Karen repeated to herself while she masturbated to climax, something she had never done before. Her whole body was on fire. Why can't I get you off my mind Jessie Carmichael? Damn it! she thought and jumped out of bed to take a cold shower.

CHAPTER TWELVE

Wednesday's work day went by quickly. Karen had ordered pizza and picked it up on her way home. She arrived just before Julie got there.

Julie quickly grabbed them each a beer while Karen dished out the pizza.

"It was a pretty busy day today," Julie started. "Too many viruses going around."

They talked about their workday and headed into the living room to sit by the fire.

Karen was fidgeting and restless. She couldn't seem to get comfortable

Slowly Julie started the conversation, letting Karen take it where she needed to go. "So, my friend, you implied the other day that you needed to talk. If there is anything I can help you with, I will."

"I appreciate you coming Julie. I know I can tell you anything, and you won't judge me."

"That's what true friends do: be there for each other. Ever since we met, Karen, you have always been there for me. Rhonda and I both respect you and cherish your friendship."

"I know. The same goes for me. I look up to the two of you as a couple and admire your relationship and the true friendship you share."

"Thanks, I appreciate that."

"I have some questions and concerns, Julie. And I need your complete honesty, brutal or not."

"Fair enough. I ask for the same from you."

"Of course, absolutely," Karen committed herself. "I can't believe I have never asked you this before, but when and how did you know you were a lesbian?" Karen asked nervously. She knew this evening was going to be difficult.

"I have known I was different, although not necessarily gay, since I was a young child, around eight or nine years old. I have always been attracted to women. When I was thirteen years old, my best friend Joy and I decided to experiment sexually. We started out kissing, then touching and feeling each other everywhere. That was the day I was certain I was a lesbian. Afterwards I tried to date guys, tried to deny what I had felt with Joy, but being with a guy wasn't for me. I did not enjoy the experience, and it certainly did not make me happy. Being with a woman is what makes me completely happy."

"You knew it that early in life! Wow, I'm surprised and impressed." Karen smiled along with Julie.

"Don't be, it wasn't easy. I got angry with myself and tried to change because of what society preached was right and what was wrong. I struggled, trust me. It wasn't always as wonderful for me as it is now."

"I never knew all this about you. Why haven't we shared this part of your story before now?"

"I guess we needed to have this discussion when it was meant to happen. We were waiting for just the right time in our relationship." Julie patted Karen's hand for reassurance.

"I suppose so. Then it comes as no surprise to you that I am having a hard time dealing with my true feelings for Jessie?"

"No, I have known for some time now. I was just waiting for you to finally realize it for yourself."

"I have always admired the relationships of my lesbian friends, especially yours of course, but I really had no idea why. I have gone out with some very nice guys, good-looking, pleasant, all that, but I have never wanted to sleep with any of them."

"And now you are having sexual thoughts about Jessie, and it terrifies you?" Julie added.

Unable to look her friend in the eye, as if she were ashamed of herself, Karen blushed and stared down at the floor.

"Karen, look at me," Julie said softly.

Karen slowly looked up at Julie with tears in her eyes. "Julie, I am afraid. This is so new to me. I want Jessie so bad that it hurts. I want to spend all my free time with her. I want to learn everything there is to know about Jessie. I want to meet her family, I want her to meet my family, and yes, I want to sleep with her, touch her, kiss her, I want all of it," Karen blurted out, relieved to finally say it out loud.

"Karen that is wonderful. I am so happy for you." Julie got up and pulled Karen to her feet. She gave her a hug. Karen held on tight. Julie felt her friend sobbing on her shoulder. "Why are you so upset?"

"I'm just not sure I can have what I want." Karen grabbed some Kleenex to dry her eyes and blow her nose.

"I don't understand. Why not?"

"I have more to consider than just my feelings."

"Well, I know Jessie is not the problem. She wants you badly, but she doesn't want to rush you."

That made Karen smile. "She has let me know that. She has been very sweet. I'm afraid I have not really given her any positive response other than our friendship."

"What is holding you back?" Julie questioned again. "I don't mean to be hurtful at a time like this. However, Jessie is quite a catch. She will not wait around forever. Rhonda told me just last week she overheard Connie on the hockey team ask Jessie out for drinks after the game tomorrow night." Julie did not want Karen to lose this opportunity for happiness.

Karen was a bit surprised. Julie was right. Jessie would not wait forever. "I have to ask you another question . . ."

"Ask away." Julie gave Karen the okay to proceed.

"Do you regret the way your life has turned out, in reference to being gay I mean?"

"Tough question. If you had asked me this question twenty years ago, my answer would have been different. Today my answer is NO. I have no regrets. I love my life. I needed to experience everything I went through to make me who I am today. I believe I am a much stronger and better person for it. I have a life with Rhonda that I would not trade for anything. And my life is just that Karen. It is MY life!"

"You are always so sure of everything," Karen admired. "I respect you for that."

"Honestly, sometimes I am not so sure. Still, this is my life. I deserve to be just as happy as anybody else," Julie said with conviction.

"Then answer me this: Do you often encounter rude comments and gestures like we experienced the other night in the parking lot?"

"Not nearly as much now as we used to years ago. Times have changed. Things are getting better for sure, but there are a lot of inconsiderate, ignorant people out there."

"We live in such a small conservative community. I just . . ."

Julie interrupted. "Karen you can't let other people take your happiness away from you."

"I wasn't going to tell you this, but remember that I was so quiet at work on Monday?"

"Yes, why?"

"Well, Sunday morning after I left your place and had been home for a few hours, all I could do was think about Jessie, lying there with her arms wrapped around me. I was so completely happy, like I have never been before."

"Wonderful! What happened?"

"Joan called me. She was upset because Roger had received a call from John Saunders, your neighbor."

Julie was familiar with John and Martha and their attitude towards homosexuals. "This can't be good." Julie shook her head.

"He accused me of being a lesbian and of sleeping with Jessie at your place. I didn't know how to react. My first instinct was to defend myself and try to explain about the misunderstanding. But the more I thought about it, the more I wondered what if I am a lesbian? Roger detests homosexuality. He wanted to get Jessie fired. What if I lose my family and friends? My family means everything to me."

Julie smiled gently. "Karen, I learned this the hard way – if you call people friends that will walk away from you because you are gay, then they were never really true friends anyway. Your real friends will love you just the same, just like you have always loved Rhonda and me. You have always been a true friend."

"What about my family?"

"What about them? You know that Joan loves you and Sophie worships you. You will always have them. If Roger has a problem with it, then it is Roger's problem, not yours."

"I have a real hard time with that." Tears ran down Karen's face once more. "I can't see me doing something that will hurt my family members."

"Step back and see what your family member is doing to you." Julie could see Karen was torn up inside. She also knew that her friend was so faithful to her family that Karen may never let herself be free to be completely happy and true to herself. Julie reached over and took Karen's hands in hers. "Karen, you are in your mid-thirties. You need to start living your life for yourself and not for everybody else. Isn't it time to have complete happiness and a companion with whom to share life's experiences? Don't you think you deserve that?"

Karen nodded, but the tears still flowed. "I know that I deserve happiness. Yet, I struggle with hurting others to have what I want. Therein lies my dilemma."

"People will always disagree on many things in life such as religion, politics, and yes, same sex relationships. That's what makes the world go around. If we were all the same, it would be a very boring world." Julie smiled.

Karen stared into the fire, rethinking all they had discussed. She knew she still had a great deal of soul searching to do.

Julie softly spoke. "True love is a remarkable gift, Karen. Don't throw it away because you are afraid. Welcome it and embrace it. Don't let it slip through your fingers. Jessie won't wait forever."

Karen once again had tears streaming down her face, torn inside with turmoil and indecision. She was unable to speak.

Julie stepped out to get more Kleenex. "Karen, what are you feeling?" Julie was genuinely concerned.

"Honestly, I feel emotionally drained and very exposed, but extremely grateful that I have you for my friend."

"I am really glad we had this conversation. It was long overdue."

"Yeah, I think so, too," Karen admitted.

"Are you going to be okay if I leave you now, or do you want me to stay a bit longer?" Julie offered.

"No, it is already after nine o'clock. You better head home. It started snowing about an hour ago. I will be fine." Karen got up and headed for the closet to get Julie's coat. "I can't thank you enough, Julie."

"I am glad I could be here for you. Hopefully I was of some help."

"Oh, I just remembered." Karen ran to the kitchen. "You can have this back." She handed Julie 'Desert Hearts'.

They both began laughing.

"Did you watch it?" Julie asked.

"Definitely. Once I started, I couldn't turn it off. You were correct in saying it was a great movie, but you are a shit for even thinking of having me watch that with Jessie and the two of you!!! Do you know how uncomfortable that would have been? Never mind, of course you do!" Karen swatted Julie on the arm.

"I can't seem to help myself. Nice to see that you have your sense of humor back, by the way." Julie felt better leaving Karen in this frame of mind.

They said their good-byes.

Karen watched Julie from the front window as she brushed the snow off her car and then drove away. Karen was exhausted. Before long she was lying in bed with a thousand thoughts swirling around in her mind until finally sleep came.

CHAPTER THIRTEEN

On Thursday morning the freezing rain made for a very tense drive into work. When Karen arrived, she was grateful that Julie had picked up their usual beverages at Tim Horton's. Julie and Karen looked out for one another and covered each other's backs when necessary. On any given day Karen was a hard worker, but today she was going above and beyond her usual workload to help Julie out whenever she could. It was her way of showing Julie how thankful she was for their talk the previous evening.

By lunch time the sun was shining. The roads were in decent driving conditions. Karen went out and picked up a beautiful bouquet of flowers along with a bottle of wine and delivered them to Julie's home. She knew where Julie and Rhonda kept the spare key hidden, so she let herself into the kitchen. She put the flowers in a vase with a card that read: "Julie, you're the best! Love Karen."

Jessie was also pleased to see the roads were somewhat cleared by noon. She had an errand to run. She had ordered something for Karen that was ready to be picked up, and she wanted it for the following night. With the errand done, she scooted by the hospital to see if Karen was available for a quick drink on her lunch break. She had never done this before, but sometimes spontaneity was fun.

Julie was on duty and told Jessie that Karen had gone out.

"Why are you smiling?" Jessie asked.

"No real reason. I'm just remembering that when Rhonda and I first dated, we used to stop in on each other just to say hi."

"Ha-ha. The difference is, Karen and I are not dating," Jessie reminded her.

"Not yet." Julie looked at Jessie and gave her a wink. "I have to get going, but I will let Karen know you stopped by."

"Thanks, I appreciate that. See you tonight at the game."

Karen had gotten back to work just in time to wash her hands and switch with Julie, so she could go for her lunch. Julie had finished filling Karen in on all the patients and updating the charts. She put her sweater on and turned to Karen. "By the way, you had a visitor when you were out."

"Was it Joan? She probably wanted to see if I am still angry with her," Karen replied.

"No, it wasn't Joan. It was Jessie. She came by to see if you had time for a quick drink with her." Julie was more than happy to give Karen the message.

"Jessie?"

"That's what I said: Miss Jessie Carmichael."

"She has never stopped by before to see us. How sweet is that?" Karen smiled from ear to ear. Simply hearing Jessie's name got her excited.

"Actually she came by to see you. Notice that she didn't stick around to spend my break with me," Julie rubbed in teasingly. "Anyway, I have to go. See you in a bit."

Karen loved Jessie's thoughtfulness. She felt the heaviness weighing on her heart lighten. It was replaced by sheer joy.

Karen had decided to drop by to see her mom and dad on her way to the game and ended up staying a little longer than expected. The game was nearing the end of the first period when Karen arrived.

The Rideau Rockets were losing two to nothing.

Julie spotted Karen as soon as she came into the arena. "Why so late?"

Karen got settled beside her. "I stopped by my parents. Mom needed some pictures rearranged and then wanted a couple of pieces of furniture moved. One thing seemed to lead to another. I didn't think she was ever going to let me go." Karen laughed. "I see our team is not doing so well."

"They are playing fine. They just can't seem to get a break. The other team is good, although ours is the better team."

Karen looked to find Jessie in the players' box. Jessie was already looking up at her. They waved to each other. Instantly Karen was in a much better frame of mind.

Just then the buzzer rang. The teams went off to their dressing rooms while the ice was cleaned.

"What a wonderful surprise I had when I got home tonight." Julie leaned over and gave Karen a big kiss on the cheek. "There was no need for that, you know."

"I wanted to let you know how special you are to me." Karen rubbed her friend's back in a friendly gesture.

"I'm not sure, if I was more of a help or a hindrance. If nothing else, I am a good listener."

"You definitely have made me look harder at some of my ways of thinking. Besides, a talk like this makes our friendship even more special." Karen leaned over, nudging Julie with her shoulder, grinning widely at her.

"I love you, do you know that?" Julie asked.

Karen giggled.

"I tell you I love you, and you giggle! It's not every day I proclaim my love to someone."

"I'm giggling at the thought of people hearing us. They would think we were dating or having an affair."

Julie's eyes got large. The two of them laughed out loud at the thought. "Six months ago you would not have had such a thought. Now look at you! You have journeyed a long way, girlfriend." They gave each other a high five.

Just then the teams came back out onto the ice. This time they showed more enthusiasm. Within minutes Jessie scored the Rocket's first goal. The Rockets ended up winning four to two. As they were leaving the ice at the end of the game, Jessie was all smiles, her stick raised over her head, beaming excitement for the win.

A while later Karen and Julie made their way down from the bleachers. The girls were coming toward them. Seeing Connie made Karen a bit uncomfortable after Julie's remark last evening. However, Karen remained her bubbly self.

"Excellent game!" Karen gave Jessie a hug, just like she always did. "You turned the game around in the second period." She looks so adorable, Karen admired. Jessie wore her usual ball cap with her red hair curled up around it. It feels so good to see her, even if it is only for a few minutes.

"Thanks, but I didn't do it alone." Jessie motioned towards Rhonda and Connie.

Karen was going to joke around and say it was because her good luck charm had shown up. Connie's presence made her change her mind.

"We are going out for beer. Would you like to join us?" Jessie asked Karen hopeful. Jessie didn't really want to go, but Connie had asked her several times, and she was running out of excuses.

Rhonda had injured her thumb and wanted to go home. "Some other time okay?" Along with Julie she headed off.

Although Karen wanted to spend time with Jessie, she didn't want to interfere with their plans. "Not tonight Jessie. Maybe next time. Thanks for the invite, though."

Jessie turned to Connie. "Why don't you go ahead, get us a table and order the beer. I will be there shortly."

"Sounds good to me. I will see you at Kelsey's." Connie headed out, pleased to finally have Jessie alone for drinks.

Jessie looked at Karen, who was smiling. "So, I hear you dropped by the hospital to see me today," Karen said a bit flirtatiously.

Jessie blushed and grinned like a school girl. "I thought with a little luck we could spend a few minutes together. A girl can hope, can't she?"

"That was very sweet of you. I hope you try again sometime."

"You don't want me to give up on you, I knew it!" Jessie slapped her hand on her knee.

Karen enjoyed the easy banter back and forth. "Lucky for you that we are still on for tomorrow night. You are coming, right?"

"Absolutely. I will be giving the students their test in the morning. They can hardly wait," Jessie joked. "I hope to get them all graded tomorrow night and have the rest of the weekend free. Did you change your mind about dinner? Would you prefer that I pick something up rather than you cooking it? "

"Of course not. I am looking forward to it. Just remember the fixings for the Caesars."

"It's all taken care of."

"Great! I will see you tomorrow. Now get going. You don't want to keep Connie waiting."

Jessie rolled her eyes. "Very funny. Ha-ha."

They walked out to the parking lot, neither of them really wanting to part.

On the drive home Karen thought about Connie and Jessie having drinks together. Jessie has so much to offer. I couldn't ask her to give me more time. It wouldn't be fair. I can just see Connie turning herself inside out, trying to win Jessie over. Listen to me, damn it; I do believe I am jealous!

Jessie was quite a catch. Was she ready to commit herself to Jessie? She was certain she was. Still she needed time to come to terms with potentially losing her family. She needed to see Joan, Roger and Sophie and get this whole issue out in the open once and for all. In the meantime Karen looked forward to her upcoming evening alone with Jessie. She planned on letting Jessie know that she was indeed interested.

When Jessie got to Kelsey's, Connie was sitting at a table in the back corner with a pitcher of beer for them to share. Connie had already started, and Jessie poured herself a glass.

"What a comeback we had tonight. It felt good, didn't it?" Jessie wanted to keep the conversation light and simple. She knew Connie had the hots for her, but she really wasn't interested.

"You played a great game, as usual I might add," Connie praised.

"Thanks, but as I say to my students, it takes everyone on the team to make it work. There is not one player who can do it alone."

"You are too modest."

Connie was not one of the stronger players on the team, but she was committed, showed up for all the games and gave her best when she played. These were important elements in any sport.

"It's not that I am modest, but perhaps you don't give yourself enough credit."

"You are very kind, Jessie. I like that about you. There is a lot I like about you." Connie gave her a wink.

"I just say it like I see it." Jessie felt the mood change. Connie had asked her out about six times already, and she hadn't wanted to decline again. But honestly she just wanted to have her beer and get going.

Jessie led the conversation back to the game and the upcoming playoffs. For a while they discussed each other's work and their interests. After two beers Jessie ran out of things to say. Connie was laughing and seemed to be having a good time, but Jessie felt it was enough for one night.

"I had better get going," Jessie said, implying it was time to leave.

Connie didn't want the evening to end. She finally had Jessie alone and was enjoying the one on one. "There is still beer in the pitcher. We can't let that go to waste."

"I already had two, and I have to drive."

"I suppose you're right. It's just that I am enjoying our conversation. Can I order you a coffee then?" Connie offered.

"No, thanks. I have had enough. It is going to be a long day tomorrow. I need to get some sleep," Jessie explained politely.

"Can we get together at some point over the weekend?" Connie asked hopeful.

Jessie had no interest. "I already have plans," she tried to get out of it without hurting Connie's feelings.

Connie stalled, trying to keep Jessie longer. "Oh, what are your plans?"

In all honesty Jessie didn't have plans. Although she was hoping to make some with Karen. "A friend and I are going out with another couple for dinner and a movie." Jessie hated to lie, but she saw no other way out. "Connie, really, I have to get going. It was nice having drinks. Perhaps we can do this again another time." Jessie put some money on the table for the beer.

"Okay, another time then." Connie gave in. "I enjoyed your company."

"Thanks, I enjoyed yours, too." Jessie smiled and turned to leave.

As Jessie drove home, she knew Karen was the one for her. Connie was clingy. Definitely not Jessie's type. The only one Jessie was interested in was Karen. Nobody else but her would make her completely happy.

Friday morning the sun was shining. Karen felt that this was going to be a great day. The drive to work was smooth sailing. Once she arrived at the hospital things changed. The whole morning was extremely busy. Both Karen and Julie were glad to see their break time arrive.

Julie was a bit ticked off at a fellow nurse who was shirking her duties. Usually Julie didn't let things like this get to her, but it seemed a bit too obvious today. Julie already had enough on her own plate. "I can't believe how slow Sylvia is today," Julie complained.

"She must be tired or something. Sylvia is usually not that slow," Karen agreed.

"She is really holding me back from my own job. I feel like I am doing double duty."

"Then take a load off your feet for a few minutes." They found a booth to sit. "Do you and Rhonda have plans this weekend?" It always made Julie feel better to talk about Rhonda.

Julie smiled. "No, not really. Nothing much anyway. What about you?"

Karen was beaming. "Jessie is coming over this evening for dinner. Other than that we have nothing planned for the rest of the weekend. They're calling for a snow storm Saturday. I am planning to stay in and watch a movie. Actually I should have asked you to bring that movie in for me today, so I can watch it again." Karen felt so much more relaxed and comfortable saying what she really felt since Julie and she had opened up to each other and shared their personal feelings.

"If you want, you can drop by the house and pick it up. Since you are off a little early today, just help yourself to it. It is still sitting on the stand just inside the front door."

"If I have time I may just do that."

"Jessie's coming for dinner? Any special occasion?" Julie moved her eyebrows up and down in a playful manner and then leaned in close to Karen. "Is tonight the night?"

Karen blushed and punched Julie in the arm. "You are so pathetic; you have a one-track-mind."

"Hey, when you are on the right track, why be derailed?"

"Ha-ha. Regardless, the answer is no. Tonight Jessie is marking her students' papers, while I am cooking dinner for us. Besides, I am not quite ready for that step just yet."

Karen's reluctance wasn't surprising for Julie. "Well, I can always hope for you. Once you cross the line, you won't want to go back. You will know that being with another woman is precisely what will make you happy."

Karen knew Julie only wanted complete happiness for her. "I just wish I were as certain as you are. Besides, I really would like to talk to Joan, Sophie and Roger about me coming out of the closet before I actually take the next step. I want to 'get my ducks in a row' so to speak."

"Yes, you are not the type of person to just act and suffer the consequences later. Anyway, remember what I said about procrastinating and then finding out that you are too late. You need to live life for yourself, not for everybody else. Life is too short, girlfriend," Julie reminded Karen.

Karen got up. "I appreciate that. I haven't forgotten anything we discussed the other night. I will keep you posted on my progress."

"I am counting on it. I live for this stuff, you know." They both laughed at Julie's comment and headed back on duty. "Thanks for getting my mind off work for a while. That was a very refreshing break thanks to you." Julie grabbed Karen's hand and gave it a squeeze.

Things seemed to go better for Julie the rest of the morning. Before too long it was lunchtime. Karen took her break first.

After work Karen picked up the groceries for dinner and a few extra things, because the local forecast was calling for that snow storm to hit on Saturday around late morning to mid-day. Since she had a few minutes left, she dropped by Julie's and picked up the movie 'Desert Hearts'. Karen recalled how much she had enjoyed it and how it had made her feel. She got all warm and self-conscience as she replayed the effects it had had on her body over in her mind – feelings she wanted to experience once again . . .

CHAPTER FOURTEEN

Jessie was enjoying her day. She only had a morning class in the gym. The rest of the day was spent with tests. During the first of three classes where tests were given, Jessie outlined her course for the following week. But often her mind wandered. She wanted to get out to Karen's as early as possible. During her second and third testing periods Jessie started grading the papers from the earlier classes to save time. By the time school was out, she had finished grading the papers from one class and got over two thirds marked of the second class. She wasted no time, quickly loaded up her briefcase, stopped by her apartment to pick up the pre-packed bag with the drink ingredients, grabbed the clamato juice from the fridge and was ready to go.

On her drive to the country Jessie chuckled to herself about the little gift she had gotten for Karen. She was pretty certain Karen would like it.

Karen was looking forward to spending the evening with Jessie. She figured Jessie would not be arriving much before five o'clock. As soon as Karen arrived home and put the groceries away, she decided to take a quick shower to get rid of the hospital smell. She always felt that she smelled like medicine and alcohol when she left work.

Karen had just gotten out of the shower and was not quite finished drying herself off when she heard the doorbell ringing. Surprised she wondered who it could be. She figured it was Joan stopping by on her way home. Karen quickly finished drying off, wrapped the bath towel around herself and headed down the hall. She looked out the window and saw Jessie's car in the driveway.

Karen wasn't sure what to do. Here she was in a towel, her hair a mess and still wet. She couldn't tell Jessie to wait a minute and leave her outside in the cold. She hadn't expected Jessie quite this early. It was only four o'clock. Karen had no choice but to invite her inside.

She went to the door and opened it, holding on for dear life to the towel. "Hi, Jessie, ah, welcome," Karen said blushing. As soon as she saw the expression on Jessie's face, she felt completely exposed.

Jessie took one look at Karen and had a mixture of feelings rush through her. Seeing Karen in nothing but a bath towel excited Jessie. Instantly she wanted to pick her up and carry her to the bedroom where they would spend the remainder of the evening together, romping around in the bed sheets.

"I guess I am earlier than you expected. Sorry about that." Jessie was all smiles, when she entered the house.

"A little. Anyway, I am glad you are here." Karen was very welcoming even though she was not prepared.

"You said to come as early as I wished. So I did." Jessie held a full bag in one arm and a briefcase in the other. "Would you mind taking this bag while I remove my coat?"

Instinctively Karen reached out for the bag. The towel loosened and was about to fall on the floor. Karen grabbed it, and Jessie started to laugh.

"Well, it almost worked. You can't blame a gal for trying." She had a devilish playfulness in her eyes.

"You're enjoying this, aren't you?" Karen retorted. "Very funny. On that note, I am going to go and slip into something more comfortable while you come in and make yourself at home." Karen headed down the hall.

Jessie watched her as she walked away. "Ah, come on. What could be more comfortable than that!" She giggled.

It wasn't too long before Jessie was in the kitchen making them both a Caesar to start their evening off on a relaxed note.

Karen wasted no time making herself presentable.

When she entered the kitchen, Jessie handed her a glass. "Here, try this."

Karen took a long sip. "Ohhhh, this is good. You sure have a knack for making these Caesars!"

"Thanks. I worked hard at perfecting it. You look great in this outfit, by the way. But honestly I preferred the other one."

Karen blushed and turned three shades of red in a matter of seconds. "Personally I am much more comfortable with this on, but thanks."

"Just know that if at any point you want to switch back, it would be okay with me." Jessie continued to tease Karen. Actually, Jessie loved Karen's current outfit, as well. She wore a pair of navy lounge pants that flared out slightly at the bottom of the legs, along with a yellow long sleeve, low cut V-neck cotton shirt that fit slightly loose around the body. On her feet she had a pair of soft deer skin moccasins. You could tell that Karen was comfortable and relaxed. The soft fragrance of her perfume had Jessie all stirred up inside. She wanted to reach out and pull Karen closer.

As they both took a couple more sips from their drinks, Karen sensed that Jessie was checking her out. At this point she was thankful to have more on than her towel, although it did make her feel good that Jessie had appreciated what she had seen.

Karen sat her drink down. "Why don't we get a spot set up for you in the living room by the fireplace? We can bring in the card table for you to work on. That way you can enjoy the warmth of the fire and the comfort of a soft seat on the couch," Karen suggested. She enjoyed the easiness of their relationship, but was also looking for an opportunity to share her feelings.

"I came earlier than expected, so I can finish grading these papers tonight. I hope you don't mind."

"Not at all. You are welcome here anytime."

"I appreciate that. Where might I find the card table?"

"Oh, it is just down the hall, leaning against the wall in the first room on the right."

Jessie went to retrieve the table and set it up. She was unloading her briefcase, when Karen came in and turned on the fireplace.

"Wow, how many papers do you have there?" Karen pointed to the stack.

"I have twenty-four left," Jessie answered. "It's just my luck that most of my students decided to actually attend classes today. They must have enjoyed the topic we were studying."

Karen remembered and began to giggle. "Ah yes, human anatomy! After all, what would be more exciting?"

"Oh, so you do find the human anatomy exciting? I was beginning to get a little worried," Jessie joked. "In case you need to have anything explained, I could help you out . . ."

Karen laughed. "Have you forgotten that I am a nurse?"

"Touché."

Karen left the room shaking her head. She returned with Jessie's drink. "Now that you are all set up, I will let you get started. I am going to go make us dinner. Call me, if you need anything."

"This is excellent. Karen, I really appreciate that you let me invite myself. I didn't want to spend another Friday evening alone."

"There is no need for us both to spend our Friday evenings alone. We could make this a weekly plan, maybe switching between each other's places. If something else comes up for either of us, we agree to cancel, and that's okay." This suggestion was out of Karen's mouth before she even realized it.

"I like your way of thinking." Jessie was elated with the suggestion. "Perfect. Next week it will be at my place."

They both toasted the idea.

"Okay, now get started marking those. I will call you when dinner is ready."

"Oh, I love it when you take charge," Jessie joked.

Karen went to the kitchen. She turned the radio on low and turned to her 'California Roast', pre-seasoned fresh pork tenderloin wrapped in chicken breasts. She went out on the back deck, fired up the barbeque and started to prepare the veggies and the salads.

Jessie was making progress in her marking. She felt completely at home. Jessie could hear Karen humming to the music while she was cooking. The pleasant sound warmed her heart.

Karen set the table and decided to eat by candlelight. She wanted to let Jessie know she was interested in her, but not completely ready to cross the line just yet. The buzzer reminded her that the roast would be done in fifteen minutes. Quickly she stir-fried the vegetables and boiled water for the rice. Dinner was coming together nicely.

Just then Karen heard Jessie. "What are you making? It smells great. My stomach is growling in here."

"It won't be much longer. Are you at a good spot to stop for dinner soon?" Karen inquired.

"Not a problem. Just let me know when."

"About ten more minutes."

The final buzzer rang. Karen went outside to retrieve the roast and turn the barbeque off. The winds had picked up, and the snow was falling fast.

She finished the sauce for the vegetables and sliced up the meat. Just then Jessie came into the kitchen. "Good timing," Karen told her.

"My stomach has a way of letting me know when food is ready to be eaten." Jessie patted her belly.

"I hope you like what I made."

"If it tastes half as good as it smells, there will be no problem."

"Would you like some wine with dinner? I have a bottle of white already opened, if you are interested." Karen went over to the table, lit the candles and dimmed the lights.

"Wine would be great." Jessie watched Karen move smoothly around her kitchen and dining room. The fact that they were eating by candlelight seemed to suggest that there was more to this evening than what met the eye. She very much enjoyed the vibe she was getting.

Karen forced herself to look away. "Will you grab the salads please? I will get the wine." She caught a glimpse of the snow falling outside. "In case you haven't noticed, it has started to snow. The winds have picked up in the last half hour. How are you coming along with the papers?"

"I am over two-thirds done. It shouldn't take any more than an hour to have them all completed. I should head home as soon as I get them finished," Jessie said as she was eating her salad. "I am impressed with these kids. They are very smart. So far, most of them have received a grade of seventy-five percent or higher."

"When you talk about your work and your students, I can tell you have a passion for what you do."

"I am living the dream I've had since I was seven years old. My parents keep telling me that all I ever wanted was to be a PE teacher. I am very lucky. I love it."

"Wow, good for you for following your dream. I envy you and your ability to be who you truly are and to do what makes you happy."

"You, on the other hand, tend to put the happiness of others before your own." Jessie reached over and touched Karen's hand. "Making others happy is a terrific quality, Karen. But making yourself happy should be your number one priority."

Silence hung in the air.

Karen was not sure what to do or say. Slowly she took her other hand and placed it on Jessie's. "I am working on that." Karen hesitated a moment. "Jessie, I am not sure how to ..." Just then the buzzer went off, interrupting their moment. Karen got up and went into the kitchen.

Jessie desperately wanted to hear what Karen had been about to say. She picked up the salad plates and carried them into the kitchen.

Karen served up the vegetables with sauce over a bed of rice, placing some meat on the side.

"This looks wonderful," Jessie complimented again.

"Thanks. I hope it tastes as good as it looks."

"I'm sure it will. Anything you have cooked for me so far has been great."

"Flattery. I love it."

They sat back down at the table.

"In that case, where would you like me to start? I could flatter you all night." Jessie reached across the table and placed her hand over Karen's once again. She looked more serious than Karen had ever seen. "I mean that, Karen. You have had me at your mercy since I first met you."

"Ah, you are so sweet. I appreciate that, but stop it or you will have me in tears." Karen intertwined her fingers with Jessie's. The warm soft touch of Jessie's hand made Karen's mind race. Her whole body began to tingle and come alive. The sensation was unbelievable. Not sure of herself and what she might do, Karen pulled her hand away slowly. "I guess we had better eat this before it gets cold."

Jessie sensed Karen's uneasiness. "Let's eat then, shall we?" she said smiling. Karen's soft gentle caress left her longing for more. Jessie savored this time alone with Karen. "This is incredible!" Jessie moaned in delight with each bite. "You have really gone to a great deal of trouble here."

"It was no trouble. Besides, I wanted to make something special for you."

"Aw, thank you. I'm grateful."

"Good. I'm glad you like it. So what are you going to make for me next Friday night?" Karen asked, intentionally putting Jessie on the spot.

Jessie wasn't a big fan of cooking. She had shared this fact with Karen before. "You are going to have to wait and see."

"Should I expect take-out?" Karen teased.

"Are you okay with take-out?"

Karen laughed. "Let's agree that our Friday evening meals are to be without any pressure. How is that for making your life easy?"

"Hey, I'm all for that. I'm easy when it comes to food."

"Only when it comes to food?" Karen questioned playfully.

Jessie smiled.

Before Karen knew what happened, Jessie quickly stood up, leaned over and placed a kiss on Karen's cheek.

"You could make me easy in other ways," she whispered into Karen's ear.

The warmth of her breath was extremely arousing.

Karen leaned into the whisper, and Jessie's face gently massaged her ear.

Jessie slowly sat back down, suddenly realizing she may have gone too far. "I apologize. I don't want to push you or upset you ... I was being my stupid impulsive self and ..."

"Don't worry Jessie. It's okay ... I'm okay." Karen wanted to set Jessie's mind at ease. "I was teasing you. I started it. If anybody needs to apologize, it should be me." Karen paused. "But I'm not apologizing. Because I am not sorry it happened." Now it was Karen who was embarrassed and blushing.

Karen got up and headed towards the kitchen with a load of dishes.

Jessie picked up a couple of items from the table and followed her. In the kitchen she turned Karen around so she could see her face. "Do you realize what you just said?"

Karen was not certain where to go from here. "I do, yes." Karen wanted to be honest with Jessie. On the other hand she feared things might go too far. There was still the issue of Roger she wanted to get resolved.

"Then can you please explain it to me? Because I thought I heard you say you were okay with the fact that I just kissed you." Jessie's pulse was racing. The excitement of there being even the remotest possibility of a future with Karen made Jessie want to cry.

Karen could see the tears forming in Jessie's eyes. She loved her for that. Jessie could be such a clown one minute and a sincere sweetheart the next. That was one of the things Karen loved about her. Jessie and Karen were very similar this way.

"I did say that, but let's not get too far ahead of ourselves, please." Karen studied Jessie's face. It was obvious that Jessie was thrilled to hear what Karen had said. Suddenly Karen needed her space. She needed time to think about what she was doing. "Can we please continue our evening as planned? You go finish your papers, and I will clean up."

Jessie was fine with this idea. Hell, she would have been fine with almost any idea at that point. Karen had just made her a very, very happy woman. "No problem. I will go finish marking, but first I want to leave you with this." Jessie knew she was pushing her luck. But she wanted to show Karen how she really felt. Gently she pulled Karen close to her and wrapped her arms around her. Leaning down she placed her lips on Karen's, taking the chance Karen would push her away.

But Karen didn't. Instead she responded.

Karen had never felt lips so soft. She wanted to taste them and explore them.

Their lips parted, and their mouths opened. Karen was trembling in Jessie's arms. Still she wanted to take things slowly and easily. Gradually she pulled away.

Jessie cleared her throat. "I had better get to work." She smiled from ear to ear. "Although I am not sure I will be able to concentrate." She giggled and headed for the living room.

Once Karen was alone, she grabbed onto the counter until she regained strength in her weakened knees. I have just shared a long, deep, amazing, sensual kiss with another woman, she thought. My God, that was powerful . . . While she reveled in the pleasure she just had experienced, she knew one thing for sure: she wanted more, much, much more.

Karen poured herself another glass of wine. She cleaned up the dining room and did the dishes. Looking outside, she was shocked to see how much snow had fallen and how fierce the wind was blowing.

The snow was whipping off the roof. "Jessie, I hate to interrupt, but it is really storming outside. Do you want to head home before it gets worse?"

"I have only three papers left. It won't take me long. I'm a pretty good driver, don't worry." Jessie went back to her papers, not showing any real concern for the weather.

Karen made them both a cup of hot tea. She took hers and sat in a chair in the living room. Enjoying the warmth of the fire, Karen watched Jessie who was sitting on the couch. The fireplace created a golden glow around her. Karen found herself stirred by Jessie's beauty. Jessie was wearing a black polyester track suit that had a fine line of grey reflective striping down each leg and both arms. The striping glimmered in the firelight, giving the appearance that Jessie had shimmering coals travelling up and down her body. Under the jacket Jessie wore a plain white low cut cotton top.

Sitting there watching Jessie, Karen had many thoughts going through her mind. I know she is marking papers on human anatomy. Oh, how I would love to check out her anatomy up close and personal! I want to make love with her, ravish her . . . Karen realized she had never in her life ever had that thought about anybody before. She felt the effect these thoughts were having on her body. She wanted to caress Jessie, and for Jessie to caress her in return. Karen finally realized she wanted it all.

If only she didn't have this issue with Roger hanging over her head! She needed her family, and Roger had always been a big part of that. She had to make sure Jessie went home, because she could not trust herself to hold off and be true to her plan.

Just then Jessie sat back and drank her tea. "Finally, I am finished," she announced. "That took me a bit longer than I had expected, but I am really pleased with these kids."

Jessie looked up. Karen was deep in thought. "Is everything alright?" Jessie asked with concern. Was Karen still struggling with their kiss in the kitchen?

Jessie's voice brought Karen back to reality and away from her arousing thoughts. "Yes, I'm fine," Karen replied even though she wasn't. She wasn't fine with having to wait any longer to finally give herself completely to Jessie. But Karen knew she couldn't give in to her own needs just yet. Her body had gotten quite heated from her daydream, and she could feel her face was flushed. "I am sorry. I was a little sidetracked. What were you saying?"

"I was saying how pleased I am with my students. They made me proud," Jessie repeated.

"They have a good teacher."

"Yes, I guess they do," Jessie agreed with a big smile. "Thanks for the tea by the way. It is just what I needed."

"No problem."

Jessie gathered up her items and put the table back where she had gotten it. The whole time Karen was continually watching Jessie's every move, wanting to reach out and pull her close. Karen wanted once again to have her lips on Jessie's warm and wanting mouth.

"I suppose I should think about heading home soon, There is just one more thing I need to do before I leave." Jessie headed for her bag she had left in the foyer when she had arrived.

Karen was worried about Jessie driving home in such bad weather. "You know, Jessie, you are welcome to stay over. I have a spare bedroom. It really doesn't look very nice out there," Karen offered, although she secretly hoped Jessie would refuse the invite, knowing she could not trust herself.

"I will be fine. It has only been a couple of hours since it started," Jessie said without hesitation. She pulled a package from her bag, came back in and sat beside Karen. "I hope you like it." Jessie was excited like a child who could hardly keep from spilling the beans on a secret.

Karen's eyes lit up in surprise. "What is this about? All I did was made you dinner." She giggled and gladly took the nicely wrapped parcel. It didn't take Karen long to unwrap the present. She eagerly ripped the paper off, anxious to discover what Jessie had chosen for her – a trophy that on one side read "#1 FAN" and on the other side: "My Good Luck Charm".

The gift emphasized how perfect Jessie was for her. Karen's eyes filled with tears. "I have never received a trophy before. This is so sweet. I love it!" She held it close to her heart. "I will cherish it always." She was so touched by Jessie's thoughtfulness, she was crying and laughing at the same time.

Apparently Jessie had picked the perfect gift. Karen was genuinely pleased. Jessie had wanted to make Karen happy and let her know she was appreciated.

Karen opened her arms, welcoming Jessie in and giving her a huge hug, a hug that lasted a long while. They stood in the living room holding each other, giving each other a silent reassurance that one day very soon they would be together.

Karen was the first to let go. Before Jessie had a chance to move, Karen took both hands and placed them on Jessie's cheeks. She gently directed Jessie's face down to hers and planted a soft kiss on Jessie's lips. "I adore my gift, and I adore you. If you are going home, you better head out now before it gets any worse out there."

Jessie was thrilled that Karen had taken the initiative. "I'm just going to go out to start the car. I will be right back." Jessie was all smiles.

Jessie opened the door and was shocked to see how much snow had fallen. She started the car, grabbed the snow brush and cleaned the car off. She came back inside. "Wow, you were right, it is bad out there."

"You can change your mind. You are more than welcome to stay," Karen offered once more.

"No, but thanks anyway."

"Please call me when you get home, so I will know you arrived safely. Then I won't worry all night."

"I promise. I had a fantastic evening. Everything was wonderful. Great food, great company, great kisses!" Jessie winked and pulled Karen closer in a playful hold. "I need one for the road."

Karen loved the playfulness and the physical contact. They gave each other a long kiss good night, and Jessie headed out.

"Drive carefully!" Karen yelled to Jessie as she was getting in her car.

Once inside Karen locked the door and took a long deep breath. She had an aching desire to make love with Jessie. Her body burned with longing. Karen was relieved Jessie was gone. Now she would be able to keep herself on track with her plan. She needed to confront her family as soon as possible.

Karen's body was crying out to be touched like it never had before. Quickly she headed down the hall, once again in need of a very cold shower. All she could think about was Jessie and the deep kisses they had exchanged. Her breathing had quickened, and her body was on fire. Oh my God, the effect that woman has on me is unbelievable! Karen thought to herself.

Karen let the cold water run over her and started to caress her body to be sure to give every inch a splash of refreshing coolness. Her hands traveled and stopped to linger on her firm breasts and taut nipples. Karen's body trembled at her own touch. She pulled her hand away and took a deep breath. She decided it was the safest to put her hands on the wall of the shower and lean into the spray. As she stood there and let the cold water slowly bring her body temperature down, she thought of Jessie out in the snowstorm. Standing there she said a quick prayer for Jessie's safety.

Jessie spun her tires and made three attempts to get out onto the road. The third time is a charm, she thought to herself as she finally made it out of the driveway.

Jessie had forgotten there were no street lights in the country. The snow was falling in huge fluffy flakes and coming down very hard. She could barely see two feet in front of her. The car was moving along at a snail's pace. A little nervous Jessie started to talk out loud to herself, hoping that hearing her own voice would calm her down. Her vision was limited. She could neither see the road, nor its margins. Think smart, and don't panic! she told herself. Look for the mailboxes, they will tell you where the curbside is.

Everything was white and blended together. Every time Jessie attempted to put on her high beams the giant white flakes of falling snow were a mesmerizing beauty and with only the low beams on she could not see far enough ahead to make out where she was on the road. There were no other tracks to follow. Her hands started to vibrate. She had to find a safe spot to turn around and go back.

Suddenly she noticed an opening where the soft glow of the street lamp outlined someone's driveway. Thank you God! Jessie exclaimed. She managed to get herself turned around and headed back in the direction of Karen's house.

After a moment she recognized where she was and realized she had not travelled that far. At least now she had her own tracks to follow and give her a guideline of where the road was. The snow was not letting up at all. Heading in this direction the wind was much more noticeable. Jessie was relieved when she saw Karen's driveway. She accelerated and got off the road. Halfway down the driveway she got stuck. She didn't care. Jessie was thankful to be off the street.

With a deep breath she turned off the engine and just sat in the car for a while. She needed some time to calm down and stop shaking.

Knowing she was out of harm's way, in the safety of Karen's drive, Jessie managed to regain her composure. It was eerily quiet. She began to appreciate the beauty of the nature surrounding her. A myriad of snowflakes glistened like diamonds in the lights that lined Karen's driveway. Each snowflake was a little miracle, unique and absolutely perfect . . . just like Karen.

CHAPTER FIFTEEN

Karen dried off, put on her two-piece short and top pajama set and stared at herself in the mirror. "I am a lesbian," she said out loud. "There is no doubt whatsoever. I love how I feel when I am with Jessie. I want to be with her . . ." Hearing herself speak the words aloud made it real for Karen. She smiled to herself, knowing for certain what had been hidden deep in her heart.

Suddenly Karen heard the door bell ringing over and over. Oh no, Jessie's been hurt, she's driven into the ditch! Karen's thoughts raced. She hurried down the hall. Opening the door, there stood Jessie all covered with snow and shivering. Her nose and cheeks were rosy from the cold.

"Get in here!" Karen ordered. "Are you alright? Did you have an accident?"

Jessie was thankful to see Karen. Knowing for certain she was safe, she took a deep breath and stepped inside. "Everything is fine now."

Karen noticed that Jessie was still shaking. "Look at you. You are soaking wet and snow covered. Let me take your coat."

"Would you please hold me for a moment?" Jessie asked softly. She needed Karen's arms around her to help calm her.

Karen tossed the coat. Immediately she took Jessie into her arms. "Everything is alright now. You are safe," Karen whispered in Jessie's ear as she continued to hold her. She gently kissed Jessie on the forehead. "Come in, let's sit by the fire and get you warmed up."

They went into the living room. Jessie sat in the chair closest to the fire. "I'm sorry Karen, but there is no way I could drive home in that weather. You were right, it is nasty out there," Jessie explained.

"I'm just glad you had enough sense to come back! You know you are welcome to stay."

"Yes, however we still have one problem." Jessie pretended to be pouting and put her bottom lip out. "I don't have any pajamas." She broke into a laugh.

"I can fix that problem easily," Karen assured.

Jessie started to tease. "And just how do you intend to do that? May I suggest that you share half of the ones you are wearing?"

"I'm glad to see you are feeling more like yourself again." Karen got up off the couch and mischievously tossed a cushion at Jessie. "Smartass!" She headed for the kitchen.

Jessie got up, pretending to chase after her.

Karen let out a squeal, which caused Jessie to break into loud laughter.

"Are you for real? Did that noise just come out of you?" Jessie followed her into the kitchen, still laughing. "You squeal like a school girl."

"There is nothing wrong with my squeal!" Karen defended herself, very much aware that Jessie was devilishly close to her.

"No, you're right, there isn't. I only wanted to tease you." Jessie knew she was taking a chance. Intentionally she placed a hand on either side of Karen onto the counter, pinning Karen so she had nowhere to go.

"What are you trying to do, pick a fight?" Karen joked. "Well, guess what? I fight like a girl too!" As Jessie let go of the counter to applaud Karen's cleverness and sense of humor, Karen quickly moved into an area where she couldn't be cornered.

"You do fight like a girl. You tricked me."

Karen smiled, quite pleased with herself. "Listen, I was going to have another glass of wine. Would you care to join me, or would you prefer a hot cup of tea to take that chill out of your bones?"

"I choose the wine. Seeing you in your jammies has caused my chill to vanish rather quickly."

A rosy blush slowly spread on Karen's cheeks.

Jessie had grown to love the fact that Karen enjoyed flattery.

"I know I'm repeating myself, but you sure are a smooth one, Jessie." Karen got out two glasses and poured their wine.

"Not really. I only say it because I mean it." Jessie reached across to take her glass and slipped her other arm slowly around Karen's waist as they headed back towards the fireplace.

Karen enjoyed the closeness and the touch of Jessie's arm around her. She set her drink down. "Relax for a few minutes. I will be right back." She headed down the hall.

Jessie took advantage of having the whole couch to herself and sprawled out full length. Now she noticed how exhausted she was. Her body was still tense from the traumatic road trip. She took a few long deep breaths and started to relax. With eyes closed she remembered Karen in her cute pajamas. A smile stretched across her face. She was pleased to be where she was safe.

Meanwhile Karen fluffed up the pillows on the spare bed and tidied up the sheets. She made sure she put out clean towels and a face cloth and set out a new toothbrush and other necessities. It was important to her that Jessie felt at home. She went fumbling through her T-shirts and came up with one that fit a bit snug on her, figuring it would be baggy on Jessie, but not too bad.

Karen returned to the living room without Jessie hearing her. She watched Jessie as she lay there. Not wanting to startle her, Karen spoke softly. "I have found you a T-shirt you can wear tonight."

Slowly Jessie opened her eyes. "Thanks, I appreciate that." Jessie began to sit up, winced and grabbed her shoulder. "Ouch."

Karen sat beside her. "Let me help you." She pulled Jessie upright. "Now turn your back to me," Karen directed. She reached out and began to massage Jessie's neck and shoulders.

Jessie moaned in pleasure. "That feels great!"

Excitement sparked in Karen. "Shall I continue?"

"Absolutely, if you don't mind." Jessie moaned again with delight.

"You are tight from the stress of your drive. Let me work it out for you."

"Are you sure you are not a masseuse besides being a nurse?"

Karen laughed. She was getting as much pleasure and enjoyment from giving the massage as Jessie was receiving it.

Jessie turned to look at Karen. "You sure have a way with your hands . . ." Jessie said softly.

Instead of an answer, Karen held up the T-shirt. "Why don't you put this on? I am sure you will feel more comfortable."

Jessie took the T-shirt and got on her feet. "Good idea." She walked down the hallway to the bedroom.

When Jessie returned, Karen glanced up. Her heartbeat stopped for a second. There Jessie stood, wearing nothing but a solid white V-neck T-shirt and a pair of panties. Karen could see the light brown circles and hard nipples beneath the white cotton. She couldn't speak for a moment and once again blushed noticeably.

Karen swallowed. "That certainly looks much better on you than it ever did on me." She stared at Jessie, looking her up and down and up again.

Jessie could tell Karen liked what she saw. She sat down close to her. "Thanks for setting everything out for me. And the bed looks comfy."

There wasn't a lot of wine left. Karen poured them each another half glass and emptied the bottle. She felt nervous with Jessie sitting so close to her wearing so little. Her desire for Jessie was overpowering. Leaning in close, Karen slowly took Jessie's arm and placed it around her shoulders. They nestled perfectly together.

Jessie was thrilled that Karen had enough motivation and longing to initiate the cuddling.

They sat in silence for a while, taking pleasure in the comfort of each other, enjoying the glow from the fire and listening to the strong winds whistling outside.

Softly Jessie moved her thumb back and forth over Karen's arm. Karen loved the feel of her touch. Jessie was feeling so comfortable and relaxed, she began to yawn. By the fifth yawn she apologized unnecessarily, and Karen knew Jessie was exhausted. Their wonderful quiet moment of togetherness was coming to an end.

Karen rose from the couch and gave Jessie a hand up. "It sounds like you need to go to bed."

"I'm sorry. It's just that I'm content," Jessie explained.

"Content is good, right? You aren't bored, are you?"

Jessie pulled Karen closer. "No way. This is total contentment." She gave Karen a kiss on the forehead and held her tightly as they swayed back and forth in front of the fire.

"I have enjoyed our time together tonight," Karen said.

"Me too," Jessie agreed. "I don't want this night to end."

Karen smiled and continued to hold Jessie close. "You are so sweet. I have never met anybody like you, nor have I ever felt this way about anybody before."

These words made Jessie's heart dance. "Oh, Karen, you don't know how long I have waited for you to return my affections." Jessie tilted Karen's face up and slowly covered Karen's mouth with her own.

Their lips parted, tongues touched, and then began searching deeper and harder. Karen responded. Deep down from within her throat came a low seductive whimper, which intensified Jessie's arousal.

Karen's head was spinning. She needed to catch her breath. Lost in Jessie's affections, Karen put both hands on Jessie's chest and pushed herself back just enough to end the kiss.

Jessie searched Karen's eyes wondering what had gone wrong. She did not want it to end. Hopefully she had not frightened Karen or pushed too hard.

Karen slowly caught her breath. "I think it's time we called it a night."

Jessie knew the moment was over. Obviously Karen needed more time. "Karen I'm sorry if I pushed you too hard, I . . ."

Karen put her finger on Jessie's lips to silence her. "Don't be. You did nothing wrong." Karen could hear a little voice inside her telling her: Listen to your heart. Live for yourself and what makes you happy, not everybody else.

Those words kept repeating over and over, as Karen routinely walked around the house and closed everything up for the night.

Jessie stood in the hall watching Karen turning off all the lights, taking care of the fireplace and locking the door. Then they headed down the hall. The gentle light from the lamp in the spare room was the only light that guided them other than a soft glow that came from what Jessie assumed was Karen's room. Jessie was thankful for the light. She was not used to the black darkness in the country.

At the doorway Jessie turned and said goodnight.

After tonight Karen knew for certain that Roger would have to accept her for who she truly was or they would have to agree to disagree. She looked at Jessie with eyes that were full of desire, then she walked over and turned off the lamp.

Much to Jessie's amazement, Karen slipped her hand into hers and led them both into her bedroom.

"Karen, I want you to be sure."

"I am very sure of what I want," Karen reassured Jessie. She was trembling with excitement and felt butterflies in her stomach. "I am just uncertain of what or how . . ."

Jessie pulled Karen close. "Don't worry about a thing. I'm a teacher. Let me teach you."

Instantly Karen's body was covered with goose bumps. "I hope I don't get a failing grade."

"I doubt that very much," Jessie spoke softly.

Karen's hands were shaking. Jessie held them in her own for a moment to calm her. Karen's eyes searched Jessie's, looking for strength and guidance. Jessie did not let her down. Jessie slowly and gently slid her hands onto Karen's waist and effortlessly slipped Karen's top over her head.

Karen's breathing deepened. She stood there trembling with anticipation.

The glow from the nightlight allowed Jessie to see the smooth silkiness of Karen's skin. She softly ran her hands along Karen's back then slowly made her way to gently cup her hands over Karen's breasts.

Karen had to catch her breath. Jessie's touch on her skin was so exquisite, like nothing she had felt before. Everything inside her came alive.

Jessie lowered her mouth over Karen's and kissed her, gently, slowly at first, and then deeper and harder. Karen's tongue began searching for Jessie's as they responded to one another's desire. Nervously Karen continued. With trembling fingers she fumbled with Jessie's T-shirt. Finally, it was off. Karen stared at the beauty of Jessie's naked breasts. They were as pert as Karen had imagined.

Jessie led Karen to the bed. She took time to place little kisses on Karen's neck. A soft moan escaped Karen's lips. She wanted this. She wanted to be taken. She wanted Jessie to do whatever she wished to do with her. Karen was willingly at Jessie's mercy.

Jessie took her time and left a trail of light kisses down Karen's neck, across her shoulder and back again. Her mouth made its way down Karen's chest, exploring Karen's breasts, licking and flicking her nipples with her tongue, making them firm and taut.

Karen moaned in pleasure. Her hands caressed Jessie. She wanted her close; she loved the feel of their nakedness together. The awareness of skin to skin gave her the comfort she needed. Karen shivered as Jessie continued to tease her nipples. Her breathing changed to quick short gasps.

"Are you okay? I want you to be okay."

Karen took Jessie's face in her hands. "I am more than okay. I am wonderful." She loved the fact that Jessie was so thoughtful and concerned about her.

Jessie quickly and expertly slipped off Karen's shorts. Karen was very much aware of her complete nakedness. Jessie was on top of her now. With every moment the intensity of their lovemaking became stronger. Jessie's hands explored every inch of Karen's breasts while her mouth devoured Karen's. Then she began kissing her once again down her neck, to her breasts, playfully exciting her nipples with her tongue as she had earlier. Jessie's tongue gently danced over Karen's belly making it quiver. Karen's breathing quickened. Jessie had one hand occupied fondling Karen's breasts while her other hand began to explore. She slowly parted Karen's legs and teased the inside of her thigh with a featherlike touch.

Jessie wanted to satisfy Karen completely. She ran her fingers along the inside of Karen's thigh and gently slipped inside of her. Karen whimpered. Jessie found her very damp and moist and eager. Encouraged by Karen's wetness Jessie explored her deeper. Her fingers began a slow rhythm that Karen answered with the movement of her hips.

Karen responded passionately to Jessie's touch. All her senses were alive. She wanted more; she moaned for more. Karen wanted Jessie to have her, all of her.

Jessie slowly removed her fingers and carefully spread Karen's legs farther apart. Her face was close enough to inhale Karen's sweetness. Oh, how well she knew what Karen wanted! Expertly she took her time, teasing Karen with her tongue along the inside of Karen's thighs, first one and then the other.

Again Karen's breathing quickened. She felt the warmth of Jessie's breath on her throbbing vagina. Suddenly Jessie's tongue was inside of her. It was hot and wet. Jessie slowly moved her tongue up and down, in and out. Jessie's warm breath and hot moist tongue found places that Karen had no idea existed.

Jessie grabbed Karen's buttocks and got into a rhythm that Karen found extremely gratifying.

Jessie could hear Karen's whimper and knew it was out of pure pleasure. Karen quickened the pace of her hip movements. She wanted it faster and harder. Jessie knew Karen was ready. She wanted to be holding her, when Karen climaxed for her first time. Slowly she removed her tongue and replaced it with her fingers.

Karen cried out in ecstasy. Her body was on fire. She held on tight to Jessie, quivering with aftershocks. "Oh, Jessie ..." Karen whispered and began to cry.

"Shhhhh, I'm right here." Jessie held Karen as she sobbed.

They lay there in silence, holding each other for a long while, both drawing comfort in the arms of the other. Karen was nestled in under Jessie's arm. With her free hand she cupped Jessie's breast.

Karen was the first to break the silence. "I had no idea making love could be so beautiful." Her finger softly circled Jessie's nipple.

"If you are in love with the person you are in bed with, it is natural for it to be beautiful. All you want is to please your partner completely." Jessie's breathing got a little heavier under Karen's gentle caresses.

"You certainly did that for me." Karen looked up and placed a kiss on Jessie's cheek.

"I'm glad."

"So am I!" Karen smiled. "There is only one problem."

"What is that?" Jessie looked puzzled.

Karen leaned up on one elbow. With her other hand she ran her fingers along the edge of Jessie's panties. "I was so lost in my own gratification that I never had the chance to reciprocate."

At the sense of Karen's touch, Jessie trembled. Karen watched Jessie's face as she continued to tease her tummy.

Jessie just lay there. With every movement of Karen's hand her grin got wider and wider. Karen quickly repositioned herself and slipped Jessie's panties off. Jessie was amused and turned on by Karen's playfulness. Karen leaned over Jessie and began nibbling on her breast. The sensation of Karen's warm breath sent shockwaves through Jessie's whole body.

Then, with rapid flicking motions of her tongue, Karen sent Jessie into a heightened state of arousal. Jessie's nipples responded. Firm rosebuds bloomed instantly. Karen dragged her hot wet tongue down Jessie's belly and did not stop until she slipped it slowly inside of her.

Jessie had never been one to make much noise when making love, but with this move by Karen Jessie lost it. "Oh fuck!" she exclaimed and gasped for air.

Karen continued with her tongue, slowly searching every inch inside of Jessie.

"My God, girl! I love it, don't stop!"

Karen felt she was taking Jessie to places she had never been before. She wanted to give her an experience unlike she had ever had. She continued to drive Jessie crazy for a very long while. When she finally removed her tongue, she quickly and easily slipped her fingers into Jessie's hot wetness and covered Jessie's lips with her own. A quickened pace set by Jessie allowed Karen to bring Jessie to complete orgasm.

Again they lay totally satisfied cuddling each other. They both drifted off to sleep from sheer exhaustion.

A few hours later when Karen awoke, their soft warm bodies were still entwined. As Karen lay there with her arm around Jessie's waist, her hand was nicely cupping Jessie's breast. She held Jessie as close as possible, once again feeling the contentment and comfort she gave her. Over and over Karen relived the events of the night before in her mind.

When Jessie finally awakened, it was mid-morning. Karen was gone. Jessie stretched and took in the morning sunshine beaming through the bedroom window. The storm was over. The heavy winds had ended. Jessie lay there thinking how wonderful she felt. The evening had been completely spontaneous for both of them.

Smiling, she rose and took a hot shower. She put on one of Karen's bathrobes and followed the aroma of fresh brewed coffee to the kitchen. Karen was not there. Jessie started to get a bit concerned, wondering about Karen's state of mind. Did she have any regrets? Where was she? Jessie poured herself a cup of coffee and strolled to the window to see the outcome of the storm.

While Jessie stood at the window, she spotted Karen carrying a pail and scoop. In a ski jacket, big snow pants and boots she made her way through the yard filling up all the bird feeders after the storm. Her head was covered with a black toque pulled way down her forehead. Jessie's heart melted. She has such a caring soul. No wonder I love her, Jessie thought to herself.

When Karen looked up and saw Jessie at the window, Jessie held up her coffee mug and smiled at her.

Karen signalled for Jessie to pour her a cup. A couple of minutes later she was back inside.

Jessie met her at the door. "Good morning."

Karen was unloading the heavy garments she wore. "Yes, it is a great morning! You should hear the birds out there; they are starving." Karen's cheeks were red from the cold.

Jessie could not help herself. She pulled Karen to her and kissed her long and slow, very seductively. "Thank goodness they have you."

"What? Who?" Karen had lost her train of thought in Jessie's kiss.

"The starving birds, thank goodness they have you."

"Go ahead, make fun all you like, but I will still feed them and make life easier for them. And I enjoy doing so." Karen knew Jessie was teasing her.

Jessie laughed. "Nice hair," she teased again when Karen removed her toque.

"Ha-ha, aren't you the funny one this morning!" Karen loved Jessie's playful wit. "I really didn't expect you to be up already. I thought I would be able to grab a quick shower before you rose from that peaceful sleep you were in when I got up."

"What time were you up?"

"Around seven. I usually get up early. Besides, I wanted to get the walk shovelled and feed the birds. We got an awful lot of snow last night."

"I didn't realize it was as bad as it was until I headed for home."

Karen lifted her hands in the air. "I tried to tell you, but you wouldn't listen. All you were concerned about was getting those papers graded."

"Hey, I give you that, but if I had listened to you, the night would not have turned out as great as it did." Jessie pulled Karen close, wrapped her arms around her and just held her.

Both took comfort in the fact that they were finally able to hold one another.

"How about that cup of coffee I poured for you?"

"I would love it."

At the same time she retrieved Karen's coffee, Jessie topped up her own.

"Let's sit in here this morning," Karen headed for the front room where they could feel the added warmth of the morning sun. "I don't know if you had plans for today, but Joe, who plows my driveway, will not be around until much later. He has a copy of my work schedule and knows that I am off this weekend," Karen explained. "If I switch shifts or get called in, I always let him know so he can get my driveway cleaned early. Sorry, but I think you are stuck here for most of the day. Maybe even until early evening."

Jessie laughed out loud slapping her knee as she often did. "I love this! I get to call in a snow day!"

"What are you talking about? Today is Saturday," Karen asked, a bit confused.

"I had scheduled our last volleyball practice for today at two o'clock. Finally I get to call and cancel due to bad weather. Now I remember how good it feels."

"I didn't realize you had plans today. I can still try to call Joe."

"No, really this is great!" Jessie was genuinely pleased to spend the entire day with Karen and not having to rush off. "That is unless you have other plans and need to leave?"

"Not at all!" Karen was thrilled that Jessie would be sharing the day with her.

They both drank their coffee and watched the birds happily flitting about in the morning sun. Both were entranced in their own thoughts, grateful of how the weekend had turned out.

Jessie glanced over and noticed a serious expression on Karen's face, while she was continually staring out of the window.

Karen was mulling over the events of the night before. How can something so satisfying and pleasing not be right? she thought. In fact, I know it is right for me! I have never felt so complete and so wonderful. Jessie and I are perfect together. Karen's frown turned into a smile. No doubt, she was a lesbian. And she liked this realization.

"Tell me what you are thinking about." Jessie spoke softly.

"Actually, I was thinking about us."

"What about us?"

Karen blushed. "I was thinking about how wonderful you make me feel."

Jessie kneeled on the floor in front of Karen. She took her hand. "You deserve to feel wonderful." Jessie kissed Karen's hand with warm soft lips, and then looked up into Karen's eyes. "I am just thankful that I am the one who makes you feel this way." Jessie swallowed hard. "Honestly, I have never had such strong feelings for anyone before. I knew from the first time I laid eyes on you that I wanted you."

Karen ran her fingers through Jessie's hair. "You are so sweet. But I too have had my eyes on you since last fall." Smiling Karen kissed the top of Jessie's head. "And look at us this morning! You certainly made it worth my wait," she teased. "Now, I hate to spoil the moment, but shouldn't you go and call your team?"

Jessie jumped to her feet. "Oh yeah, I had better get hold of them and reschedule for tomorrow. We need the practice. Our last tournament is on Monday in Trenton."

"Then volleyball is over for the season?"

"Yes. Next is badminton and then tennis," Jessie explained. "I can't believe that I almost have my first full year of teaching behind me. It seems unimaginable."

"Well, from what I have heard, you are very respected. It sure is a great way to start your career. While you are making your calls, I am going to grab a quick shower." Karen rose to her feet. "If you need the phone book, it's in the stand just under the phone."

Karen headed down the hall.

Jessie pulled on her boots and coat and quickly ran out to her car. She grabbed her briefcase which contained the list of players and their phone numbers. Back inside she began making the calls. By the time she finished she had been able to reach all but two players, and with them she left detailed voice messages stating practice would take place on Sunday afternoon. Karen had not returned, yet, so Jessie began preparing breakfast for the two of them.

Karen could smell the bacon cooking and was pleased that Jessie was comfortable enough to make herself at home. Having Jessie around was most enjoyable. Karen loved it.

Karen entered the kitchen. "Something smells great!"

"That would be the bacon." Jessie smiled and greeted Karen with a glass of juice and a kiss on the cheek. "I hope you don't mind. I wanted to surprise you." Jessie noticed Karen was back in her adorable pajamas.

"Why would I mind? I love it. Let me know when, and I will put the toast down." Playfully she patted Jessie's behind.

"Any time now would be good. I scrambled the eggs, and they are just about ready."

They enjoyed their uninterrupted time together over breakfast. A few hours passed with them laughing, flirting, teasing, talking, and getting to know more and more about each other. Jointly they cleaned up and did the dishes, not wanting to be apart from one another.

Karen watched Jessie moving around in her home, and it was as if she belonged there. Jessie's eyes seemed to dance with delight. Every time she laughed, it completely melted Karen. She yearned to make love once again. She knew more than ever what she wanted. Too much of her life had passed her by.

When Jessie turned her back to Karen for a second, Karen took advantage of the opportunity. She moved closely behind Jessie and placed both hands on Jessie's hips. Slowly she turned Jessie around and untied the belt on the bathrobe Jessie wore. The robe fell open and reveled Jessie's nakedness. Karen smiled. A look of pure delight came over her face as she took in the view of Jessie's fit body. Slowly she slipped her hands around Jessie's waist and drew her closer. The feel of Jessie's soft skin instantly had Karen hungry for more.

Jessie was surprised by Karen's forwardness. However, she was very pleased to discover this side of her. "Are you frisking me?" Jessie wore a seductive smirk.

"What if I am?" Karen asked.

Every hair on Jessie's body stood at attention as Karen gently caressed her. The excitement travelled quickly over her entire body. "Uh, then feel free, don't let me stop you." The smile on Jessie's face widened. She was beaming. The thrill of having Karen seduce her was beyond what she had ever imagined.

"Actually, I believe I am ready for another lesson from my favorite teacher," Karen flirted. "I am extremely eager to learn more."

"Are you joking? You are an A+ student. You learn very quickly. In fact, I think I could take a couple of lessons from you."

Karen laughed and led Jessie to the bedroom. As they stood there, she slid the robe off Jessie's shoulders slowly and seductively. The look on Karen's face was one of pure desire. She stood there in awe consuming the vision. In the morning light Jessie's figure took on an angelic glow. Karen took much pleasure in the new direction their relationship had taken. Making love to Jessie gave her the feeling of wholeness.

With expert hands Jessie quickly removed Karen's garments. Her gentle touch had Karen trembling with excitement. They kissed softly and slowly, while they made their way to the bed.

Desire that had been locked up deep inside Karen for so long now became unleashed again. Passion took control of her. Her caresses had Jessie begging for more. Karen tantalized Jessie, with a skilled tongue that caused every fiber of Jessie's being to tremble and convulse in ecstasy.

For hours they explored each other, giving each other pleasures beyond what either had ever anticipated. They pleased one another over and over again, their bodies damp with sweat.

"I have to say, you are amazing in bed," Jessie tried to catch her breath.

"I'm glad you think so." Karen beamed. She could not believe how wonderful she felt both inside and out. "I do want to thank you Jessie."

"Thank me for what?"

"For many things. But mostly for your patience and persistence. I know that sounds contradictory, but they both played important roles in getting us to this point. Seriously, I have never felt so complete and so comfortable in my own skin." Karen nestled in closer to Jessie's warmth as her own body was cooling down.

"Well, you didn't make it easy on me, that's for certain!" Jessie clowned.

"I am just thankful you didn't give up on me. You are special, and I want to make sure you know it."

Jessie turned more serious. "Karen I have never met anybody as caring, as sweet and as sincere as you are. You are genuine and honest; I love that about you. That and your great sense of humor." Jessie kissed her forehead. "May I also add your exceptional lovemaking skills!"

Karen blushed in a mixture of pride and embarrassment.

They snuggled for a while longer. Suddenly Karen thought of something she had always wanted to try. "You lay here, I will be right back." She started to get up.

Jessie pulled her back down on top of her. "Be sure to come back, okay?"

"I won't be long." She covered Jessie's mouth with hers and gave Jessie a long hard kiss.

After Karen left Jessie lay there staring out onto the snow covered yard. In the distance she heard the sound of snowmobiles. It triggered a memory of Tom and her years ago out having fun on their machines. She remembered her home in Mattawa and was aware that she felt very much at home here, too.

It wasn't long before Karen returned. In one hand she carried a bowl of red, luscious strawberries, in the other a large tub of Cool Whip.

Jessie sat up with excitement. "You are a woman full of surprises ..."

"Better than being predictable all the time."

"This weekend you're definitely not!"

"I have always dreamed of this. Will you help me make another of my dreams come true?"

"I'll do my absolute best." Jessie winked and reached for the strawberries.

Karen removed her robe and crawled into bed alongside her. Jessie took a plump strawberry and dipped it into the whipped cream, covering it almost completely as well as her fingertips. Karen grinned as Jessie approached playfully with the berry. She opened her mouth and let Jessie feed her, then took Jessie's fingers and inserted them into her mouth one at a time. Tantalizingly slow she licked them clean. With every lick Jessie moaned and once again became aroused.

Karen took her turn feeding Jessie. Getting a bit more playful, their mouths were covered with Cool Whip, and they took turns licking it off one another. The kissing intensified with each arousing touch. Jessie dipped her finger into the tub and made a trail from Karen's chin down her neck. Then she positioned herself on top of

Karen. Starting at the neck she licked the whipped cream off and placed gentle kisses all over Karen.

The tickling sensation caused Karen to giggle with pleasure. Her skin was quickly covered in goose bumps. Jessie's tongue slowly followed the trail downward, then to one breast and around the nipple flicking and sucking. The other breast received the same tantalizing treatment.

Karen moaned in sheer pleasure. Jessie followed the trail of Cool Whip down Karen's belly and watched it quiver as she excited her. Once again she parted Karen's legs and devoured the Cool Whip she had placed there.

She was driving Karen wild. "My God!" Karen's whole body trembled as a quake of excitement travelled from head to toe and everywhere in between.

Pleasing Karen excited Jessie. The wetter Karen was for her, the wetter Jessie herself got. She slipped her fingers easily inside teasing her, torturing her until Karen's excitement became unbearable. Only then she gave her what she wanted.

Jessie was a willing recipient, when Karen took her turn indulging in the whipped cream experience.

It wasn't long before both lay in complete ecstasy and exhaustion. They drifted off to sleep and woke up to Joe honking in the driveway.

Both jumped out of bed and raced to put on their clothes. Karen was the first dressed. Quickly she slipped on her boots and fumbled for Jessie's car keys. Karen rushed out, waved at Joe, got behind the wheel of Jessie's car and backed it out onto the road, so Joe could get to work.

Karen smiled when she smelled Jessie's fragrance inside the vehicle. It comforted her in a funny kind of way.

It didn't take Joe long to finish up. Soon Karen backed the car into the driveway closer to the house. She waved to Joe, and he went on his way. Karen was grateful she didn't have to speak to him, because he probably would have been able to see sex, sex, sex written all over her face.

She giggled and rushed inside.

Jessie met her at the door.

"We were almost busted," Karen said.

They both began laughing.

Karen noticed Jessie's expression had changed. "What is it? What are you thinking?"

"It's just . . . What if we had been busted . . .? Would you be okay with it?"

"I am fine, Jessie. Or at least I think I am. My biggest fear is Roger, my brother-in-law. I need to talk to my family. Hopefully Roger will still love me afterwards."

"Roger is Sophie's dad, right?"

"Yes. I believe Joan and Sophie will be okay, but Roger is questionable. He always makes rude comments about my gay friends. So far I have put up with it. Never have I let him know how much it hurts me to hear those nasty words."

"Not everybody gets it. Times have changed, but homosexuality is still a difficult situation for many people."

"I know, trust me. I have given this a lot of thought during the last six months. I have finally decided to live my life for me, no, for us. I want complete happiness and companionship and lots of lovemaking until the wee hours of the morning. I want to make up for lost time."

"Well, at this rate you should be all caught up by next Saturday." Jessie chuckled.

Karen slapped her.

"Hey, I didn't deserve that," Jessie protested. "You are one hell of a horny woman."

Karen's face flushed. "I guess I had it bottled up all these years. Now that I know how great it feels, I just can't seem to get enough of you. Is that so bad?"

"Not at all. I loved every minute of it, and I wouldn't want it any other way." Jessie leaned down and placed her lips on Karen's.

Their lips locked. When they came up for air, Jessie was breathless. She placed her hands gently on Karen's cheeks, looked deep into her eyes and told her something she had only said to one other woman in her life before. "I love you."

Karen searched Jessie's face. The love Jessie held for her was clear to see. Karen had waited her whole life to have this. Jessie was her special someone. "I love you, too, Jessie."

Karen easily persuaded Jessie to stay over again. However, Jessie made Karen promise that they would actually get some sleep. Jessie had a couple of physically demanding days ahead and required some strength and energy. Of course they retired early to the bedroom for one more session of lovemaking before they both drifted off to sleep in each other's arms.

Sunday morning Karen had a difficult time saying good-bye to Jessie. "I am going to miss you terribly."

"Same here. But I will call you later." Jessie gave Karen a deep long kiss. "That will have to keep us going until we can see each other again." She smiled and kissed Karen on the forehead.

CHAPTER SIXTEEN

About half-way into practice Jessie began to feel tired. Without doubt caused by overexertion in the past forty-eight hours. Thinking of the reasons for her fatigue made Jessie smile. She couldn't help but be overjoyed. She was truly in love. Jessie could not remember ever being this happy. Her love for Lynne had never felt like this, not even close. Maybe Lynne had done her a favor after all, when she had left her ...

Jessie managed to find enough ambition to complete the exercises with the team and call it a day.

Karen, basking in her contentedness and beaming with joy, puttered around the house most of the day. She wanted to call Joan, but she was unsure how to handle the whole situation with her family. Instead she decided to enjoy the day and deal with Joan and Roger later.

Jessie called, and they talked for over an hour, simply sharing the events of their day. Neither of them wanted to be the one to end the conversation. Karen wanted to continue talking simply to hear Jessie's voice. It made her feel close.

Early Monday morning Karen ran early for work. She stopped at Tim Horton's for treats for her co-workers, a coffee for Julie, and, of course, her French Vanilla Cappuccino.

Julie had arrived just before Karen.

Karen greeted her with a bubbly cheerfulness. "Good morning, Julie!"

"Good morning to you, too." Julie took her coffee and a box of donuts from Karen and watched her closely. She looked fantastic. Something had changed.

Karen hung up her coat and was putting on her work shoes when Julie pulled her chair up close beside her.

"There is something different with you this morning. You have this special glow . . . Oh, my God!" Julie exclaimed all giddy.

"What is it? What's the matter?"

"You got laid, didn't you?"

Karen was still beaming from ear to ear. "What on earth would give you that idea?"

"Just look at you! You look radiant!"

"Does it really show? Gee, Julie, I feel like I am wearing a billboard saying 'Look at me, I finally got laid!"'

They both laughed aloud.

Julie gave Karen a huge hug. "I am so happy for you. I have waited a long time to see you like this."

"So have I. I cannot believe how fortunate I am to have found someone so perfect for me."

"I knew it, I just knew it. Wait 'til I tell Rhonda. She will be just as pleased as I am for the two of you."

"Thanks, Julie, for everything. You are a great friend."

Julie headed off to grab the phone that was ringing. She turned back and said, "I love you kiddo!"

Karen stood there smiling. She should have known that her friend would be able to see right through her.

The rest of the day whisked by. After Karen was home and had her dinner, she called Joan to announce a visit for the following evening.

"Hi Joan, we haven't seen each other for a while, and I wondered if you were all going to be home tomorrow evening. I thought I would drop by."

"Yeah, we would love to see you. By all means, come anytime. I think today was the end of Sophie's volleyball, so she should be home, as well."

"Good, I look forward to it."

"Me, too. I have to go pick up Sophie, but we will talk tomorrow night. Love you."

"No problem. See you then. I love you, too." Karen hung up. I hope she still loves me after tomorrow, she thought to herself,

She was still contemplating that thought when her phone rang. "Hello."

"Hey, good-looking, how are you?"

Karen beamed when she heard Jessie's voice on the other end. "Better now that I am talking to you."

"You are such a flirt," Jessie teased.

"Only with you and besides, you love it."

They laughed together.

"You're right, I do. Which brings me to my next question."

Karen interrupted. "Wait a second. Before we go any further I want to know how your team did at the tournament."

"We won!" Jessie practically yelled into the phone.

"Excellent! You must be so proud."

"I am very proud and pleased with all of them. What a wonderful day we have had. There is only one thing that would make it even better."

"What could be better than bringing home the trophy?"

"Celebrating my victory with you."

"Just come on over. If you aren't too exhausted that is . . ."

"Actually, I am pumped and exhilarated from the day. The girls are thrilled! Give me half an hour, and I will be there." Jessie hung up, eager to see Karen.

It wasn't long before Jessie's arrival. Karen was watching for her and opened the door to greet her once she reached the front step. They were both so happy to see one another.

Jessie lifted Karen and spun her around, giggling like a school girl. "I am thankful you were home tonight. I wanted to see you so badly.

On the way home from Trenton all I could think about was celebrating with you tonight."

"I love the idea." Karen smiled, as her lips found Jessie's. They locked onto each other's mouths for a long while.

Jessie's eyes were closed. When the kiss ended, Karen could see pure joy on Jessie's face.

"Mmmm, that was nice." Jessie's eyes slowly opened.

Karen took pleasure in simply watching Jessie. "I put wine in the fridge to chill. Would you like to toast the win?"

"Sure, I would love some." She slid her hand into Karen's as they walked to the kitchen together.

Jessie took the wine and opened it while Karen got out the glasses.

"I would like to make the first toast." Jessie lifted her glass in Karen's direction. "To my personal good luck charm. You have made me one very happy woman."

Karen blushed. "And I have the trophy to prove it!" she said proudly. She lifted her glass to Jessie's and took a drink. "Now, here's to the best female coach whose team kicked ass today."

They continued making toasts back and forth, getting a little sillier each time. Before they knew it, their glasses were empty.

"Awe, that was fast!" Jessie complained.

"Another glass?" Karen winked.

"What about driving home?"

She slipped her arms around Jessie and pulled her close. "You don't have to drive home tonight. I can find you another T-shirt to wear, although I don't see the reason when it only stays on for a few minutes," she said mischievously.

"I thought you would never ask." Jessie squeezed her tight.

Karen couldn't believe how comfortable the two of them had become with each other. Everything felt right when she was with Jessie. She was Karen's soul mate, the one she had dreamed of for so long.

"More wine then?"

"Yes. Shall we move this party to the bedroom?"

"No arguments here."

They locked everything up and turned off the lights. With the wine bottle and the glasses they headed for the bedroom. Anticipation built in each of them as they both knew what they were looking for from each other. They undressed and got into bed. Karen leaned over and settled in under Jessie's arm. Jessie held her while they talked and sipped wine.

"I won't be home tomorrow evening," Karen remarked. "I am going over to Joan's."

"Do you still plan on telling your family about us?"

"Yes, I do. I am not the type of person who can hide things from them."

"I respect that. I am the same way. I have been very fortunate that my whole family has been very loving and supportive of me and my lifestyle. I don't know what I would do if I didn't have them."

"I hope, I am as fortunate as you. My family has always meant everything to me."

"I hope so too, for your sake." Jessie placed a kiss on the top of Karen's head. "May I propose something?"

"It's a little soon for a proposal, isn't it?" Karen joked, knowing that was not Jessie's intention. "Seriously, go ahead, propose away!"

"I would like for you to come with me to Mattawa this Easter. I really want you to meet my family. I know they will love you."

Karen hesitated, not wanting to disappoint Jessie, but wanting to hold on to tradition. "Can I think about it? I usually host Easter dinner here for my family and do the turkey and all the fixings. It has become a tradition. Actually, I was hoping you would join us."

"I already promised my mom I would come home. I haven't been home since Christmas."

"I understand."

Jessie took her finger, slowly and tenderly making circles around Karen's nipple. She watched how abruptly firmness set in, causing the nipple to stand out. Lowering herself, she nibbled gently on Karen's earlobe.

The sensation of Jessie's warm breath on her ear drove Karen crazy. With excitement she turned to Jessie and let her tongue dance down Jessie's neck and over her bare shoulder, placing gentle kisses along the way.

Their lovemaking was slow and graceful. Exhausted they fell asleep in each other's embrace.

Karen's alarm clock awoke them. Karen looked over to Jessie lying there in her bed and smiled. This is living! she thought to herself as she got up to shower for work.

She made coffee and set out two bowls of cereal. Cheerful for finally having a companion she loved, Karen was preparing lunches for the two of them, when she suddenly stopped, looked up and said a quick prayer. She was thankful for the happiness she felt and worried if her family would still love her, understand how special Jessie was to her and welcome her with open arms.

Just then Jessie made her presence known.

Startled and embarrassed Karen turned around. "How long have you been there?"

"Long enough to know I make you happy." She planted a playful kiss on Karen's cheek making her giggle.

"I'm so used to being alone, I . . ."

"You don't need to explain anything. I think it is sweet. And I adore the fact that you carry on conversations with God no matter where you are."

"When you put it like that, I sound a bit off the wall." Karen wrinkled up her nose, and Jessie quickly kissed it.

"Aren't you?" Jessie asked and braced herself for the punch in the arm that she knew she was about to receive.

After they had enjoyed their breakfast together, Karen headed off to work, leaving Jessie to get herself out the door on time.

Karen's fragrance lingered in the air in every room that Jessie entered. She wanted to bottle it and take it with her. The thought made her smile.

Jessie had a great day at school. Everyone congratulated her on the team's win. She also got to hand out the good test results from the week before.

Later that evening she called Tom to share the great news.

"Hey, Tom, how is it going?"

"Things are fine here. Seems to be warming up a bit. Hopefully spring is right around the corner."

"I'm ready for it. Although I was thankful for the large dumping of snow last Friday night."

"Oh, why is that?" Tom asked.

"I happened to be at Karen's and couldn't make it home. So as luck would have it, I had to stay the night."

"Luck as in 'got lucky'?" Tom teased.

They both laughed.

Jessie cleared her throat. "You bettcha."

"Hot damn, you finally won her over. What's not to love, right?"

"Exactly."

They laughed.

"Actually Tom, Karen is the best thing that has ever happened to me. I have never felt this way, not even about Lynne."

"Wow, this sounds pretty serious. I hope you are sure. I don't want you to get hurt again. It has taken you a long time to bounce back from Lynne."

"This is different. I don't just love Karen. I am 'in love' with her. Now I recognize the difference."

"Holy shit, are you getting all philosophical on me?" Tom had never heard Jessie so serious about anything. "She must be something special, if she has you all stirred up like this. Will we get to meet her this Easter?"

"Probably not. She usually hosts a family dinner. Karen's family is as important to her as mine is to me."

"Then maybe Sharon and I will take a trip down to Brockville and check in on you and this new female companion of yours."

"I would love to have you come for a visit!" Jessie was excited at the thought. "How are Mom and Dad doing?"

"They miss you. You are definitely the favorite child," Tom joked.

"Do you blame them? Look at my competition!"

"Ha. Nice one. You are on top of your game tonight."

"Yeah well, on that note, I had better let you go. Be sure to say hello to everyone for me."

"I will. I love you Sis. See you soon."

CHAPTER SEVENTEEN

During her entire day at work Karen wondered what the evening would hold. Would she know what to say? And what would be the best approach? She ran a few scenarios over in her mind.

She saw Julie only briefly. Julie let her know that she and Rhonda were extremely happy for her and Jessie.

As it got later in the day, Karen's nerves were getting to her. The anticipation about the evening had her on edge, so she didn't eat much for supper.

On her drive over to Joan's she convinced herself that honesty was the best policy. This was her family, and she needed to tell them the truth.

She parked the car. After a deep breath she headed towards the door. She knocked lightly.

"Come on in," Joan hollered.

As soon as Karen entered the kitchen, she started feeling nauseous. She realized that this was going to be more difficult than she had expected.

"Hi, Joan." She gave her sister a hug, holding on longer than normal.

Joan picked up on it. "What's up?"

"Where is Sophie?"

"Upstairs, she will be right down. And Roger's not home, yet. He went out for a couple of beers with the guys. From what he told me work was not that great today. He should be home any time."

Karen breathed a sigh of relief. Roger could be very obnoxious when he was drinking. It was not the most pleasant side of him.

Just then Sophie bounced off the third last step and landed in the kitchen doorway. "Hey, Aunt Karen! How are you? You look great!"

"Yes, you do look great. Whatever it is you're doing, keep it up because it looks good on you," Joan agreed with Sophie.

Karen smiled. Instantly she thought of Jessie who made her feel good. The thought helped to calm her nerves. She decided to tell Joan and Sophie before Roger arrived.

Karen exhaled slowly. "Well, that is kind of why I am here tonight . . ."

Just then Roger's truck pulled up. Karen cringed but knew she had to continue. Roger opened the door and let it slam behind him. They all greeted him as he grumbled something on the way to the fridge to grab a beer.

"Bad day?" Joan asked.

"Terrible actually. Everything that could go wrong did." Roger's expressions showed he was disgruntled and tired.

Karen decided to change Roger's mood by talking about something pleasant. "So, Sophie, I hear your team won the final volleyball tournament on Monday!"

"I know. How great is that! Miss Carmichael told us that this was the first time in nine years that our school has won the trophy!"

"Very impressive, Sweetheart," Joan praised.

"Yeah, considering you have a dyke for a coach." Roger said nastily. He was in a very bitter mood, and it showed.

All three of them were disgusted with Roger's comment and reacted with strong vocal retort towards him.

"What!" Roger defended himself. "She is a dyke. All she needs is a good fuck from a man to turn her around." Roger guzzled the rest of his beer.

"Roger, watch your mouth in front of our daughter!" Joan exclaimed.

Karen saw red. She felt the need to stand up for Jessie. Without any hesitation she ventured forward knowing it would be unpleasant. "You could say that about me then, too, Roger."

Roger looked dumbfounded. "What exactly does that mean?"

"Well, this is the reason I wanted to talk to everyone tonight. I am seeing someone very special. In fact, I am in love with . . ." she hesitated. "I am in love with her."

"What exactly are you saying? That you're a lesbian?" Roger questioned harshly. "Honestly, Karen, you can't be serious."

"As a matter of fact yes, I am." There! She said it. No turning back now.

Joan and Sophie just stood there, waiting for an opportunity to interject.

Roger was getting more furious with every breath. "What the hell is going on with you, Karen? This is not at all like you!" Roger raised his voice to Karen which he had never done before. She had always held a special place in his heart.

Karen knew Roger had issues with homosexuality. But for some reason she had thought he would understand. This was clearly not the case. It was not going at all like she had hoped.

Just then Sophie spoke up. "Yes it is. It is totally like Aunt Karen!"

Both Roger and Karen looked at Sophie and responded in unison. "What!?"

Sophie tried to explain herself. "Sorry, Aunt Karen. I don't mean it in a bad way. But I have always thought you were gay. It doesn't matter to me. I love you no matter what."

Joan piped up. "So have I."

Karen's eyes widened. She was shocked to be hearing her family tell her this. "And yet nobody has ever said anything to me. Why?"

"What would we say?" Joan asked. "Karen, I think you are a lesbian?"

Karen swallowed. This was tough. "To be honest, I never fully realized it myself until I met Jessie."

"Jessie is trouble," Roger remarked coldly.

Joan ignored him and gave Karen a hug. "I am glad you have finally found someone who makes you happy."

"So am I, Aunt Karen." Sophie gave her a hug.

Roger knew better than to tell Joan what to do, but he could still order Sophie around. Watching his daughter hug Karen caused him to snap. "Get your dyke hands off my daughter!" he ordered.

The room fell silent.

"Dad, what is wrong with you? It's Aunt Karen."

"I don't care. I don't need her type putting any ideas into your head."

Joan defended her sister. "Roger, you are overreacting!"

Karen and Roger's eyes locked. Karen could see the hate Roger felt. Roger saw only what he now felt Karen stood for. And that was a homo.

Karen broke the silence. "How would you react if it was Sophie telling you she was a lesbian? Would you reject your own daughter? Would you disown her?"

"She's not and never will be. Sophie is my daughter. There is no way any child of mine is queer." He made it sound dirty and evil.

"I'm just saying: what if?" Karen was still hoping Roger would realize how hurtful he was being.

Roger was not about to even remotely entertain this idea. "That's it. That's enough! Please leave my house!" He showed her the door.

"Roger, it's me, Karen, your sister-in-law," Karen begged to reason with him.

"I said 'leave'!" His eyes were dark and cold.

Karen's eyes welled up. Tears trickled down her face. "I am still the same person who I have always been," Karen said desperately.

"Leave!"

She slowly turned and walked out the door.

"Roger! What on earth do you think you are doing?" Joan yelled.

"Sophie, get me another beer," Roger ordered.

"No, get it yourself!" Sophie stomped off up the stairs to her room.

"Joan, don't start with me," Roger warned as Joan was about to ream him out.

Joan left the room in a huff, and Roger was left to get his beer for himself.

As soon as Karen was far enough away from the house, she pulled over, turned off the car and sat there in disbelief. She began to sob. Running the whole episode over and over in her mind only made her cry harder. Karen was devastated. She felt alone and abandoned.

Once she was able to calm herself, Karen drove home and poured herself a strong drink. She thought about calling Jessie, but she didn't want to get her involved, nor did she want Jessie to think she was weak. Karen needed to handle this, she was just very uncertain as to how.

On numerous occasions before sleeping with Jessie, Karen had gone over in her mind all of the 'what ifs' of admitting she was gay. But once she had decided Jessie was the one she wanted, there had been no turning back. Karen deserved to be happy. She loved her family, and now Jessie was a part of that family. They needed to understand that.

Jessie had just finished making herself a grilled cheese sandwich when the phone rang.

"Hello," Jessie answered.

"Hi . . . Miss Carmichael?" asked the voice on the other end.

"Yes. To whom am I speaking?"

There was a short silence on the other end. "Miss Carmichael, it's me, Sophie. I normally would never call you at home, but it's about Aunt Karen."

Jessie was immediately concerned. "Is she alright? Has she been in an accident or something?"

"I probably shouldn't be calling you, but I love my aunt, and as I understand, you do, too."

Jessie became a bit uncomfortable talking about her love life with a student. "Sophie, I don't mean to be insensitive here, but I don't think this conversation is appropriate for us. Does Karen know you are calling me?"

"No, she doesn't. I just thought you should know that my dad was pretty hard on her tonight. I don't want Aunt Karen to be alone. She was very upset when she left. Personally I am very happy for her. I was hoping you would be able to go see her and make sure she is okay," Sophie expressed with genuine concern.

Jessie realized Sophie was calling more as a friend than a student. "I appreciate the call, Sophie. Thanks for letting me know. I will leave right now. I'll call you tomorrow when your dad is at work and let you know how Karen is. Thanks again." Jessie hung up the phone, shoved the sandwich into her mouth, grabbed a bottle of water from the fridge and ran out.

Karen heard a car pull up. Not wanting to talk to anyone, she looked to see if she recognized who it was before deciding whether to answer the door or not. It was Jessie.

When Karen opened the door, her eyes were red and puffy from crying. With the Kleenex in her hand Karen had tried to disguise her tears, but she knew Jessie was very much aware of her state of mind.

Jessie stepped inside, quickly tossed her jacket, and without a word she drew Karen close to her. She held her in silence for a long while. Karen sobbed on her shoulder. Jessie reassured her that she was there for her with a soft "shhhhh", as she gently stroked her hair.

Jessie managed to get Karen to the kitchen and sat her at the table. "I'm going to make us some tea. Then I want you to tell me everything," Jessie insisted.

Karen shook her head, still sniffling. "Okay." She filled Jessie in on how hard Roger had been on her. She made it very clear that Roger had been drinking with the boys, and that he had had a difficult day at work.

"Karen you can't possibly be making excuses for him. Drinking or not, bad day or not, that does not give him the right to treat you like that."

"I am just trying to explain that he is not normally this insensitive. You have not gotten to know him, yet. I don't want you to pre-judge him because of this."

"Has he not pre-judged me?" Jessie looked at Karen in disbelief. Karen's ability to accept Roger's meanness and let him get away with it angered Jessie.

"I am just saying that two wrongs don't make a right. I need you to help me get through this, Jessie. Unfortunately I don't handle anger and hurtfulness very well."

"I know, Sweetheart. You are so kind-hearted, I admire that." Jessie lowered her voice, kissing Karen on the forehead.

Karen wanted Jessie close to her for moral support and comfort. She did not want to be alone.

They called it an early night and headed to bed. Jessie held Karen as they lay talking. Karen did not understand how things could go so terribly wrong, but they had, and now she must figure out a way to deal with her situation. With Jessie by her side, she knew it would be possible for her to stand her ground.

The next day was very emotional for Karen. Jessie had agreed to stay with her until Karen felt she was okay to be on her own. Jessie was on March break for the week and was staying in Brockville instead of heading home.

Jessie called Sophie and informed her how much her aunt was hurting. She reassured her student that she would be there for Karen. In time she was certain Karen would be fine. However Jessie stated that she would be grateful, if there was anything that Sophie and her mom could do to reassure Karen they still loved her.

Karen took her break with Julie and filled her in on what had taken place during her visit at her sister's house.

"That asshole!" Julie fumed.

"You know Roger, Julie. He normally isn't this rough."

"Karen, come on! Not once has he ever acknowledged Rhonda or me whenever we have run into him. He knows what good friends we are with you. Yet he can't bring himself to say hello to us. He just doesn't want himself associated with anyone who is gay."

"You never told me that before." Karen was genuinely surprised to hear this.

"We didn't want to interfere. It's your relationship with him that counts. After all, he is your brother-in-law, and you always spoke highly of him."

"Well, I am starting to see Roger in a whole new light. What makes him think he is better than anyone else?" It was not Karen's nature to speak badly of others, especially family members. To admit her feelings about Roger was hard for her.

Their break was ending. Julie gave Karen a comforting hug. "Things will work out somehow, don't get too discouraged."

That evening, when Karen arrived home from work, she was thrilled to see Jessie. It was heartwarming to have Jessie waiting to greet her. She came through the door, and right away she could smell the aroma of dinner wafting from the kitchen. To come home to this kind of welcome put the first smile of Karen's day on her face.

Jessie took Karen's coat and hung it up.

"Thanks, Honey." It made Karen feel good just to be able to say it. "What smells so great?" She put her arms around Jessie's waist and cuddled up close to her.

Jessie wore a huge smile. She had feared that Roger's reaction might have sent Karen running away from her. Thank God this was not the case.

Jessie lowered her mouth onto Karen's, engaging in a very seductive, lengthy kiss until it was interrupted by the buzzer on the stove. Karen tried to keep Jessie from leaving, but the buzzer persisted.

"Sorry, I have to get that. You don't want your dinner burned, do you?"

"No, but I don't want to stop kissing you either." Having Jessie there was good for Karen. Jessie's kiss made everything inside Karen come alive.

They both headed for the kitchen, holding hands like two kids in love.

Jessie had made Karen a nice hot meal for dinner – scalloped potatoes and ham with corn, along with homemade garlic-cheese dinner rolls. Jessie turned the buzzer off and pulled the rolls out of the oven, passing the tray playfully under Karen's nose.

Karen inhaled the aroma and closed her eyes as she enjoyed the wonderful smells in her kitchen, created by the woman she loved. Nobody had ever done anything like this for her before.

"Ummmmm," she sighed with pleasure.

"Wait until you taste it. My mom taught me how to cook when I was a young girl," Jessie bragged.

"I thought you didn't like cooking?" Karen grabbed a couple of plates with utensils and turned toward the table only to discover it was already set. "You know, if you keep this up, I will never let you go home."

Jessie laughed. "A girl can hope, can't she?" She winked at Karen as she tossed the rolls into a bowl. "Okay, everything is ready. Would you like some wine?"

Karen thought for a moment. "I think I will have a glass of cold milk tonight. I've had a long day. A glass of wine might put me to sleep."

"Milk it is. Have a seat. I am waiting on you tonight."

Karen was feeling a bit guilty not doing anything to help out. "Jessie, you don't have to wait on me. Don't get me wrong, I love it, but it is not necessary."

"I am off this week, and today I have enjoyed myself completely. It's been fun, really," Jessie reassured Karen.

Karen took a mouthful of potatoes. "Delicious! I don't remember the last time I had scalloped potatoes." She took a bite of a dinner roll. "You said you couldn't cook, and that is not true."

"I said I didn't enjoy cooking. Besides, today was different, knowing it was for you."

Karen smiled. They enjoyed their dinner together and shared the events of their day. Later they both cleaned up and retired to the living room with tea.

Karen set down her tea, went to Jessie and gave her a big kiss. "I am very grateful for all of this."

"Just how grateful are you?" Jessie inquired.

"I promise I will show you before the night is over," Karen flirted.

They both giggled and wrapped their arms around each other. They stood there, swaying, each drawing comfort from the other in the glow of the fire.

"Jessie, I have decided to drop by my parents' tomorrow after work to tell them about us."

"Are you ready for that?" Jessie drew her in closer.

Karen exhaled a deep breath. "I do have concerns about their acceptance after the way Roger reacted." She swallowed hard. "I was certain they would love me regardless of the fact that I am a lesbian. But now I am unsure and afraid." Tears filled her eyes. "I need them to still love me. I need my parents to love me, Jessie. What if . . . what if . . ."

Jessie kissed Karen's forehead. "Not everybody is like Roger, Sweetheart. I hope your mom and dad will love you even more for your honesty, not only to them, but also to yourself." She tried to be reassuring, knowing there was no guarantee.

"Would you stay overnight, in case it doesn't go well?"

"I will be here. You can count on it." Jessie could feel Karen's body begin to relax.

"What do you have planned for your day off?" Karen asked, now soothed she would not have to spend the night alone if things went badly.

"Rhonda and I are going to the gym. We plan to shoot some hoops and then play a little one-on-one."

"Sounds like fun. If I didn't have to work, I would come and be your personal cheerleader."

"I would love to see where you put your pom-poms!" Jessie tried to lighten the tension.

Karen loved Jessie's sense of humor. "For your eyes only, my dear." Karen placed a gentle kiss on Jessie's lips. "I will be eating supper at Mom's, but you are welcome to come over anytime. It is great knowing you will be here for me." Karen smiled widely.

"What are you grinning at?"

"It feels kind of funny letting someone know my whereabouts. I like it. This whole relationship we have, Jessie, it feels wonderful! I never thought I would have love in my life. I thought I was destined to be an old spinster."

"Now that would have been a waste with all the love you have to offer! You needed me to come in and sweep you off your feet."

They never drank their tea. Instead they ended up making wild passionate love while the evening slipped into the wee hours of the morning.

Even though Karen did not get a lot of sleep, she felt full of energy after her morning shower. She made herself a ham sandwich for lunch and left Jessie a little love note on the table.

After work Karen headed to her parents, still uncertain of what their reaction would be. She was reluctant to share the news of her sexuality with them. She did not want to risk losing her parent's love, but they had raised her to be honest, and she owed them the truth.

Karen arrived. Taking a deep breath, she headed for the door.

She was greeted with open arms by her mom. "Come in, dear. We are so glad to see you."

Karen knew immediately that someone had already told them her news. "Hi, Mom. It's good to see you, too. Is Dad here?" Karen drew comfort from the big hug her mother gave her.

"He is in the living room."

Karen gave her mom a kiss on the cheek and went to see her dad who was already on his feet. "Hi, Sweetheart. How are you holding up?"

"I wanted you to hear it from me, but I guess Joan has already been here to give you a heads up."

"Joan and Sophie came by yesterday. They love you very much ... as do your mother and I," her dad reassured her and softly placed a kiss on the top of her head.

They took a moment and let the silence linger. Everyone breathed a little easier now that they had those initial difficult, awkward moments behind them.

"Sit down." Her mom gestured to a chair.

Karen was extremely relieved that her parents welcomed her with such a loving reception. "I haven't spoken with Joan or Sophie since I left their place the other evening. How are they doing?"

"They are worried about you. They know how hurt you were by Roger."

Karen felt her face get warm, although she was not sure if the redness was caused by the embarrassment of how Roger had treated her or by the anger she still felt when she thought of their conversation. "Yes, well, it wasn't pleasant."

"Would you mind filling us in in your own words on how this has all come about?" her dad asked. "There is nothing like hearing things directly from the source."

Karen began to fidget. "As you both know, I have dated many times, but never, not once, have I had the desire to pursue any of those relationships. But from the first time I met Jessie I have been attracted to her. We met last fall, became friends, and I fell in love with her very unexpectedly. I struggled with my feelings for several months." Tears streamed down Karen's face as she explained how much she loved Jessie. Her parents could see how difficult this was for her. "Since I met Jessie, I think about her all the time. I can't wait to see her or talk to her. She makes me laugh. She makes me feel good about myself. But most of all: I am happy. My heart is whole, and I don't have that emptiness in my life anymore. My life is complete with Jessie in it." Karen looked at her parents with sincerity. "I cannot hide from my sexuality any longer. I just pray that you still love me for who I am."

"We will always love you, Karen," her mom reassured.

"Sophie speaks very highly of Jessie. She sings her praises," her father informed. "I have one more question."

Karen suddenly got a little uncomfortable, not knowing what to expect. "If I can answer it, I will." She looked down at the floor, not wanting to look at him.

"When do we get to meet this bright young woman who has stolen our daughter's heart?"

Karen looked up to see the smiles on her parents' faces, and she knew they would absolutely love Jessie. "Any time you want!"

They all stood up and had a group hug.

Karen breathed a sigh of relief, thankful this difficult conversation was behind her. "How about if we come by in a few days, and we all have a drink together?"

"That sounds wonderful," her mother answered.

"I do have one other request for the two of you." Karen didn't want to push her luck but needed to get plans rearranged.

"What's that?" her dad asked.

"It's about Easter. I usually prepare dinner at my house, but with all the upset with Roger, I do not want it to be uncomfortable for anyone. I certainly would not want to put Joan in a position to have to choose."

"Very thoughtful of you. What are you proposing?"

"Jessie doesn't know it, yet, but I am going to accept her invitation to go to Mattawa for Easter and meet her family. That way you all can still have an enjoyable peaceful Easter without the tension."

"It won't be the same without you here. Easter has always been a big deal for you. Are you sure this is what you want?" her dad asked.

"I believe so. Besides I am looking forward to meeting Jessie's family. It does mean though that Joan will have to do all the work." She chuckled.

"Thank goodness she has Sophie," her dad added.

"Thank goodness we all have Sophie. She has turned out to be quite the young lady."

Once the heavy conversation was over, they enjoyed a relaxing dinner. Karen helped with the dishes and headed home soon afterwards.

On her drive home she breathed a sigh of relief that the evening had gone well. She was very thankful to have such wonderful, understanding parents, knowing not everybody was that fortunate.

CHAPTER EIGHTEEN

Karen was disappointed when she arrived home and Jessie was not there. Hopefully she would be arriving soon. She was excited to tell her how well the evening had gone, and that her parents wanted to meet her.

As soon as Karen entered the house the phone rang. She quickly grabbed it, thinking it was Jessie. "Hello there!"

"Hi, Karen." Joan sounded nervous. She had not spoken with her sister since Roger's outburst.

Immediately Karen tensed up. "Oh, it's you, Joan," Karen managed. "I was expecting it to be someone else."

"Jessie, I guess. I hope I haven't disappointed you too much," Joan tried to relieve the tension.

"Actually, I am glad you called," Karen reassured.

Joan got directly to the point. "I just got off the phone with Mom. She said you had a good visit with them."

"I did. Although I was surprised they had already heard my news."

"Sophie and I wanted them to be aware of Roger's unpleasant outburst."

"I see. In a way I was relieved that they already knew and I didn't have to set myself up for another painful outcome. Mom and Dad were wonderful. I know they have their concerns. Although they worry for me, they still love and accept me."

"That's exactly why I am calling. Can Sophie and I come over for a visit tomorrow evening?"

At first Karen was thrilled. Then the thought of Roger came to mind. "Just you and Sophie?" Karen asked cautiously. "In that case I look forward to your visit. Around seven?"

"Perfect. And Karen, one more thing."

"What?"

"I love you." Joan was choked up. Quickly she hung up the phone.

Karen pressed the phone to her chest. Her bottom lip began to quiver. Tears rolled down her cheeks. She was grateful to hear those words from Joan. She had feared that Roger would use his influence to turn her sister and her niece against her.

Twenty minutes later Jessie's car pulled into the driveway. As soon as Jessie reached up to knock, Karen swung the door open and greeted her with open arms. She couldn't wait to see Jessie and tell her about the evening. Karen didn't wait for Jessie to take her coat off. She pulled Jessie to her and gave her a long seductive kiss.

"A girl could get used to a reception like this. Tell me: What I did to deserve this, so that I can do it more often," Jessie teased. She could see that Karen was on top of the world. Things must have gone well with her parents.

"Very funny! I missed you, that's all."

"I am later than I had expected, but I told you I would be here." Jessie smiled.

"I must make a special note: 'Jessie is the thoughtful sort'," Karen teased.

Jessie removed her coat. "I desperately need a shower. Rhonda and I played hard today. I have to freshen up."

While she showered, Karen made them both hot chocolate and waited for Jessie in the living room. She was all smiles. She felt like she was busting at the seams.

"Okay, out with it!" Jessie ordered.

"I have a surprise for you."

"I love surprises. What is it?"

Karen couldn't hold it in any longer. "Remember that we talked about the Easter weekend? Well, my plans have changed. Is your invitation to go to Mattawa still available?" Karen's eyes were wide and bright with excitement.

Jessie's mouth dropped open. Her face lit up. "Are you serious? You're not just fooling with me, right?" Jessie didn't want to get too excited only to be let down.

"I am very serious."

"Wow, yes of course! I would love for you to come with me!" She was pleased with the news. "Just what exactly happened tonight?"

"I went to see my parents, but Sophie and Joan had already filled them in. Mom and Dad were wonderful. I am very blessed to have parents who love me so much."

"After your ordeal with Roger this must be very reassuring for you. It isn't easy coming out to your parents. Fortunately I, just like you, am very blessed with understanding, loving parents."

"Exactly! I breathed a huge sigh of relief for sure. Anyway, I thought it's best if I won't host the Easter dinner this year. I told them about your invitation and that I was going to accept your offer."

"They don't think I want to change your tradition, I hope?" Jessie didn't want them blaming her for taking their daughter away.

"Not at all. It was my idea. I don't want everyone to feel awkward and uncomfortable." Karen was happy to be going with Jessie. But she knew there was a part of her that was going to find it difficult to be away from her own family at Easter. "And don't worry about my parents blaming you for anything. I had a long talk with them. In fact they want to meet you."

"They do?"

"Yes, we will go over for drinks in a few days. They want to meet the person responsible for turning their daughter into a love crazed animal." Karen had finished her hot chocolate and snuggled close to Jessie.

When Karen looked at Jessie, their eyes met, and once again their mouths devoured each other in a passionate deep kiss.

Without a word they stood up. They could see the love and desire in each other's eyes. Slowly Jessie unbuttoned Karen's blouse taking in the beauty of the woman she loved. Never would she tire of the vision standing before her. Karen's large perfectly shaped breasts heaved as her breathing intensified. Jessie's hands moved over Karen's shoulders, dropping the blouse to the floor.

Jessie could hear the quickening of Karen's breath. She ran her fingers down Karen's arms, pulled Karen towards her, and with skilled hands quickly dropped Karen's bra to the floor.

Karen caught her breath. She quivered with excitement and anticipation as Jessie started nibbling on her earlobe. Jessie's delicate kisses made a path down Karen's neck and shoulders; softly she nibbled on Karen's breasts, taking her nipple between her teeth. With her warm wet tongue Jessie gently teased the tip of the rosebuds.

Karen could hardly breathe. Her knees became weak.

Jessie slowly moved downwards. Her hands unfastened Karen's jeans and slid them off. Karen wore black lace panties that had the scent of baby powder. Jessie nuzzled her face into Karen's panties and inhaled her fragrance. She was acutely aware of Karen's sweetness and desire.

Karen ran her hands through Jessie's hair and parted her legs, so that Jessie could remove her panties.

Very slowly Jessie began parting Karen's lips with her tongue, tasting Karen's sweetness. Karen's loud moan excited Jessie even more. She enjoyed giving Karen pleasure. She was getting as much pleasure out of it herself.

Jessie motioned for Karen to lie down on the sofa. Her tongue journeyed to Karen's belly. She slipped her fingers easily inside of Karen, who was now totally at her mercy. Jessie knew how to both tease and please Karen, and she did just that for a very long time.

Exhausted and completely satisfied Karen curled up next to Jessie. "I love you," she whispered and soon drifted off to sleep.

Jessie knew Karen was both physically and emotionally exhausted. She covered her up with a blanket and watched her sleep. Karen looked so peaceful and innocent, it warmed Jessie's heart. This was the woman of her dreams.

The following day brought sunshine and warmth. Much of the snow had disappeared. A hint of spring was in the air. Karen and Jessie made arrangements for dinner to be take-out, and Jessie had accepted Karen's invitation to be there when Joan and Sophie came over to visit.

Both, Karen and Jessie, were a bit nervous when they saw the car pull in. Karen went to the door, while Jessie remained in the living room, not wanting to interfere.

"Come on in," Karen welcomed.

Everyone seemed uneasy. Awkwardness filled the room.

Sophie was the most relaxed and immediately threw her arms around her aunt.

"I hear you have been my guardian angel through this whole ordeal," Karen told Sophie. "You truly are a godsend. Thank you so much." She gave her a kiss on the cheek and a tight squeeze filled with emotion.

Then she turned and looked at Joan who had been watching the strong bond of love between her daughter and her sister.

Karen reached out her arms for Joan who had already removed her coat, and the two of them held on tight to each other. Neither of them said a word, nor did they have to. Both had tears streaming down their faces.

After a long moment, Karen whispered into Joan's ear, "I love you. I don't ever want anything to come between us." She kissed her on the cheek and rubbed Joan's arms up and down in a loving gesture.

"Nothing will ever stop me from loving you," Joan reassured. "Not even Roger." She smiled.

Jessie had witnessed the whole greeting and now felt her entrance was appropriate. When she entered the foyer, Karen grabbed her by the hand to have her join them. "I believe you both know Jessie," Karen said with a wide smile.

"Hi, Miss Carmichael. It is really good to see you." Sophie held out her hand in a cordial manner.

Jessie took Sophie's hand, but instead of shaking it, she drew her in closer and gave her a hug. "I want to thank you again for phoning me. And please call me Jessie, when we are not in school."

Joan spoke up. "I also want to thank you for being here for Karen."

"No thanks needed. I wouldn't want to be anywhere else." Jessie grabbed Karen's hand and squeezed it.

Joan watched as Karen's face lit up at Jessie's touch. It was easy to tell that Karen was happy.

"Let's go sit down, shall we?" Jessie suggested.

"Would anybody like something to drink?" Karen asked.

Both Sophie and Joan had ginger ale, and Jessie and Karen had tea.

"I am so glad to see both of you," Karen started. "I have thought about you often in the last few days, but I didn't want to call."

"We understand completely." Joan wished she could defend Roger in some way or make excuses for him and his behavior, but in all honesty there was no excuse for the way her husband had treated Karen.

"Can I ask how Roger is doing?" Karen was genuinely concerned. She loved Roger like a brother. There had never been any harsh words between them before. "Has he spoken about my visit? How is he dealing with the situation?"

Joan and Sophie looked at each other, not knowing how to answer.

Karen could sense the uneasiness. "It is okay if you don't want to answer. I worry about him."

Sophie spoke up. "I don't know why you worry about him, Aunt Karen. He was horrible to you."

"It wouldn't be like Karen if she didn't. She has the biggest heart of anybody I have ever met," Jessie said with pride.

Joan smiled. "You're right, Jessie. I don't know how she does it. She always finds it in her heart to forgive others. That is why she makes such a great nurse. I think she's a damned saint."

"Not quite." Karen laughed. "But thanks for saying so."

"Roger is still being a jerk. We don't talk about that evening. In fact, we don't talk much at all," Joan explained.

"Joan, I could never forgive myself, if my sexuality came between you and Roger."

"Don't worry, Aunt Karen. He is just sulking because we aren't talking to him."

"He told me last night we are making him feel like an outcast. I looked at him and said 'Really! And how do you like it?'" Joan admitted. "I think he will come around. I just don't know when. He has always thought the world of you, Karen. He still loves you. He just needs time to figure this all out."

"I don't know Roger at all, but it has been my experience that men have a harder time accepting homosexuality than women do. For Karen's sake, I hope Roger figures it out, but I wouldn't count my chickens," Jessie explained.

"Yeah, I have never seen Dad react like that about anything before. I think Miss Carm... I mean Jessie ... is right. Let's not count on Dad coming around any time soon," Sophie agreed.

"Well, we didn't come over here to talk about Roger." Joan wanted to change the subject. She had noticed that Karen's expression had gotten sadder as the conversation had taken on a negative tone. "We wanted to get to know more about the woman who has stolen my sister's heart. I am very glad you are here tonight, Jessie. I see by the way Karen lights up when she speaks of you how much you mean to her."

"I am glad to be here, too. Karen has always spoken so highly of her whole family. I am happy to get to know you."

The rest of the evening went extremely well. Jessie had questions for Sophie and Joan just like they had for her. Jessie told of her one and only previous love and stressed how love was a serious commitment for her. They also had light-hearted moments and laughter. Karen, Sophie and Joan shared some stories of each other over the years. Conversation came easily for all of them. Karen was beaming as she watched how Jessie fit in with her sister and niece.

When Karen explained her reason for not hosting the Easter dinner, Joan accepted her explanation; although she joked it wouldn't be so easy for Karen to get out of it the following year.

It was getting late and time for Sophie and Joan to leave. They all headed towards the door.

"Thanks to both of you for coming over." Karen sent Joan and her niece on their way with big hugs and kisses. "I feel much better knowing you still love me."

Jessie stepped forward and felt comfortable enough to extend hugs to both of them. "Karen really needed this. And I have enjoyed getting to know you better."

Just before leaving Joan turned around and looked directly at her. "Jessie, I must tell you that I have never seen my baby sister in love before. Karen deserves to be happy, and you have given her that. Thank you."

"The pleasure is all mine." Jessie turned to wink at Karen and noticed the tears streaming down her face.

"Okay, we are going now. Come on Mom, let's give them some space," Sophie ordered, acting like the adult.

As soon as the door closed, Karen let loose. But now the tears were happy tears. So all Jessie needed to do was to be there and hold Karen in comforting arms.

When Joan and Sophie got home that evening, Roger was watching TV and enjoying a beer. He seemed to be in a fine enough mood, so they filled him in on their visit to Karen.

Joan took a deep breath. "Roger, we need to talk."

"Why now? You have hardly spoken to me."

"Sophie and I have just returned from seeing Karen."

"I should have known." Roger stood. "I don't want to talk about your lesbian sister."

"Well, you're going to, so sit back down!" Joan ordered.

"Please listen to what we have to say, Dad." Sophie stood alongside her mother.

"Apparently I don't have a choice," Roger grumbled.

"No, you don't. We saw both Karen and Jessie tonight. Karen is happier than I have ever seen her."

"Yes, she is, Dad. She beams whenever she looks at Jessie. Why would you not want that for Aunt Karen? She deserves happiness."

"I want you to stay away from your Aunt . . ." Roger started.

"I am over sixteen. I can make my own decisions. You can't keep me from seeing her," Sophie countered with confidence.

"I damn well can. I am your father, and you will do as I say."

"Not that Sophie needs it, but she certainly has permission from me to see my lesbian sister any time she wants to. I am proud of Karen and who she is."

"You mean what she is," Roger spoke with disgust.

"We are not arguing with you. We only wanted to let you know that your lesbian sister-in-law, with all her own struggles right now, is concerned about how you are doing. That is the Karen you know and love. She is the same person she has always been. Think about that!" Joan grabbed Sophie by the hand and headed for the kitchen.

Roger swallowed hard. He did not share with his wife and daughter that he had been considering going to see the principal of Thousand

Island Secondary School where Jessie taught to demand her termination, because she was a lesbian and his daughter was in her class. He hadn't been able to follow through with it, but he had made it to the school parking lot. He just could not understand how two people of the same sex could be sexually attracted to one another. It hurt him to think of Karen this way.

The next few days flew by quickly. The weather continued to be sunny and warm. It put smiles and happy faces on everyone. It had been a long winter. Everybody was ready for spring to arrive.

The last few Thursdays Jessie's teammates had seen her arriving and leaving with Karen. Things like this did not go unnoticed by the regulars. Rumors started, and Jessie took some playful harassment in the locker room about it. All she could do was smile, blush, and, of course, brag to those she knew were fine with it. The only one who didn't find any of this amusing was Connie. She was not at all pleased that Jessie had chosen Karen over her.

On the weekend Jessie and Karen got together with Rhonda and Julie for a fun evening of board games. They had a blast. Karen felt the most free and comfortable with their foursome than she ever had before. She cuddled with Jessie, patted her on the bum while walking by and kissed her gently on the cheek. Both Rhonda and Julie noticed how the two new love birds flirted with each other over the course of the evening.

That night in bed Julie commented on the evening. "Rhonda, isn't it great to see those two finally together?"

"I am glad to see that Karen is finally out," Rhonda admitted. "I know that Jessie is thrilled. She told me when we went to the gym that Karen is the best thing that has ever happened to her. She really loves her."

"Didn't I tell you last fall that I thought they had eyes for each other?"

Rhonda smiled. "Yes, you did. You are quite the matchmaker. Now come here and give me some of that lovin' you keep talking about. There is no reason why Karen and Jessie are getting all the action."

Julie giggled and played hard to get. But before too long Rhonda won her over.

Jessie was back to work. With only a few short months to go, her first full year of teaching would soon be behind her. Smiling she thought, this is one year I will never forget, for so many reasons. She loved her job and most importantly she loved Karen.

On Jessie's first evening at home alone she called Tom. It had been some time since their last conversation. The phone rang about four times before Tom picked up.

"Hello there, stranger," Tom answered recognizing the number on the phone.

"Why did it take you so long to answer? And you're out of breath! Are you and Sharon fooling around?"

Tom laughed. "I wish! No, we were just coming in with the groceries. I have tried calling you a few times, but you never seem to be home."

"I got your messages. I will give you Karen's phone number. You can call me there."

"Does that mean you are living there now?" Tom asked, not wanting his sister to be moving in too quickly.

"Not exactly, but I do spend a great deal of time at Karen's place. Neither one of us is happy when we are apart."

"Can you hear yourself?" Tom asked. "Jessie, I hope you are not setting yourself up for disappointment. Your heart is more fragile than you may remember."

"This time it's different, Tom. Karen and I are like two peas in a pod. We suit each other perfectly. By the way, she is joining me after all for my visit home this Easter."

"Dad told me when I was over there a few days ago. They are excited to meet her." Jokingly Tom added, "Does this mean you don't want Sharon and me to visit you in Brockville in a few weeks?"

"Of course not! I want you to see where I work and the town where I live. Besides, if I didn't want you to come, I would just tell you so." She laughed.

Tom always found Jessie's sense of humor a delight. "I know I can count on you to tell it like it is, no matter how much it may hurt me."

"You're tough, you can handle it. Besides Sharon has a shoulder you can cry on if you need it."

"Ouch, this is getting painful."

"Honestly, Tom, I would never intentionally hurt you. I love you too much, Big Brother."

Tom loved it when Jessie referred to him that way. "Now you're trying to make up for it."

"Yeah, so?" Jessie and Tom both laughed. "How is my favorite sister-in-law doing?"

"Sharon is great and as beautiful as ever."

"She can hear you, can't she?" Jessie laughed.

"Yes."

"You big suck. Are you looking for brownie points tonight, wanting to get lucky?"

"Every chance I get."

"You're the one I take after! I knew it wasn't Mom or Dad."

"That's right. Take after me, Sis, and you will get lucky often. The ladies just can't seem to resist our charms."

"Okay, that's enough for me tonight. I don't want to get into any details. Let's save that for another time."

"Agreed. Besides Sharon has that glow in her eye. I'd better go now before the mood passes." Tom turned towards Sharon who raised her eyebrows playfully.

"Okay, I will see you soon. Easter is not that far away."

CHAPTER NINETEEN

Quite some time had passed since Karen had seen Roger. She began to really miss him. She had seen Joan and Sophie on a couple of occasions, but Roger did not appear to be budging. Karen appreciated that Jessie filled a huge void in her life and felt truly blessed, but she missed the interaction with Joan, Sophie and Roger as a family unit. Her relationship with Jessie was wonderful; however, it had created a new void in her life.

The more excited Karen was to finally be taking Jessie to meet her parents.

"I am very nervous," she confessed on their drive over. "This is the first time I bring home a love interest to meet my mom and dad."

Jessie laughed. "How sweet. However, I can't say the same. I took lots of girls home to meet my parents." Jessie was joking, of course, trying to get Karen to relax.

Karen didn't disappoint her and gave Jessie a playful swat in the arm. "You are just nasty! Were you a loose woman before I met you?"

"I used to be in my younger years," Jessie bragged.

This made Karen smile. She looked over and saw Jessie's big brown eyes dancing with delight while the two of them teased back and forth. "Let's not tell my parents that part. I wouldn't want you to fall off of that pedestal that I built for you."

"Didn't I tell you that I am afraid of heights? Pedestals are no place for me."

As they pulled into the driveway, Karen's mom watched from the window. She could see how happy Karen was. She greeted them at the door, "Come in, come in. We have been anxiously waiting to meet you, Jessie. We have heard a great deal about you."

"Don't believe everything you hear," Jessie replied.

"Ah, Karen said you have a good sense of humor."

"Guilty." She smiled.

They sat in the living room for a couple of hours chatting and getting to know one another. It went smoothly and seemed so natural; Karen wondered why she had been so nervous. Her mom and dad made Jessie feel very welcomed. Jessie and Karen's father in particular really hit it off. He asked Jessie lots of questions about her education to become a teacher. By the way Jessie spoke, it was clear that she was proud of herself and her accomplishments.

Jessie had Karen's parents laughing often. They could easily see why Karen loved Jessie's lighthearted spirit. Karen watched as the relationship between her parents and her girlfriend developed into one of mutual admiration.

When it became time to leave, Karen's parents told Jessie that she was welcome anytime.

Easter weekend was almost upon them. The weather was warming up, signs of spring arrived. The flowers came to life, and fresh buds showed on the trees. There had been an occasional light snow flurry which passed quickly. The road sides and ditches were dirty, but a couple of good hard rains would wash the dirt away.

Karen had started packing a suitcase for her weekend in Mattawa. She hadn't been away in such a long time. Since she would not be at home with her own family at Easter, she had promised Joan she would make the pies for their Easter dinner. She needed to pack and make the pies before hockey the following evening. Jessie and she would be leaving for Mattawa early on Good Friday morning.

Jessie did not want to miss her hockey game. They were in the playoffs, and with only one or two games remaining she wanted to be part of it. The series was the best three out of five. The Kingston ladies' team were ahead with two wins, and the Rideau Rockets had one.

On Thursday Karen ran out during her lunch hour to pick up ingredients for the pies. When she returned to work, one of her coworkers was walking in from the parking lot with her.

"Hi Roberta, great day, isn't it?" Karen greeted.

"Yes, it sure is. I am glad we have a long weekend off. Do you have plans, Karen?" Roberta asked.

"I'm going away for the weekend for a change. How about you, Roberta, do you have anything planned?"

"No, thank goodness, I am looking forward to some quiet time alone with a few movies. Where are you going?"

Karen tensed up. Then she took a deep breath. "I'm going to Mattawa with a friend." She tried to keep the answer simple.

"Mattawa, is that where Jessie's family lives?" Roberta asked.

Karen was stunned that Roberta knew about Jessie. However, she wasn't about to run or hide. This was her time to stand tall. "Yes, that is Jessie's hometown." Karen smiled.

"I've heard that you and Jessie had become good friends, well actually more than friends, but that is none of my business." Roberta watched as Karen's face flushed. "Don't worry girl, you won't have any problems from me." Roberta put her arm around Karen and squeezed her shoulder. Karen looked at her and Roberta whispered, "I'm happy for you."

Karen smiled widely. "Thanks, Roberta. I appreciate that."

"But just so you are aware, some of the other staff knows, too."

Karen looked dumbfounded. "How? Who?"

"A couple of idiots who poke fun. They have always done the same with Julie."

Karen sighed. "Just for the record, I am a changed person. I am living a much richer life because of Jessie." Karen was proud of herself for making a statement.

"Good for you, Karen."

They both walked through the doors together and wished each other enjoyable weekends. Karen thought she would be on guard the rest of the day watching to see how people looked at her or if they whispered when they thought she wasn't looking. But after a short time her mind was strictly on her work and her weekend with Jessie. Karen realized she didn't need to concern herself with others.

On her afternoon break she filled Julie in on her conversation with Roberta.

Julie was not surprised. "People love talking about other people's business. Don't let the gossip bother you."

"Actually Julie, it is not bothering me nearly as much as I had expected. I don't really care what others think, because I am so completely happy with Jessie. That is, except for Roger. He is still not talking to me."

"Why do you let him get to you?" Julie asked.

"I miss him, I love him, and I care about what he thinks. I don't know why," Karen explained.

"My advice is to carry on with your life as usual as you can be sure Roger is doing. Just let it go. Don't dwell on it, or it will drive you crazy. But then, you would only have a short drive."

The remark lightened Karen's mood, and she began talking about her upcoming trip to Mattawa.

In a small town news traveled fast. Although Roger had not mentioned a word about Karen to anybody, his co-workers started to spread rumors.

John Saunders verbally abused Roger continuously. "Seen your dyke sister-in-law Karen recently?" he would ask, or he would tell a joke, "Why do lesbians suck at cooking? Because they always eat out!" Of course he constantly spoke loud enough for several people in the lunch room to hear, and the room would burst into laughter. "What do you call a lesbian with fat fingers? Well hung!" Again the laughter.

Every day was a new joke. "What's the difference between a lesbian and a Ritz cracker?" he would ask, "One is a snack cracker and the other is a crack snacker!" Again slaps on the back, with what they considered hilarious comments. On one occasion Roger found a two headed dildo in his locker with a note that read, "Know any lesbos that could get off on this double headed ding dong?" Roger saw red; he was mad at his so-called friends for harassing him. He took the dildo and threw it against the wall in anger, then he quickly retrieved it and buried it in the garbage can before anyone else arrived in the locker room.

In the beginning they had attached Karen's name to the jokes. Roger didn't give them the satisfaction of letting them see his anger. He would just give them a half-assed grin and shake his head as if to say 'grow up', but inside he really wanted to turn around and punch them in the face. He didn't like them talking about Karen, and he wanted to defend her, but he knew the truth. She was a lesbian and couldn't deny it.

After several weeks of jokes and pranks Roger felt hurt and saddened. Some of his closest buddies wouldn't sit with him on breaks any more. Roger's work environment was no longer a place he enjoyed. He began to realize the torment that Karen must be feeling.

As soon as Karen got home from work, she started making the pies. Since she did not want to visit Jessie's family empty-handed, she made four pies in total: two pumpkin pies and two apple pies, one of each for her family and one of each for Jessie's family. While the pies were baking, Karen finished packing. Pleased with herself, she headed back to Brockville to pick Jessie up for hockey.

Jessie played hard and made her team proud by scoring three goals. Rhonda had a shutout for the Rideau Rockets who won the game four nothing leaving the series now tied two games each. The final game would be the following Thursday, and the season would be over.

After the game Karen and Jessie headed home. When they entered the house Jessie smelled the homemade pies. "Mmmm, what smells so delicious?"

"I wanted to surprise you. I made a couple of pies to take to Mattawa with us."

"What kind did you make?"

"Apple and pumpkin."

"Oh, you are definitely going to win points with my brother Tom. He loves homemade apple pie. My mother always makes mincemeat for my dad and pumpkin for me."

"Oh good, the apple can go, and we can leave the pumpkin one here if you like."

"No! We are taking both of them. But ..." Jessie slyly made her way over to the counter.

"But what?"

"But can I have a piece of the pumpkin now?" Jessie dropped to one knee like she was begging. "They smell sooo good," she complimented.

Karen laughed. "No, I'm not going to take a partially eaten pie to your parents."

Jessie tried to convince her they would understand, but Karen wouldn't allow it.

Jessie hopped in the shower. When she came out, Karen was already asleep. A perfect opportunity for that pumpkin pie ...

The next morning they awoke to the sound of the alarm clock. They had set it for six a.m. so they could be on the road by seven. Both Jessie and Karen packed the luggage into the car, but Jessie made sure she offered to put the pies in so Karen would not notice there was a piece missing.

Before long they were ready to leave. Jessie took Karen in her arms and smiled. "I can't wait for my family to meet you. They are going to love you just as much as I do." She made a goofy expression, lifting one eyebrow. "Maybe not as much as I do, of course, but I know they are going to love you."

"You are so cute and charming." Karen kissed Jessie's forehead. "I admit I am nervous to meet them. Now I know exactly what I put you through with my family." She looked a bit sober when she added, "With the exception of Roger, of course."

Jessie gently placed her finger under Karen's chin and lifted her head up. "Karen, don't let Roger come between us. He is trouble for us. Do you think you can get through this weekend without letting thoughts of him bring you down?" Jessie was serious.

Karen saw the intense look in Jessie's eyes. Not wanting to disappoint her she replied. "Of course. I have been looking forward to this all week. Now let's get going." She put on a brave face, smiled and headed for the car. Karen was uncertain if she was telling the truth or not, but she would do her best to make her lover happy.

The roads were empty when they first headed out. Soon the traffic got busy due to the holiday weekend. After a couple of hours on the road they stopped in the small town of Arnprior at a Tim Horton's for breakfast sandwiches, tea, coffee, and a couple of donuts.

"Nothing like a good healthy meal to start the day," Jessie kidded.

"This isn't the healthiest choice, but it is quick and it definitely satisfies the palate."

They both agreed and toasted their hot beverages as they walked across the parking lot to the car. They had stretched their legs, gone to the washroom, gotten food, and before long they were headed back onto the highway.

Karen could see Jessie was familiar with eating and driving at the same time. In fact Jessie had it down to an art. After they had eaten breakfast, Jessie decided it was time to liven up the trip. She switched her radio station to one she recognized and cranked the dial. The tunes were a mix of pop and rock'n'roll. They knew the words to almost every song and sang along. Cutting loose and having fun, Karen was enjoying the drive. She had not been anywhere for a long time, and it felt great to be on a road trip.

Neither could believe how quickly the drive went. As Jessie was entering Mattawa, she filled Karen in on some childhood stories. She pointed out where she used to go swimming, where she went to school, where she played baseball, etc. Before Karen knew it, Jessie made a quick turn and pulled into Tom's driveway.

"This is Tom and Sharon's place. I didn't tell them we were coming today, so they will be surprised," Jessie explained.

"Maybe we shouldn't drop in unexpectedly. I wouldn't want to interrupt them." Karen felt uncomfortable showing up uninvited.

"They won't mind. Besides, would you not just show up at Joan's?" Jessie watched as Karen smiled. "Exactly my point. Come on, I want you to meet them."

Jessie ran up to the door and pushed the doorbell over and over and over.

They heard Tom from inside. "Alright, I'm coming already!" He opened the door. As soon as he discovered Jessie, his expression changed to one of complete joy. His arms automatically extended. He picked Jessie up and held on tight. "It is so good to see you, Sis." He put her down. "I had no idea you were coming today. What a great surprise!"

Tom was an attractive strawberry blonde fellow with a huge friendly smile. His freckles were every bit as noticeable as Jessie's. Watching the two of them carry on made Karen relax. She knew right away that Tom was easygoing.

Jessie turned towards Karen. "Tom, I would like for you . . ."

"Karen, is it?" Tom cut Jessie off politely and extended his hand. "What a pleasure to finally meet you! We have heard a great deal about you." Tom noticed immediately that Jessie was glowing.

"Thank you." Karen blushed. "Jessie has hardly mentioned you to me." When Karen was nervous, she tended to cover up with her wit. This was an adorable characteristic quality that Jessie loved about her.

They all laughed. Tom pulled Karen close and gave her a squeeze.

"Didn't I tell you that she has a great sense of humor?" Jessie asked.

"You did. Karen, you are going to feel right at home here. Come on in. I want you to meet Sharon."

They went inside. Tom hollered up the stairs. "Honey, come on down. We have company."

Sharon quickly made her way down the stairs. "Hi, Jessie!" Sharon threw her arms around Jessie, then turned around and threw her arms around Karen. "You must be Karen. I'm so glad to finally meet you."

"I'm happy we finally meet, as well." Karen returned Sharon's hug and enjoyed the warm welcome.

"Let's sit down," Tom invited.

"We haven't been to Mom and Dad's yet. I should call and let them know we have arrived safely," Jessie explained. "We stopped here first. I wanted Karen to meet the two of you." Jessie, bursting with pride, took Karen's hand and followed Tom and Sharon to the kitchen.

Karen was self-conscious holding hands in front of two people she had just met, while Jessie seemed completely at ease.

Jessie used the phone to check in with her parents.

"Are you two hungry? I could make a couple of grilled cheese sandwiches and soup," Sharon offered.

Jessie's eyes lit up. "I would love a grilled cheese, no soup though. How about you, Karen?"

Jessie offered her help and got ready to follow Sharon to the kitchen.

"Wow Karen, Jessie must be trying to impress you," Tom stated. "She normally lets us wait on her hand and foot." The room filled with laughter, when Jessie tossed a pillow at her brother.

Everyone had milk with homemade chocolate chip cookies for dessert. Karen quickly carried on as if she had known Tom and Sharon forever. It felt so natural and heartwarming. Jessie and Karen made plans to come back later and play a board game or something.

Karen was feeling more comfortable and yet a little sad, as well. She wished Roger was as accepting of her as Tom was of Jessie. How wonderful it would be if Roger were happy about their relationship. She also wondered if Joan had dropped by and picked up the pies. It was the least she could do for her sister, knowing she would have to make the rest of the meal on her own.

"You were a hit with Tom and Sharon," Jessie said. "But then, what's not to love?" She reached over and gently put her hand on Karen's upper thigh. With a seductive motion she slowly massaged it.

Karen promptly felt a surge of warmth accelerate through her body. She revelled in the way her body reacted to Jessie's touch. Karen took Jessie's hand in hers and lifted it to her lips. Softly she kissed each finger, one at a time. She then took one finger into her mouth and slowly licked it. She did the same to each finger on that hand and watched Jessie's reaction.

Jessie's breathing became deeper under Karen's caresses. Her breasts heaved up and down. The two women looked at each other, knowing what each of them wanted. But they were on their way to meet Jessie's parents. This was no time to be wet and horny.

Jessie on the other hand had other plans. Unbeknownst to Karen, she took a different route than that to her parents. She stopped in front of an old country trail where she would on occasion go parking in her earlier years. This was a safe place for them to make out.

Karen grinned. "Are you serious?" She felt like a child, doing something she knew she shouldn't be doing, but wanting so badly to do it anyway.

"Absolutely!" Jessie swallowed hard. "Let's get in the back."

"I have never done this before." Karen giggled.

It wasn't long before Jessie was showing Karen the pleasures of a back seat on an old country road.

Jessie quickly devoured Karen's mouth. Her breathing was heavy and hot. They both enthusiastically removed their pants and tossed them onto the car floor. Jessie positioned Karen flat on her back with one leg propped up on the back of the seat in front and the other towards the rear window. Without wasting any time, Jessie slid her hand inside Karen's panties and easily slipped inside Karen's wetness.

"You are so fucking wet for me, my God you excite me." Jessie was pleased.

Karen moaned in sheer pleasure. Suddenly Jessie was down on her. Her tongue searched deeper, harder. Karen cried out in passion. "Fuck me, fuck me!"

Jessie rejoiced, it was music to her ears. She took Karen to higher peaks and satisfied her completely.

Not wasting any time, Karen eagerly reciprocated the pleasures for Jessie. The two lay there in each other's arms, exhausted and out of breath. Filled with utter contentment they started to doze off.

Karen vaguely heard the sound of a tractor in the distance. It alerted her back to reality. She shook Jessie. Both hurriedly put their pants on and climbed into the front seats.

Seconds later they headed for Jessie's parents.

Within five minutes they were in the driveway. Jessie's mom and dad were very happy to see them.

The sun had warmed the day enough that they came outside to greet them. Jessie's dad came right over, opened Karen's door for her and introduced himself. "Hi, Karen, I'm John. We are so pleased that you were able to join Jessie this weekend."

Karen was happy to meet John. However, she thought to herself, if he knew I just finished doing the nasty with his daughter in the back seat of this car, would he be as happy to see me? Karen smiled to herself.

"I'm glad I was able to make the trip, as well. I have been looking forward to meeting all of you."

"Karen, I'm Elizabeth. John and Jessie will get the bags. Why don't you come on in and make yourself at home." Elizabeth led Karen inside.

After the bags were inside, Jessie took the suitcases to her room, and then joined the rest of them in the living room. "Dad, did you get the two dishes that were in the back seat?"

"No dear, I didn't. I thought there were only things in the trunk."

"That's okay. I will get them."

"I can get them, Jessie." Karen felt guilty that Jessie was doing all the work.

"No, I'm good, thanks." Jessie smiled at Karen and gave her a wink that caused Karen to blush.

Upon her return from the car Jessie had a pie in each hand. When she reached the door, she tapped it with her foot for someone to open it.

Karen was the first to jump up. She quickly got the door and let Jessie inside. "Let me help you with that."

"Thanks." Jessie handed over the apple pie and led the way to the kitchen.

Karen followed. After placing the pies on the counter they headed back into the living room.

"Karen, Jessie tells me you drink Rye and Pepsi. Can I fix you one?" John offered.

A drink sounded great. "That would be wonderful. But only if someone else is going to join me."

"Oh, have no fear. I'm having one. Elizabeth, how about you? Can I get you anything? Jessie?"

"I will help you, Dad."

"I will have a glass of wine please, John," Elizabeth answered.

Elizabeth and Karen talked about the weather forecast for the weekend; Jessie and her dad went to get the drinks. Before too long they were back with a round for everyone.

John started the conversation. "So, Karen, Jessie tells us you are a nurse."

Karen told them a bit about herself and her career. In return they shared stories of Jessie and how proud they were of her teaching career. It was what Jessie had always wanted to do ever since she had been a young girl.

The remainder of the afternoon and the early evening passed by quickly.

Karen and Jessie did the dishes after dinner, and then they headed over to Tom and Sharon's. Mattawa was a small town. Traveling back and forth to each other's place took no time at all.

The four of them laughed, joked, told stories and played scrabble into the wee hours of the morning. When they arrived back at Jessie's parents, the door had been left unlocked for them.

Elizabeth got up early and prepared the coffee. Karen was wide awake and could not go back to sleep, because Jessie was 'sawing another cord of wood' very loudly. She made herself decent and headed down into the kitchen.

"Good morning, Elizabeth," she said and poked her head into the room.

Elizabeth was happy to see Karen. "Good morning, dear. Did you sleep well?"

"Yes, fine. Thanks. I am used to getting up early. Once I'm awake, I usually can't go back to sleep. I heard someone was up, so I thought I would join you."

"That's nice, I'm glad you did. The coffee is ready, if you would like some."

"Would you mind, if I boil water for tea?" Karen asked.

"Oh, by all means. Be my guest." Elizabeth giggled. "No pun intended."

Karen laughed. "So clever this early in the morning. Are you the one Jessie takes after?"

"I can't take all the credit. That child has had a warped sense of humor from an early age. There were times when she would have us in stitches for a whole evening telling jokes one after another. We always wondered how she could remember them all." Elizabeth smiled at the pleasant memory. "I was just about to make the pies for Easter dinner. Do you mind if I go ahead?"

"No, don't let me get in your way. If there is anything I can do to help with the preparation for dinner I would be more than happy to assist," Karen offered. "By the way, in those two containers on the counter are a couple of pies for you, as well."

"Pies? Jessie brought pies?" The expression on Elizabeth's face was one of puzzlement. "Oh, you made them!" Elizabeth opened up the first container and saw a very impressive looking apple pie. "Tom loves apple pie. This looks delicious." She took the cover off the second pie and discovered an equally impressive pumpkin pie.

Karen heard a snicker from Elizabeth when the older woman looked at the pumpkin pie and wondered what was funny about it. "Is there something wrong with the pie?"

"I think you have a two legged mouse who found its way into the pie dish." Elizabeth held it up and showed Karen the pie that had one piece missing.

Karen's mouth dropped open. All she could do was laugh and cover her face. "I am so sorry. I'm embarrassed. I asked Jessie not to touch that pie until we gave it to you. I am not sure when she got into it, but she obviously did." They both had a good laugh. Karen had a sip of tea and was still shaking her head. "I have half a mind to take the rest of that pie up to Jessie and make her wear it," she joked.

Elizabeth was quick to defend her daughter. "No, don't give her the satisfaction of having the whole pie. Besides, your pie looks great. You saved me some work this year. Now I only have to make John his mincemeat pie. That was very thoughtful of you, Karen."

"My pleasure. I was making pies for my family's dinner, so I decided to make a couple extra ones and bring them with us. I usually prepare the Easter meal for my entire family, so I really have gotten away with a lot less work."

Elizabeth was impressed. She knew what a hard job it was to do it all. Elizabeth was more than pleased with Jessie's new companion. Karen was a wonderful addition to their family.

"While you make the pie, may I help by peeling the potatoes for you?" Karen offered.

The two women worked away in the kitchen, sharing different ideas for recipes.

When Jessie finally came down, she stood outside the kitchen for a while listening to Karen and her mom. Karen had won her parents over, just like she had known she would.

Jessie entered the kitchen quietly, came up behind Karen and gently placed her hands on Karen's hips. When Karen instinctively turned her head, Jessie met her lips with a soft, gentle kiss. Karen smiled and then blushed. After all, Elizabeth was in the room.

Jessie poured herself a cup of coffee, then she sat at the table and joined in the conversation. Karen gave her a hard time over the missing piece of pie, but Jessie took pleasure in the verbal beating. All Elizabeth could do was watch and enjoy the two of them banter back and forth.

Once Karen was confident the preparations were done for Easter dinner, she excused herself and headed for the shower. The girls soon left for a walk. As they strolled through the small town of Mattawa, Jessie offered some local history as well as stories of childhood days. Karen thoroughly enjoyed the educational tour along with the funny tales of Jessie's younger years. Many of the locals either waved to them or stopped and chatted, asking Jessie all kinds of questions about her career, where she was living and so forth. Everyone wanted to be brought up to date on her life. Karen could feel the genuine concern the locals had for Jessie. No wonder Jessie enjoyed her visits back home so much. It was a wonderful, close knit, small community.

Neither of them had realized how long they had been gone. When they returned the house offered up the familiar smells of a turkey cooking with all the fixings. Karen inhaled deeply. It reminded her of home and what she would be doing to get ready for her own family to arrive. Only this year it was different. Suddenly it struck her. For a moment she dwelled on what she was missing.

Right about now my family would be arriving, Karen thought sadly. Greetings, laughter, warmth, drinks … genuine love all around. No, not anymore. Not with Roger …

Jessie was so caught up in the tempting aroma that she did not notice Karen's sadness. Instead she headed straight for the kitchen.

Jessie and Karen were putting the finishing touches on the table settings when Tom and Sharon arrived. Everyone gathered to greet them at the door. They exchanged hugs, the wine was uncorked and poured, and they all settled in the living room. Sharon poured herself ginger ale. Karen took part in much of the conversation. It was easy to see how comfortable she and Jessie's parents had become.

Elizabeth stood. "You all stay here; I am going to check on dinner."

"Can you wait just one moment, Mom?" Tom asked. "If you don't mind, I would like to make a toast."

"Oh, Big Bro, getting all soft on us, are you?" Jessie teased.

Tom held out his glass. "I would first like to start by welcoming Karen to our family. I can see why Jessie is so taken with you. You are a good fit for Jessie and this family. Welcome, Karen."

They lifted their glasses in a toast to Karen whose eyes filled with tears.

She was so touched by Tom's gesture; she rose to her feet, went over and gave Tom a huge hug. "Thank you, Tom. That was so sweet of you!" Karen turned, "Thanks to all of you. You have made me feel very welcome. Jessie is blessed to have such a wonderful family." On her way back to her chair, she grabbed Jessie's hand and gave it a squeeze.

"Well, I have more. So please raise your glasses one more time." Tom reached for Sharon's hand and gently pulled her to her feet. "Sharon and I would like to make a toast to another new member of the family." He pointed towards Sharon's belly with his glass. "We are finally pregnant," he announced beaming from ear to ear.

"Finally I get to be an aunt!" Jessie hollered.

"And we get to be grandparents," John said proudly.

Everyone was thrilled. Glasses clanged, cheers rang out, and more hugs and tears were shared.

Then Elizabeth made quick work of getting the food on the table. She asked Karen to say the blessing. Karen was sure to include in her many thanksgivings the blessing of Tom and Sharon's long awaited pregnancy.

The meal was fantastic. Before long they were all complaining of how they couldn't eat another bite. At least until dessert was put out.

Tom immediately spotted the homemade apple pie. "Mom, you made apple pie! My favorite!" He usually had to settle for pumpkin.

"I didn't make it," Elizabeth confessed with a grin. "I only made the mincemeat for your father."

Karen watched Tom's confusion. He knew Jessie hadn't made the pie. He looked at Karen who was smiling. "Guilty," she said.

He got up, came over to Karen, and putting her face between his hands he planted a big kiss on her lips. "I love apple pie."

"Her pumpkin pie is very impressive too," Jessie piped up.

Tom took a bite of the apple pie and moaned out loud. "Oh, this is good!"

Karen was pleased that her pies were a big hit. Silently she wondered if they were as big a hit with her own family.

After the meal the guys headed for the living room while the women cleaned up. Coffee and tea were made. By then Tom was ready for a second piece of apple pie.

After they had been visiting for a while, Karen needed to get some fresh air. She excused herself from the room, grabbed one of Elizabeth's sweaters off the back of a chair and slipped out the patio door from the kitchen. From outside Karen could hear the soft rumblings of conversation and laughter. It made her think of her own family. She had enjoyed her Easter dinner and the time with Jessie's family very much, but she still missed her family. Easter dinner was not the same for her, nor would it ever be the same again. Her tradition of making the dinner for her loved ones was now broken, along with her relationship with Roger. She wondered if they even missed her.

With tears in her eyes she looked up into the evening sky. Karen spoke a silent prayer still hopeful that one day Roger and she could be friends again. At the same time she knew that the chance of this happening was very slim.

Tom slowly opened the patio door and came out. "Are you okay, Karen?"

"Yes, I'm fine, thanks."

When Karen turned, Tom could see the tears in her eyes. "You are crying?" he asked. "What's wrong? Is there anything I can do?"

"You are such a sweet man, Tom. No wonder Jessie holds you close to her heart."

"Jessie has kept me filled in on your relationship from the beginning. After her breakup with Lynne she had told me that she was holding out for 'her perfect woman' and would not settle for anything less. Jessie means what she says. I believe she has found that woman in you, Karen."

Karen managed a quivering smile.

"Are you not happy with Jessie?" Should Karen have second thoughts Tom wanted to be there for Jessie. He knew his sister would then be devastated and heartbroken.

Karen swallowed hard. "The funny thing is Tom: I love Jessie with all my heart. I have never felt so complete, and my life has never been so full of happiness. I just have one nagging concern that rears its ugly head every so often."

"Can I help?"

Karen hesitated. "Has Jessie told you about my brother-in-law?"

"Roger? Yes. The way he has treated you is very unfortunate," Tom sympathized.

"Roger has been a big part of my life for twenty years. I love him like a brother. You know how strong that bond can be. I am not sure if I can live without him in my life. That would be like asking Jessie to live without you in hers."

Tom's expression showed concern. "Just what are you saying?"

"Having said that, in the short time that Jessie has been in my life she has made me happier than I have ever been. I love her deeply. I have never felt this way before about anyone. I am not sure if I could live without her. I feel so torn sometimes, uncertain which way to turn."

Tom took Karen's hand in his.

Karen held on tight to take the comfort he was offering. "I promised Jessie I would not let Roger interfere with us this weekend. I needed some fresh air to clear my thoughts," Karen explained. "Can I ask you not to share this conversation with Jessie? I don't want to disappoint or hurt her."

"This conversation will be kept between us. But Karen, I will not stand by and watch Jessie get hurt."

"I respect that." Karen admired Tom for the way he watched over Jessie.

Just before they headed back inside, Karen turned to Tom. "Each of you has made me feel very welcome here, Tom. Jessie is lucky to have a family that loves her so much." She inhaled a deep breath of the cool evening air and dried her eyes. "This is all so new to me. Often I wonder what I did to deserve such happiness with Jessie. I am in love with her, Tom. Please don't ever question that. I just need to figure out a way to make it all work."

"I respect your honesty." Tom gave Karen a kiss on the top of her head. "Life isn't always easy, but sometimes you have to stand up and fight for what you want."

"I have never been much of a fighter." Karen smiled. "We had better get back inside before they send a search party after us."

CHAPTER TWENTY

After everyone had turned in for the night, Karen lay in bed saying her prayers quietly. When she finished, she rolled towards Jessie and propped herself up on her elbow. Jessie was lying on her back facing Karen. Her soft red hair was lying on her pillow in a state of disarray. She was beautiful. "Jessie, I want to thank you."

Jessie looked a little puzzled. "For what?"

"For allowing me to share your wonderful family. I had a terrific weekend." Karen smiled and placed a gentle kiss on Jessie's freckled cheek.

"I knew you would love everyone, and I know they think the world of you. Just look at the way you and my mom get along. Especially in the kitchen!"

"Yeah, that was fun." Suddenly Karen's facial expression changed. "Do you think Elizabeth would still like me as much if she knew what I was about to do to her precious daughter?" Karen quickly slipped off the night shirt she was wearing and had a devilish glint in her eye.

Jessie laughed quite loudly. Quickly she covered her mouth. She removed her own shirt. "My mom would be pleased that you are taking such good care of me," she whispered.

They made love with such lust it led them to sheer exhaustion.

Jessie and Karen had intended to get up earlier than they actually did, but they really didn't have a deadline to be home. However, Karen had to work the Easter Monday. After breakfast they loaded their bags into the car. Elizabeth and John were sad to see them leave, but saw them off with waves and smiles.

They stopped by Tom's on their way out of town.

"Are you coming inside?" Tom was pleased the two had stopped before heading back to Brockville.

"We really can't stay Tom, but thanks. Karen reminded me this morning that we still had your chainsaw in the trunk."

They went back out to the car. Tom was putting the chainsaw in the garage when Sharon joined them. "Hey girls, its cooler today, but not a bad day to be driving!" She held her arms up to welcome the sun.

"No, we have been fortunate with the weather. I will call you and let you know when we get home, so you all can stop worrying."

Karen walked up to Sharon. "I wish you the best with your pregnancy."

"Oh, that's sweet, thank you."

"Don't forget that I'm a nurse. If you have any questions about anything, feel free to call me. I am there for you."

Sharon took Karen's hands. "I appreciate that." She pulled her close and gave her a hug.

"And you have to call and keep us updated on the progress. I can't wait to be an aunt," Jessie added.

Tom stood by watching the girls sharing the excitement of his wife's pregnancy.

Karen turned to Tom with extended arms. "The offer goes to you, too. If you have any questions that Sharon feels silly calling about, don't be shy, call me."

Tom wrapped his arms around Karen and held on tight. Jessie watched the two of them, and she knew a special bond had been developed this weekend. Her heart was doing its own little happy dance in her chest. She was thrilled to have her best friend and brother connect so well with the woman of her dreams.

Before Tom and Karen separated, Tom whispered, "Be strong and stand your ground. Fight for what you believe in."

Karen kissed him on the cheek and gave him a wink.

Jessie interrupted. "Okay, break it up, it's my turn." Standing in the middle of them she turned and hugged Karen instead of Tom causing everyone to laugh.

"Once a comedian, always a comedian." Tom shook his head smiling. "Come here, you crazy clown. Give your brother a hug!"

Karen and Jessie got in the car and drove away.

The traffic was steady, but not too hectic. They arrived home in pretty good time. They backed Karen's car out of the garage and put Jessie's in to unload their bags more easily. Once they had everything put away, they closed the garage door and decided to lay down for an afternoon siesta.

For dinner Jessie cooked up a quick macaroni and hamburger dish. She had decided to stay over and head to Brockville in the morning. They were just finishing dinner, when they heard the doorbell ring.

"I'll get it," Jessie offered.

Karen looked towards the driveway and noticed it was Joan's car. "Thanks hon, it's Joan."

When Jessie opened the door, she was totally caught off guard. It was Roger who was standing there staring at her with an equally dumbfounded look of surprise.

Jessie was uncertain of what to say. "Uh . . . hello Roger," she stammered.

"Is Karen around?" Roger had only seen Karen's car in the driveway. He was expecting her to be alone. He wanted to ... no, he needed to talk with her.

By this time Karen had come to the foyer. She saw Roger for the first time since that day he had been so mean to her. To look at him now, she couldn't imagine it was the same person. He stood so quiet and unsure of himself. Karen had missed him and wanted to reach out and hug him, but she knew it would not be well received. Ironically, little did she know that it was her hug that Roger so desperately wanted and needed.

Karen swallowed hard. She wanted to be mature about this. "Roger, would you like to come inside?"

Roger glanced from Jessie to Karen and back to Jessie. "Perhaps this is a bad time. I can come by another day." He started to turn and realized he had the pie plates in his hands. "Oh, I almost forgot. Joan had these cleaned up. I need to return them to you."

Karen took the pie plates from him. "Did she ask you to bring them?" Karen was curious.

"No," Roger confessed. "Joan doesn't know I'm here."

It must have taken a great deal of inner strength for Roger to show up on her doorstep unannounced. "I'm sure you didn't come all the way over here to just return my pie plates."

"No, I was hoping we could talk."

Karen could tell by Roger's body language that he was out of his comfort zone, but he was making an effort, and she wanted to demonstrate an effort, as well. Her stomach was churning, caused by her nerves. She had to admit she had been terrified of Roger the last time she had seen him. She was uncertain about how Roger might act now that Jessie was here with her.

Although she was nervous, seeing Roger made Karen realize even more how much she had missed him. "Then Roger, please come inside," Karen invited calmly. Karen could feel Tom's words being whispered into her ear once again. "Be strong and stand your ground. Fight for what you believe in."

Hesitantly Roger came inside.

"Can I take your jacket?" Jessie reminded both of her presence.

"Yes, thanks." Roger handed his coat to Jessie without looking at her.

Karen tried to clear the air. "Roger, I believe you know Jessie."

"Yeah, we've met." He nodded his head and acknowledged her. "Jessie."

"Roger." Jessie nodded in return. She would not back down for him, but for Karen she was willing to be cordial.

Karen motioned for Roger to sit down.

After a few moments of awkward silence, Jessie offered, "Karen would you like a tea? Roger, how about you? Anything to drink?"

Karen was relieved. "I would love one, thanks."

Roger looked at Jessie. "Yes, a tea would be great." He wondered why she was being so nice to him.

Jessie headed for the kitchen. "I will clean up a bit while the water is boiling." She left the two of them alone so they could talk.

As soon as Jessie was out of sight, Roger clarified, "I had no idea you had company. I don't want to impose."

"You are not imposing. You are always welcome . . . at my home," she added pointedly, a jab he deserved.

He looked at Karen with big sad puppy dog eyes. "Yeah, about that Karen . . . you know you are always welcome at our home." Roger couldn't believe how easily the words came to him.

Karen's eyes widened. "No, I don't know that. As of our last conversation you wanted me nowhere near your home. I had to see Joan and Sophie everywhere but at your home." That had to hurt. It was the truth, and he had to hear it. Karen knew Roger coming here was a big step for him. She didn't want to scare him off, but she was going to stand her ground.

While Jessie was picking up the dinner dishes and preparing tea, she made damn sure not to make too much noise so she could hear at least the tone of the conversation in the next room. If it were to increase in volume or turn nasty, Jessie would be all over Roger so quick he would have no time to react.

Roger was not a stupid man. He was aware that Jessie had left the two of them alone to talk. He had to admit he was pleasantly surprised with Jessie's way of making herself scarce.

Roger stood up, moved across the room and sat on the couch close to Karen.

Karen squirmed uncomfortably beside him.

Roger was not proud of himself for making Karen, of all people, feel uneasy around him. He reached over and placed his hand on Karen's. They both looked at each other. "Please don't be uneasy around me, Karen. I am here to talk, not to argue." His voice quivered slightly. He cleared his throat.

Karen released a breath of relief. "I am glad to hear that. I have wanted to talk, as well. I have just been unsure of what kind of reception I would get."

"Me, too. But I had to take the chance. I wouldn't have blamed you, if you had closed the door in my face."

"I'm not like that, Roger, you know that."

"Yes, I do. It is one of the things I love about you. You are the kindest person I know." Once Roger started he couldn't seem to stop himself. He just blurted it all out. "Karen, the word is out around town about you being . . ."

Karen held up her hand. "Stop right there! I don't need a lecture!"

"No, let me finish," Roger insisted. "The guys at work all know. I have taken quite a razing and haven't enjoyed one minute of it. But I would like to explain that it has made me think of how you must feel to be verbally abused. I hate it. I can't imagine how I made you feel." Roger hung his head in shame. "I am truly sorry."

Karen was stunned. Was this really Roger? She was amazed at how he had come to understand how hurtful he had been.

"Roger, you broke my heart. I hated you for at least twenty-four hours. But I can't hate you forever. I love you. I will always love you, no matter what."

"That is almost exactly what I came here to tell you tonight," Roger said.

Karen looked puzzled. "Almost exactly?"

Roger smiled; it was so good to see him smile again. "Well, I hated you for more than twenty-four hours for sure."

Karen laughed. "What does this mean?"

They both felt the tension in the room disappear.

"After these last three or four weeks without you, my whole life has changed. I never realized before how much of a difference one person, other than my wife and daughter, could make in my life. And trust me; they have not made my life easy. Without you being there yesterday, things were so different – and not in a good way."

Jessie had the tea made, but was listening on the other side of the entrance way to make sure she didn't walk in at a bad time.

"Roger the fact remains that I am a lesbian. Spending my life with Jessie is what I want. We are meant to be together. Jessie and I are soul mates. We belong together."

Roger looked at Karen. "I said things to you I didn't mean. I love you, and I miss you."

"Does my sister know you love another woman like this?" Karen raised her eyebrows.

Roger smiled. "I've missed you. Can you ever find it in your heart to forgive me? We still have some hurdles to get over. Everything isn't going to be rosy, but we can tackle those issues one at a time."

Karen threw her arms around Roger's neck. The hug was filled with emotion. Tears welled up in both their eyes. Karen had never seen Roger cry before. It reinforced the fact that he truly did love her as much as she loved him.

Jessie decided this was good time to enter with the tea. She grabbed a handful of Kleenex and handed some to them both.

Roger stayed for his tea. Jessie felt comfortable enough to join in the conversation. They talked about hockey and the fact that the Ottawa Senators were ahead in the series over the Toronto Maple Leafs. They stayed on safe topics. No one wanted to push their luck. Roger didn't need to see them hold hands or kiss. Neither Karen, nor Jessie wanted to make him uncomfortable.

To his surprise Roger found himself enjoying the conversation with Jessie. He couldn't believe that not so long ago he had wanted to destroy her career. He could clearly see now, that move would have destroyed his relationship with Karen forever.

He watched Karen and Jessie banter back and forth over the two teams and knew that Karen was happier than he had ever seen her. She was beaming.

When Roger left that night, everyone felt like a huge weight had been lifted. Their lives were starting to be put back together, and although it had only been a month of turmoil it had seemed like a lifetime.

Karen knew the relationship between herself and Roger would never be the same as it had been, but she could settle for what Roger was offering. They would work out their differences over time.

Karen was exhausted from the events of such an intense emotional day. At the same time she felt very much alive, proud, and thankful.

They turned off the lights, locked the doors, and headed for bed.

"So, Miss Jessie Carmichael, with all that being said and done – are you ready to move in, yet …" Karen flashed her big white smile at the woman she loved, ready to unleash her desires once more …

THE END

Do you want more lesbian love stories?

Check out our other titles

Ruth Gogoll

In the Heat of the Night

A steamy summer night on the Rhine, a hot love affair . . . it wasn't supposed to be any more than that. But when Tina is in need of a lawyer, she cannot think of anyone but Mar. That's when, out of nowhere, other feelings and not just the hunt for the right paragraphs, enter the equation.
Tina doesn't want to hear about it, since the motto "It was just sex, not love" still stands between them like a wall. Will they some day be able to overcome their differences?

Kay Rivers

Tender Kisses

Michelle Carver has a stressful job as manager at Disney World in Florida. She hardly has time for her personal life and that's why her love life is limited to the occasional affair. The word "love" has been firmly eliminated from her vocabulary.
Cindy Claybourne is a student and has taken a summer job at Disney World. She realizes that she feels very attracted to Michelle and wants to get a good look at what's underneath that hard shell of hers. But Michelle doesn't go down without a fight. Cindy won't give up that easily, however and fights for her love for Michelle.
When is Michelle finally going to realize that Cindy is the right one for her?

Ruth Gogoll

The Actress

When teenage sweetheart Simone, nowadays a famous actress, reappears in Pia's life, the flames of a long lost passion reignite. But the woman she adores is held captive in a world full of illusions, leading the life of glitz and glamour, torn between fame and the great abyss every waking moment. On the big screen, she shows deep emotions, but in real life she doesn't even seem to know what real feelings are.

Simone's charm and beauty turn Pia's world upside down; She tosses all concerns to the wind that Simone might break her heart all over again. While Simone tries to drown her sorrows in alcohol, Pia embarks on the fight for the love of her life ...

Alison Barnard

A Walk in the Rain

Alison Barnard's A Walk in the Rain is the story of two women who meet when each is on the brink of world-wide fame and trying not to face her dissatisfaction with the life she has made for herself. It is a love story, but it is also about a journey to self-acceptance. By the end of it, both major characters have to challenge assumptions and prejudices in society and in themselves.

Actress Shara travels and lives with Jessa while researching her new role – that of Jessa Hanson – in the film about the conductor's life, and they fall in love. Shara's boyfriend Derek intervenes, helped by Shara's belief that she has caught Jessa in a compromising position with a former lover. They separate. "Maestra" is filmed and Jessa records a musical poem that is a tribute to the love she has lost. When Shara hears that musical piece, goes to see her. They consummate their relationship, but is Shara ready for the kind of publicity a lesbian relationship will attract?

Kingsley Stevens
Love Me

Amy Flanagan and Morgan Holdsworth meet over business. Amy works for an advertising agency and she is trying to land a large contract with Morgan, who owns a large cosmetic corporation. Even though Amy is usually strict about separating business from pleasure, she falls in love with Morgan. They start having an affair. Apparently, Morgan doesn't want to take the relationship any further, while Amy wished she could get much closer to Morgan.

Ruth Gogoll
Taxi to Paris

Ruth Gogoll's Taxi to Paris is the best selling lesbian erotic novel in Germany.
"I savored the view of her naked beauty for a moment. I walked up behind her and kissed her between the shoulder blades without kissing her anywhere else. She yelped with surprise. Then I saw her shiver from head to toe, and a relief of tiny dots covered her skin. She laid her head back. Otherwise, she didn't move. 'More,' she whispered."
In 1993 Ruth Gogoll wrote her first book, "Taxi to Paris", which has become the most bestselling lesbian erotic romance novel in Germany. In 1993, though, nobody would print it. So Ruth Gogoll founded her own publishing house, elles, which has become famous for Lesbian Erotic Romance, publishing more than 100 romances in German. Now these thrilling books are available in English.
New edition! Completely revised!

Ruth Gogoll
L as in Love

Peek into the interwoven lives of the women who gather at the Sappho Café, and meet a broad cross section of Cologne's most interesting people. Whether we're in the presence of the "perfect" couples or the women who are on the lookout for love, you'll find that Sappho always has drama on the menu – as well as a first-rate cappuccino.
So sit back and enjoy the ride.
Once you've met Sabrina, Chris, Carolin, Rick, Rebekka and all the rest, you'll be back for more "L" – as in lovely ladies, lust, laughter, lies, lightheartedness, and lasciviousness – but mostly, "L – as in Love"!

Ruth Gogoll's
Christmas Carol

is a new twist on an old classic. Christmas is coming and good-will and merriment fill the town. It's not the best of times for everyone however ...
Company president Michaela Wittling is all work and no play and Christmas is just another day. *What's all the fuss about? The lights are a waste of electricity. They all expect time off and bonuses. Humbug!*
Faithful employee Ramona Benckhoff is all worry and no play. *Will I keep my job? Will the boss find out I sometimes cut my hours short to go to the hospital?* And, the most frightening question of them all ... *Will my daughter live to see the New Year?*
Michaela thinks she has it all figured out. Ramona believes she has no hope and nothing figured out.
One very strange night changes everything.

www.ingramcontent.com/pod-product-compliance
Lightning Source LLC
Chambersburg PA
CBHW020328260626
47156CB00004B/1422

* 9 7 8 3 9 5 6 0 9 1 5 3 7 *